LITTLE MAN OF MY DREAMS,
A LOVE STORY

The story of
"Koza"

BY LOUISE BOUCK

"Little Man of My Dreams, a Love Story."   The story of KOZA.

Registry of Copyrights United States of America
Registration Number TXu 2-009-036
Effective date of Registration: April 21, 2016
Copyright Claimant Louise Irene Bouck
ISBN 13 978-1-943984-20-6 <u>Paperback</u>
978-1-943984-21-3 <u>eBook</u>
Hisgivenstories LIB Publications

This book is a work of fiction. Any resemblance to events of persons living or dead is entirely coincidental.

TABLE OF CONTENTS

"Little Man of My Dreams, a Love Story."   The story of KOZA.

ACKNOWLEDGEMENTS

Thank you to my family and friends for your daily prayers for me. Thank you to those, who were truthful in offering advice and comments for the story's refinement. A special thank you goes to Dale Bouck my first editor and husband, for his application of skills and knowledge for keeping my computer running. A big thank you goes to a new editor, Maureen Burge. Her efforts and hugs are helpful and greatly appreciated.

DEDICATION

This book is dedicated to all the people who appreciate others and things that are a little different, and to the simplicity in a child's questions and the complexity in finding an appropriate and truthful answer.

Here is a suggestion. Look for love where you found it first, and offer that love to others. Believe in the true love of our Creator and His Son, our Savior, Jesus. He always was, always will be and always remains the same. I offer this work to Him, as we all draw on the urgings of our inner spirit and live in the hope that we are pleasing in His eyes.

CHAPTER ONE
KOZA'S MOVE

I have been working for a long time preparing, and it is all settled. With you and Dad divorced and living in separate locations, I think it is time for me to launch out on my own. I have economized and saved and believe it or not I actually have enough to take Bennington's offer in New York and survive for a while if it doesn't work out."

"But where will you stay dear until you find an apartment? They are hard to come by and very expensive in New York City."

"I found one online and Dad paid the deposit. It is a nice place with even a bit of green out the front window. You can imagine how hard that was to find. I just wanted two things, to be able to park my car within walking distance, and to have a pet. The man said he would install a lockable dog door in the side door. I told him Jackie weighs almost forty pounds and he said that was the size limit. I have talked to him many times."

"Mom, this notebook is for you. It has the web address where you can see a video of the inside of my place and the outside, too. Just look for "2G" and then click on it. I looked last night and he hadn't taken it off yet. He said he wouldn't until I actually moved in.

"You are really going to do this aren't you?"

"Yes Mom I am and I will be driving and Jackie is going with me and we are going to have fun and take our time getting there."

"Well, at least it is a good time of year and the roads will be clear."

"Mother, will you quit worrying? I am a big girl!"

"I know you are dear but you have never been away from me in a big city, all on your own. What if you have car trouble getting there?"

"Mother, be reasonable. The mechanic said my old car is good to go. Oh, and I don't think I told you, but the man I leased the condo from said that it has enough furniture to live comfortably. He said he would remove anything I don't want and that I can replace things slowly. He isn't charging me for the furnishings, so I will put my extra stuff here in storage. I will get a feel for the place and see what I need after a bit and maybe I will have some of it shipped to me then or replace it with new."

"Who is going to put all this stuff in storage? I can't do that."

"It's all arranged. Dad has a friend with a truck and they are coming here Wednesday and they will pack it up and I have already rented a storage unit. Here is an extra key in case you want to put something in there or use any of my things. I won't mind. I will probably end up selling most of them eventually."

"You and your father never tell me what is going on! When did you plan all this?"

"Last weekend, and I just told you. This is the first moment I have had to talk to you. Either you have been gone or I have. You know everything that is happening. Here look in the notebook. It has my new address in it, and here is the name of the place and the address where I will be working. The next page has the name and location of my storage unit. It is just six blocks from here. I still find it hard to believe that I am going to be working for Bennington's accounting dept. Do you have any idea how lucky I was to land that job? They must have had a million applicants!"

"Don't exaggerate dear." They walked outside together with Jackie prancing about eager to leave. "I knew I couldn't persuade you to stay but I had to try. I hoped that you would take the full time job here and then I would get to see you once in a while."

As soon as Koza had started packing the car Jackie had figured out that a trip was being prepared. Of course she had no idea how far they would travel or how her life would change.

"Koza, wait just a minute. I bought something for you to use on the way. I was sure you would go when Benningtons offered you the job. I almost forgot to give these to you." Her mother dashed in her front door and returned quickly. "This is a safety harness for Jackie. I figured you would take her if you could. She will have to ride in front. You have the back seat full." Her mother opened the front door and Jackie immediately jumped in. This part goes around her like this and then this part goes through the seat belt and locks so that she won't slam forward if you have to stop suddenly. That's not all, I bought this, too. It sticks to the inside of her window. When the sun is streaming through, she can still look out but it stops most of the heat and glare." Koza was already seated behind the steering wheel. Jackie was leaning over kissing Koza eager to get moving. Her mother closed the door making sure Jackie was clear of it.

"Mother, that was so thoughtful of you. You thought of everything!" She hurried around to her daughter's side of the car and opened the door. "Thank you Mom. I appreciate all the love you have given me and the education you and Dad encouraged that made this opportunity possible. I love you Mom. I will call you."

"Be safe Koza, and drive carefully. Call me each night so I can see on the map where you are. I won't sleep a wink if you don't call me," she threatened as she gave one last hug, and leaned in further to give Jackie a pat. Jackie barked with joy as the car began to move. She loved to ride.

Koza backed slowly out of the driveway and suddenly felt very sad. She looked back at her mother standing in the driveway waving and waved back. This was the end of an era and the beginning of a new and exciting life.

"I'll be fine! " She called out her window and turned the corner heading her car toward the freeway. The next time I visit her she will be living in the back of her little book store. I feel bad saying goodbye to her and this house. I grew up here. Today marks the end of my childhood. No, that's not quite true. Their divorce did that.

"Jackie, we are in for a big adventure! I have a beautiful Condo waiting for us with a wide green belt in front of it with trees and groomed green grass. At the end of the grass is a gate that lets us into a small park. My new job pays way more than I let on to Dad or Mom. I hope I can do all that they require. My job at Grayling gave me a wide variety of experience to fall back on. I hope it is enough." She and Jackie were both excited.

After a few blocks she pulled to the curb and offered the panting dog a drink from a special travel bowl she had placed on the floor of the front seat. Her vet had recommended that she give Jackie a couple drops of Dramamine, for motion sickness, as they started out. It will relax her and keep her tummy from getting bothered. She had slipped the dropper in the side of Jackie's mouth before she offered her the drink. Koza sipped her ice tea and took a deep breath.

"There Jackie, I think we are really ready."

Days sped by, and she missed her exit and had to find her way back to the highway on surface streets. They stopped for meals and rest. The traffic became intimidating at times. She was more than a little glad when she finally left the manager's office holding the keys to her condo. She held Jackie's leash tightly.

"You will have to stay with me until you learn this area, Jackie." She walked the grass with her until Koza was sure that Jackie was starting to understand where her boundaries were. She had taught her about never crossing into the street alone, when she was little. This exercise in caution would be repeated many times over the next few days until Koza was sure that she would not lose Jackie and that she would not leave the wide green area with many trees.

Koza's heart fluttered with excitement as she inserted her key in the front door and swung it wide open. A pleasant, clean, fresh scent greeted her. She strolled through the rooms still holding Jackie's leash. She noticed the dog door but didn't unlatch it.

"This is our new home Jackie!" The dog was wagging and almost as excited as she was. The manager knocked on her open front door. Jackie barked but continued to wag. She had met this man and he had petted her, she felt that he was a friend.

"I brought you this big cart to use. I am sure you have a car full of boxes to move in. Everyone does when they arrive. When you are done with it, just roll it back beside my office."

"Thank you so much. This place lives up to my expectations and then some. It is really nice."

"Good, I am glad you like it. Is there anything else you might need? I will be gone for a few hours, but you can call me later at the number I gave you if you think of something."

"Thank you again." Koza closed the door but didn't lock it. She took the cart, her purse and Jackie back to the parking garage and began the job of unloading her car. Several trips later, she left Jackie inside and just carried her keys. When she returned she found Jackie sleeping. She was already comfortable. She could tell that this was where Koza would be with her. The boxes held the scent of the rooms they had come from. Her bed was in the corner and she was in it.

CHAPTER TWO
THE ACCIDENT

Kozarina Kinny entered through the side door to the parking garage and greeted Sandy and Mandy. The twin girls were playing an old fashion game of jacks in the middle of the cement lane of the parking garage.

"Good morning girls."

"Good Morning Koza," they replied in unison without looking up.

"Would you do me a favor?" She asked.

"Yes, if our mother says yes."

"I would like it very much if you would come and play in my parking space after I leave. You would be much safer there. I am sure your mother would approve."

In the few months that Koza had lived in her new Condo, she had made many acquaintances. She enjoyed her job and found it was challenging but nothing that surpassed her training and ability. Koza excelled in many areas of life.

She had not spent a week in the new condo before she had rearranged the living room furniture and ordered a desk that fit against the back of the couch and allowed her to face the living room window when she worked at it. Her large laptop took center stage. It contained all the stories she had written starting in high school. Even with double majors in college and a part time job, she still made time to write.

The bottom drawer of the desk held a separate drive that protected copies of all her files. Koza was cautious as well as conservative. Already the décor in her place reflected her taste. Simple coordinating tans and deep browns against white walls with just a pop of soft yellow and ice blue for accents flowed through the rooms. Just one day spent shopping had enabled her to completely change the look of the place. A soft tan suede slipcover over the flowered couch, a puffy butter yellow comforter for her bed, and two new clear glass lamps with light blue shades sat on the round dark wood tables on either side of the couch. Also a pair of pillows, one for the dark brown rocker and one for the couch, an abstract art piece with just the right colors for her bedroom wall, a cozy throw in white for the end of the bed and another for the arm of the couch was all it took. She looked back at her home and smiled as she left locking the door. She was happy.

As Koza got in her car and was putting on her seat belt, she could hear wheels screeching. Someone is driving too fast, she thought. They will never be able to stop! They will hit the girls! She started her car and backed it straight up, blocking the path of the oncoming car. A split second later it careened around the corner and hit her broadside, lifting her car up and then sliding back as it dropped down. The two little girls had jumped up and were standing on the stairs with eyes as big as saucers.

"Are you alright?" Koza called. They nodded but didn't speak. "Go home girls. Gather your jacks and go down the stairs and go home." Koza rubbed her neck and felt the growing bruise on her left shoulder as she stepped out of her car.

She heard a woman's voice shouting at her.

"What were you doing, backing out without looking? Look at my poor baby car! It is ruined!" She wailed. It was then that Koza realized that the woman was very intoxicated. She could barely stand up.

"Do I know you?" asked Koza. "Your face seems familiar."

"Everyone knows me. I am Madelyn Clay of Clay Devine Designs!" She said it theatrically, using her hand to create a flourish, but with a pronounced slur.

"I saw your picture on the news this morning. You had a big fashion show last night. I hope that you are not injured."

"I think I am fine, just a little shaken. Would you help me to my door? I seem to be a bit dizzy. It must have been the accident. Did I bump my head? I think I bumped my head, and please don't call the police. I will pay for your car repair. I can't stand the bad publicity."

"Let's get in the elevator," said Koza. "There we are, on one already. Now which way do you live? Can you tell me?"

"Of course I can tell you! I live there, the second house with the pink flowers by the door."

"Is someone here to help you or call the doctor?"

"Briggs is here."

As she shifted Miss Clay's weight to the other arm, Briggs, the butler, the man who was skilled and trained to always take care of anything Madelyn needed; opened the door and helped to steady her as he took her in and sat her in a plump, overstuffed chair. The entire room looked as if it had been plucked from a fifties movie. It was obvious that Madelyn liked drama.

"Maddie, I demand to know where you have been! Do you realize that it is eight, o'clock in the morning?" The stern question came from a little person. The man standing beside her could look straight into Madelyn's eyes, although she was seated.

"What are you doing here? How did you get in?"

"I came in the same way I always do when you aren't around. I came through the dog door. I didn't want to disturb Briggs if he was resting. I am sure that he waited up all night for you, too. He always does. We both do. Now tell us where you went when you left your show. Were you driving around in traffic in that condition? Why didn't you call your limousine? I am amazed that you are not in jail, or in an accident!"

"That takes us to why I am here," said Koza. "She did get in an accident. She drove into the side of my car in the parking garage. I deliberately backed out when I heard a car coming that sounded out of control. I could hear the tires squealing! Two little girls were not far down the lane, and she would have hit them if I hadn't blocked the way."

"What girls? I didn't see any girls," mumbled Madelyn.

"I knew that you couldn't see them in time to stop. That's why I backed out in front of you. They were frightened but uninjured. I spoke to them as I was putting my manuscript in the car. I asked them to move their game of jacks to my space after I left so they would not be in the lane."

"Briggs have you fed the animals and let them out yet?" Maddie asked, still seeming disconnected from what had just happened. She seemed unable to absorb the facts.

"They have been fed but I usually wait until nine to signal their release. By then most of the residents are gone for the day."

He pushed a button and almost instantly, a full grown lioness and two golden labs bounded into the room and out the extra-large dog door.

"No wonder that dog door is so big. I can't believe what I just saw. Was that a lion?" asked Koza.

"Don't be alarmed, she has special filing done daily on her claws and Maddie got her when she was tiny and she was raised with the dogs. She thinks she is a big dog. She is rambunctious but harmless and loving," said Jay.

"Jay, please write this young lady a check for the damage to her car, she did help me home without calling the police. I am going up to take a bath." With exaggerated steps she climbed the stairs clinging to the banister, entered her room, closing the door rather loudly.

"I am Jay Spencer, Madelyn's brother. I didn't get your name."

"My name is Kozarina Kinny. I really need to call a cab and get my manuscript to the publisher. We have a contract meeting this morning at nine. I don't think I will make it on time but I want to try. I can't believe it. She nearly killed two little girls and she didn't even acknowledge it!"

"Don't be angry with her. She is too drunk to realize very much of anything right now. When we explain to her tomorrow what has happened she will be shocked at her own behavior. This was the biggest night of her life. She just presented her new fashion line to an audience of international buyers that couldn't order fast enough. She was surrounded with total approval."

"This could have been my biggest day, if I hadn't missed my signing. I need to call my agent and explain that I was in an accident."

"It could have been a lot worse. Thank you for the quick thinking, of course we will fix your car and make sure you get where you need to go while it is being repaired."

"Thank you for that." Suddenly barking and growling filled the courtyard along with the cry of a cat." That's Jackie, my dog. I know her bark." Her heart filled with fear at the thought that the lion may have attacked Jackie. She ran out the door and across the grass in the direction of the sound. The growling continued, and then they heard a woman's voice shrieking. They couldn't understand the words but it was obvious that she was somehow involved in the situation and gravely distressed.

"What is it Mrs. Dodge? Are you alright?" Jay's face displayed his feelings of concern.

"Two big dogs came over the fence from the park and grabbed my cat, Puddin. They killed her and your good Jackie tried to defend her. She has always played so nice with Puddin. They have been friends since the day you moved in. They bit her, too." Both women knelt beside Jackie. She was still looking toward the wooded park and growling with the fur in the middle of her back standing on end. Her shoulder and neck wounds were bleeding. Mrs. Dodge was crying as she tried to sooth Jackie.

"There, there, dear, you are going to be alright. Don't growl now girl, they are gone. I hope she will be alright. Do you have a veterinarian where you can take her? I can give you the information for mine if you don't have one yet."

"Yes, of course. I am so sorry about your cat."

"They killed her and took her away!" She said, as she picked up a small piece of her cat's fur from the grass and held it as if it were a delicate flower. Jay walked Mrs. Dodge to her door and asked if she had someone she could call to be with her.

"Yes, I think I will ask my sister to come over. She doesn't live very far. She loved Puddin, too. Wait and I will get you my veterinarian's number."

"Thank you, but I don't think that will be necessary." He heard her sob as she shut the door. Koza struggled to pick up Jackie.

Jay looked in the direction of the incident. Then he spotted Koza carrying her dog. She stopped at her door and realized she didn't have her keys. They were still in her car ignition. Her purse had been left behind too.

"How can I help?"

"I need my keys, I can't unlock the door."

"There are benefits to being small. I can help, give me just a moment." Jay hurried around to her side door that opened to the kitchen. A standard sized dog door challenged Jay's limber body, but he made it through. "Everyone should have a lion," he mumbled to himself as he crossed the living room to open the front door. He took Jackie in his arms and cradled her like a baby, talking to her softly. "We will get you fixed up girl. You were brave to defend your friend. You are such a good girl." He placed her on a throw rug and removed her collar.

"Koza, please bring me a clean soft cloth, a pan of warm water and some antiseptic solution." As soon as the supplies were placed beside him, he went to work with gentle hands carefully parting the fur to better observe the wounds. "The only one that is deep is this puncture here on her neck. We will need to watch it carefully to make sure that it doesn't get infected. Is it alright if I leave her collar off for now?"

"She will be fine without it, until that heals. Thank you so much for helping her. You must have worked with animals. You knew just what to do and how to calm her."

"Yes, Maddie has always surrounded herself with animals and I felt it was wise to learn the basics. Do you have any canned beef broth that we can offer her?"

When Koza brought the soup, Jay stuffed half of a tiny pill in Jackie's mouth and held the bowl near her mouth for her to drink.

He picked Jackie up and placed her on the far side of Koza's bed.

"There that should do for a while. I think she will rest now."

Jay is quite strong for someone small, Koza thought.

"I made a pot of coffee earlier if you would like a cup," Koza offered as she put away the first aid items and dropped the rug into her washer with some detergent and turned it on.

"Thank you. Will you join me?" She poured two cups, and reheated them in the microwave, placing a small pitcher of milk on the table.

"Do you like sugar?"

"No thanks, I like mine black," he said as he washed his hands at the kitchen sink and dried them with a paper towel. He watched as she added a small trickle of milk to her cup and placed a plastic bonnet over the pitcher before putting it back in the refrigerator.

While her back was turned he dropped a tiny white pill in her coffee. He had noticed her hands trembling as she collected the things from the floor. It had been a stressful, frightening morning for her. She needed rest. They sipped their coffee and made small talk for a few minutes and then he said if she promised to rest beside Jackie while he was gone, he would go to her car and retrieve her purse, keys and briefcase before they were stolen.

"Your presence will be a comfort to her," he suggested.

"I think I will, just until you come back," she said, as she lay down beside Jackie gently stroking her head. "I need to call my agent and my new publisher and explain why I am not there. Also I need to call my boss and say I won't be in until Monday, and I want to call Madelyn and see if she is alright. I have too much to do to nap, but I feel so tired that I …

She had drifted off to sleep mid-sentence. Jay pulled the soft white throw over her and left quickly heading to the parking garage. He pulled the keys and had to pick up the contents of her purse from the floor where it had landed. Her briefcase was closed holding the manuscript safely inside.

After noisily backing Madelyn's red Ferrari into a nearby space, he was able to pull Koza's car up and clear the lane. He couldn't help wondering why Madelyn had driven to the second floor, when her space was the second one on the first floor. I could take her car down there, he thought, but I'm not sure that I should. It sounds like the fan blades are tearing up the radiator. He noticed the large amount of liquid on the garage floor.

As an afterthought, he pulled Madelyn's keys and collected her tiny hand bag from the floor of her car. I will drop these through her mail slot on the way back to Koza's condo, he thought. Jay tried to remember everything she had said as she drifted off to sleep. They will both sleep for a while. That will give me time to try to put things right again.

He searched the top of her desk and found the number of the publisher's office in their letterhead. A letter from them lay on her desk setting up the appointment for nine o'clock that morning. He became aware that many of the things that Koza owned were brown or tan. She had been wearing a dark brown skirt and cream color blouse, with brown leather pumps. I like her brown hair and dark brown eyes with gold flecks. I noticed them when she knelt beside Jackie in the sunlight. She is very attractive.

The phone rang startling him. He realized that he had been musing over her and not making the needed calls. On the other end of the line a woman's voice spoke curtly. "I am calling to speak to Miss Kinny. Is she available?"

"No I am sorry she isn't. Is there something I can do to help you?"

"Who are you and where is Miss Kinny?"

"Miss Kinny has had a personal emergency this morning and will be unavailable the rest of today."

"She can't just be unavailable. She is late for a very important meeting. This is her publisher's office. Who did you say you are?"

"I am just a friend. Miss Kinny has been given a sedative by her doctor and will be asleep for quite a while."

"What's the matter with her? Why is she sedated?" A man took the phone and identified himself as, John Maxwell, her agent.

"Where is Koza and where is that manuscript? She is about to blow the whole deal. She has to get the final edited version to us now and sign the contract. She can't keep publisher's waiting!"

"I really don't think we should discuss her personal life. Do you? If you wish to send a courier for the manuscript, I will see that they get it. Do you have her home address?"

"Yes of course we do. I am sorry. I didn't mean to sound as if we were not concerned about her. Is she alright?"

"She will be tomorrow."

"Thank you. The courier is on the way." The agent hung up and Jay started to wonder if he had done the right thing. The phone rang again.

"Are you sure that you have the final copy that we need?"

"Yes, I am sure." Click, the agent hung up again. Well, he isn't big on manners. An agent shouldn't allow himself to get flustered no matter what happens, thought Jay.

Jay called the law firm that he and Madelyn used, and talked for a moment to Jane, the secretary. His call was put through immediately to Mark Harris.

"Mark I have several new things you can help us with this morning, in addition to what you are already working on."

"Jay, you sound tense. What has happened?"

"Madelyn slammed into the side of a woman's car this morning. Madelyn was still loaded from the celebration last night. By the way, thanks for coming."

"It was fun. My wife put me in the poor house as usual." They both laughed as he continued. "Was anyone injured?"

"No, but had the woman not deliberately blocked Madelyn's path, she would have hit two children."

"Did they call the police?"

"No. It happened in the parking garage and the woman actually was nice enough to help Maddie home. The problem is that the woman was heading to a meeting to sign a contract with a publisher for her first book. Now she has missed the meeting. She is quite upset about it. What do you suggest?"

"First, you are sure that no one was injured?

"Yes, no one was hurt."

"That's good. Madelyn needs to quickly make restitution for the damage to the woman's car and probably give her a substantial some on top of that. I can help with the book contract. Give my secretary the information she will need and I will read through it whenever I have time. Set an appointment. Has the manuscript been sent to her agent?"

"Yes, in fact they are at the door, hold on a minute." He signed the clipboard and accepted the receipt handing the manuscript to the young woman.

"That was their courier."

"Jay is there anything else?"

"Well she was shaking like a tree in the wind so I slipped her a sedative. Just one of those the doc gave me for Maddie. I just thought you should know."

"Jay, you can't go around slipping that stuff in people's drinks just because you think they need it. You better hope that she doesn't figure it out. She could take legal action against you for that. I can't talk more now Jay I need to be in court soon. Please talk to Jane and set something up."

Jay's call was transferred back to the secretary and after a few moments of discussion he ended their conversation, sighing heavily. He was bone weary. Maddie has got to change her behavior before she kills someone, he thought.

Slipping his Italian leather shoes off, he placed them by the front door; noticing that he had scraped the toes of them on the cement sidewalk when he wiggled his way through the small dog door.

Koza was starting to stir. I hope that I haven't given Jackie too much. She is still lying just as I placed her. I only gave her half. It is easy to give dogs medicine. They don't complain about it later. She washed it down with the beef broth we gave her just before I put her on the bed. I wish Jackie would move a little.

Jay went into the kitchen and hung his tuxedo jacket on the back of a chair, pulled his bow tie off and unbuttoned the top two buttons of his crisp white shirt. He was still wearing his formal attire from the night before.

After rolling up his sleeves and pouring himself another cup of coffee, he felt able to go to work. He checked the cupboards pulling out a few things and then the refrigerator. Her kitchen is well stocked, she must be a good cook, he thought, as he prepared everything for omelets. He stirred a small bowl of dough and spooned it into greased muffin tins, sprinkling the top with brown sugar. Next he dumped the condensed strong coffee down the drain and prepared the pot for a new batch.

After setting the table, he dialed Briggs.

"How's Maddie?"

"She is still asleep, Sir. She did the usual flop on her bed and is still in her gown. I pulled off her shoes and covered her. I think she will sleep most of the day."

"I just walked over to the garage and saw her car," said Jay. "It needs to be picked up right away. I backed it into the closest space.

She should not have been on the second floor. Her space is on the first. She must have missed it and instead of backing up, I think she was heading up to the roof to turn around. Also we need to have Miss Kinny's car picked up and repaired. I dropped her car key through the slot in the front door, along with Maddie's purse and keys. Did you notice them?"

"Yes, of course."

"I want you to buy Miss Kinny a new car. It must be something nice, metallic brown, with a good sound system and sensible, with four doors and a tan leather interior but not too large. Can you arrange to have her car towed and the new one in space "2G" by two o'clock today?"

"I'll do my best sir."

"You always do. I wouldn't trust my sister to anyone else. Thank you Briggs, tell Maddie she needs to give you a raise." Briggs chuckled. He always says that when Maddie has created another of her melodramatic situations, he thought. Maybe this time I will ask for that raise. He took a large reusable canvas shopping bag and walked swiftly to the parking garage where he completely emptied Koza's damaged car, of any personal belongings, not missing a thing. On his return he tapped on her front door lightly and set the bag next to it.

The house was quiet until the shower kicked on. Koza was up and in the bathroom trying to pull her head together. I can't believe that I slept. I never nap. I feel strange, she thought as she let the water run down across her hair and face. Jackie was still in the same spot. Jay hurried in feeling concern. She had not reacted to the tap on the front door. Maybe you can't use that stuff on dogs. What have I done? He worried. He leaned over the bed and gently stroked the black fur. She raised her head and moved just the tip of her tail before putting her head down and closing her eyes. Good she is alright. He breathed a sigh of relief, returning to the kitchen and switching on the coffee, just in time to pull the muffins from the oven. His dark hair was mussed. He had a habit of running his fingers through it when he was talking on the phone.

Jackie limped to the kitchen door to go out. He slid his hand to her nose. It was cool and wet, no fever. As he watched through the window, he saw her make her way to the spot where they had found her. She frantically sniffed the ground and searched the area for information. She would miss Puddin.

When she finally made her way back to the kitchen door, she could smell something good. Jay had used hamburger, rice and an egg to make a pan of dog food. He had a generous portion cooling on a plate. The rest he had stored in the refrigerator.

Koza came in the kitchen catching him off guard. Her bare feet, with pink toe nails, were showing beneath a bright yellow terry cloth robe. She hadn't made a sound crossing the carpet. The scent of her shampoo was that of a sweet spring meadow. It surrounded her. Her long, wet, brown hair hung down her back in soft natural waves. It looked darker now that it was wet.

"I made fresh coffee," he said as he poured her cup full and placed the little pitcher beside it. The burner was on and he began to add ingredients to the sizzling pan.

"That smells wonderful. What are you making?"

"Omelets and I hope you don't mind, I made a batch of dog food for Jackie with the hamburger that was in the refrigerator. I couldn't find any dog food. It's just meat, cooked rice and an egg. I make it for Maddie's animals once in a while."

"That's wonderful, but why are you still here? You don't need to do all that. Really, we are fine now, but I must admit my head feels a little strange, not exactly dizzy but close. Did you put something in my coffee to make me sleep?"

"I won't lie to you, Koza. Yes I did. The doc gave me some pills to use when I know Maddie is too nervous about work to sleep. Sometimes she goes days without rest. I noticed you were shaking and I thought a nap would help. Many people get upset when they see Maddie's lion and you got that shock on top of the accident, and then Jackie got hurt. That was terrible!" He had automatically shortened her name. Her father did the same thing. She liked it.

"I should be furious with you, but I know you meant well."

"Just so you know Maddie's bunch is never without their trainer. That's why they were not involved in that situation this morning. When Briggs pushes the release to let them come through, it is really just a buzzer that notifies the trainer that it is alright to let them. If he is busy he can override the release. He has access to the courtyard through a separate door. They have played with Jackie many times. Tonga won't hurt her. That lion thinks she is a dog."

"Now, about your car, I took the liberty of getting it towed to the repair shop. Briggs collected your things from the car. They are here in this bag. Maddie will pay the bill and she has a surprise for you, for not calling the police. It would have ruined everything. The fashion industry is very fickle. She can't stand bad publicity."

"Thank you Jay, for all you have done. None of this was your fault."

"Don't look so glum. I spoke with your publisher's secretary and your agent Mr. Maxwell. They sent a courier to pick up the manuscript. Here is your receipt. Your agent is hammering out the contract with them and it will be sent to my lawyer's office. You have a meeting with Mark Harris tomorrow at ten thirty. He will read the contract today and go over it with you tomorrow; to be sure it is favorable for you, before you sign it. Now I know that I took many liberties with your personal business, but I knew that with contracts, it is best to get it done before one of the parties changes their mind, or their best offer. I hope you don't mind me stepping in to handle the mess that Madelyn made for you."

"You certainly are the take charge type, aren't you? Actually I don't mind at all and honestly, I am so new at all this that I didn't consider that the publisher's contract should be read by a lawyer before I sign it. I was about to make a serious mistake. Thank you, Jay for everything. You would make a marvelous secretary!"

"My secretary would laugh at that. I am Jacob Spencer, at your service. Here, eat up. The eggs are done."

"Are you, "The Jacob Spencer, of Spencer's People? But you are..."

"What little? I know. I use my father for the photos. Actually we look a lot alike other than the fact that he is taller than I am, and twenty years older. The first photo in an advertising campaign I published brought calls from people wanting to hire little people. I can't understand why they thought that all our personnel were small just because I am. My mother is a little person and so is my brother, Adam. He works with me on the accounting end of things."

"That's how you knew just what to do. Your company trains people to do that very thing. They pick up the pieces and make order for those who are in need of help."

"Exactly," he said smiling.

She sipped her coffee and smiled. Her smile was beautiful. In fact everything about her was naturally beautiful. Here she sat in front of him with wet hair, and a face freshly scrubbed with no makeup and he couldn't find a thing that wasn't to his liking. He realized that he didn't want to rush off as he had planned. There was no place that he would rather be.

"Here have a muffin. You had that little mix in your cupboard. I added a few things to it."

"These are wonderful, and you are wonderful. I can't thank you enough for using your skills to help me sort this morning out."

"I was able to handle some things, but not everything," he said, dropping his eyes to his plate. "I worry about Maddie. She lives too much in the creative world and has trouble dealing with reality. Just think what this day would be like if you had not been there to keep her from killing those children! Whatever she does she totally submerges herself in it and has trouble letting go of it." He paused for a moment before continuing.

"Here is an example. She took her design team to Africa for inspiration for an exotic line she was envisioning. That's where she found the lion cub. The mother had been killed by a hunter. The cub was in a small cage at a rescue compound. She fell in love with it and felt sorry for it, I guess. She brought it back here as soon as it cleared the waiting period and had all its shots. While she was waiting for the cub to arrive, she bought the condo next to hers and had it made into a jungle. She kept two rooms, a bedroom and a bathroom for the trainer. The kitchen is still there but has been surrounded by jungle. The floor is dirt and it is open to the sky. She has large trees

24

in there. Orchids climb up the tree trunks. It is amazing. A small waterfall supplies a stream for the animal's fresh drinking water. The trainer said the cat was lonely so she gave him permission to get two big dogs. He picked the two golden labs. Tonga was raised with them. The dogs are Congo and Chase. He is the one that is always last.

Jay looked at her and laughed. "I have babbled my way through your entire breakfast. Your plate is clean. I am glad that you were able to eat."

"Now it is your turn to talk and my turn to listen and eat."

"Let me pour us both another coffee and you can tell me all about yourself." He handed her the little pitcher and began to butter his muffin. He glanced around the kitchen and noticed the bouquet of flowers in a vase near the sink and his eyes rested there. I wonder who sent them. He hadn't considered that she might be involved with someone. She wasn't wearing a wedding ring or engagement ring. He had already noticed that.

"I'm not sure where I should start," said Koza "I was born and raised in Michigan. My parents still live there, but they are divorced. My mother opened a small book store and gift shop in Port Huron and my dad still works for General Motors. He works for their corporate office in the finance division. My parents stayed friends. They go to lunch together once in a while and she still buys his shirts when she finds some on sale. My father is a little color blind and so am I. Navy blue and black look the same to me."

"I noticed that you like dark brown and tan," said Jay.

"Yes, I guess I figure they are safe colors, not too showy."

"What's wrong with being showy?" She laughed and shrugged her shoulders, feeling the tenderness in the muscles but didn't let on to Jay.

"If you will finish dressing, there is something I want to show you, and then I need to be on my way. I want to check on Maddie before I go to my place and get some rest. That party of hers lasted all night. Fancy affairs aren't really my style but I go to watch over her. I did a poor job of it this time. I thought she had gone in the ladies room but instead she had slipped out the side door. She had someone bring her Ferrari. She went there in the limo. I don't know how she got her car there or how she avoided an accident in New York traffic. How she managed to avoid being spotted by a cop, I'll never know. I must thank you again for saving her from hitting the children that was quick thinking."

"Well, I didn't really think. I just acted instinctively." Koza looked frightened at that moment. "I should have considered that she might be badly injured when she hit my big old Oldsmobile."

"If you had considered all the possible ramifications it would have been too late to do anything. You did the right thing, don't second guess yourself now. Koza, please go slip into something while I clear this away." He waved his hand in the direction of the plates and stove.

When she returned in a pale pink sweater and jeans, she found the kitchen sparkling and the dishwasher purring away. Out the window she saw Jay and Jackie walking slowly under the trees. He was even carrying a "doggy doo," pick up bag. This man is too good to be real, she thought. He is smart, fun to be around, good looking and he can cook and cleans up! Jackie sure likes him. I think he is cute.

"Are you ready?" He asked as he led Jackie back in. He had disposed of the little bag into the proper container outside.

"Yes, I just need to find my keys."

"Your purse is disorganized because it spilled. I hope that I found everything. If I didn't, it will be in the bag that Briggs brought with the things that he retrieved from your car before they took it away for repair."

"Here, I forgot to give these back to you," he said, as he pulled the door shut and made sure that it was locked. He handed her the ring with her condo keys on it. "The key for your car went with it to the repair shop."

CHAPTER THREE
POOR PUDDIN

As they entered the garage she was thinking about the damage to her car and Maddie's, but when they stepped out of the elevator on level two, a metallic brown car was being pulled into her space. Her mouth dropped open as the young man stepped out of the car smiling and handed Jay the keys.

"I hope this will do sir."

"Thank you, Briggs."

"What do you think Koza? Will this be alright to drive?

"Yes, of course, but you didn't have to rent a car for me. It will only be a few days of taxi rides. I can manage that long."

"Do you like it? You won't need to manage. This car is a gift from Maddie. He tossed the keys for the new car to Koza. She appreciates what you did and how you handled it."

"I can't take this. It's too much. She doesn't owe me anything. We all make mistakes and need help once in a while. You are repairing my car and did so much for me this morning. Really, I can't take such a gift."

"You must, it is here and paid for, just enjoy it," he said, as he hurried in the elevator and closed the doors.

My car is a brand new car! She glanced at the odometer and it read 7.5 miles as she slid on the smooth tan leather seat. It is beautiful. This even smells new. What would Mom and Dad say? I can't take such a gift for doing what is right can I? She returned to her living room just long enough to get Jackie and her purse. "Jackie we are going for a ride." I should at least allow myself the pleasure of a ride before I decide. Maybe I should call Dad when I come back.

As she drove out onto the street, Jackie moved up to the front seat and was now riding shotgun. Koza made a mental note that she had forgotten Jackie's harness and bowl. They must be in the bag of things that Briggs collected.

"I am so glad that you were not with me when all that happened. You would have been badly injured or worse," she said. Jackie was wagging and not concerned with the words that Koza had said. She just knew she was getting a fun ride with the person she loved most in the entire world.

"You like to ride in front, don't you Jackie? Do you like this new car? I do," she said. "I wonder if I dare keep it."

After enjoying the car more than she felt she had a right to, she returned it to the garage. As she approached the grass, she slipped her shoes off. I love the feel of this soft grass almost as much as the leather on the seats of the new car, she giggled to herself as she walked toward Mrs. Dodge and someone else sitting on a blanket under the trees.

"Hello, Mrs. Dodge. How are you? I am so sorry about you losing your sweet Puddin this morning."

"Hello Koza, She had a good friend in Jackie. How is she? Is she alright?"

"Yes, the man I was with knew just what to do. Jackie is feeling better already."

"Forgive me. I am being rude. Koza I would like you to meet my sister Helen. She has agreed to stay with me for a few days. Helen this is Koza, the woman that has Jackie. I told you that she tried to protect Puddin but she couldn't against two big dogs." A tear escaped Mrs. Dodge's eye and she wiped it away.

"It is nice to meet you Helen."

Mrs. Dodge bent forward and picked up two tiny blue eyed kittens.

"These little ones were left in a basket by my door about an hour ago. Someone rang the doorbell and when I went to answer it, there they were. They have so much fur that it is hard to see their eyes. Did you get these kittens for me?"

"No, I didn't, but they are darling. I had a fluffy cat when I was young. They are beautiful. Someone must have heard what happened and wanted you to have them. I'm glad. It was a nice thing to do. Well I think I better clean up after Jackie and get to work. It was nice meeting you Helen."

"It was nice meeting you, too, and Jackie. Ruby told me what a sweet girl she is."

"Maybe I'll see you later," said Koza.

When she entered her front door, the phone was ringing. She picked it up and talked to her agent, John Maxwell. His news brought tears of joy to her eyes as he related the crux of the contract, mentioning things like a jacket design clause and international publication rights, as well as movie and TV rights.

"When will they have a copy of the contract for my lawyer to read?" She asked.

"I have one in my hand." She gave him the information on the lawyer's office that Jay had provided, feeling grateful for all that he had arranged. He must do things like that for Maddie all the time. She thought as she explained about the ten thirty meeting in the morning and that she thought that he should be there.

"Please get a copy of the contract to him today, as soon as possible, so that he can go over it before the meeting."

"I will have it delivered right away and I will pick you up in a cab at your place at about ten and that will give us plenty of time so we don't have to rush."

Koza was thinking of Jay, when she hung up the phone. I wish I could ask him to be there with me in the morning, but he has already done so much that I can't ask him for anything more. Anyway he said he had an important meeting in the morning. I wonder when I will see him again. She couldn't help smiling when she thought of the funny grin that crossed his face in the garage as he closed the elevator doors. He could be a bit mischievous, I think. I saw a twinkle in his eyes that comes from monkey business.

The next morning, outside the tall skyscraper, Koza didn't recognize the woman reflected in the polished windows as they approached the huge brass trimmed doors. Her stomach was full of butterflies and her cheeks were flushed with excitement. In spite of that, the woman in the glass seemed cool and collected. In a dark brown business suit and heels, she looked very professional.

Her briefcase held another copy of her manuscript as well as questions she had jotted on a pad. She wanted so much to hold it together and look professional, but when they passed the ladies restroom off the lobby, she was forced to dart inside. She promptly lost her toast and coffee. A glance in the mirror revealed gray smudges under her eyes from lying awake most of the night, filled with anxiety and wonder at the event she was about to attend.

As she dabbed makeup under each eye and refreshed her lipstick, she was thinking of Jay and wishing that he could be beside her in that meeting. She dashed out the door and joined John Maxwell who was looking at a long list of names and suite numbers in a black case on the wall near a bank of elevators.

"Harris and Harris," she read. "That's it," she pointed.

"Tenth floor," said John. "I'll bet it's the corner suite. Lawyers make a lot of money."

Suddenly, it dawned on her that Jay said he had arranged an appointment for her with his lawyer. He never indicated what the fee would be. She swallowed hard knowing the meager amount in her checking. I'll have to make some kind of an arrangement, she thought. The elevator stopped twice to disperse people to other floors before arriving at the tenth. The door opened to reveal a hall with white carpeting, white walls and a heavy glass door with "Harris and Harris" on it in gold letters.

As they approached it, John took her hand and said, "You are the boss here. Play the part." He smiled broadly, frowned, and then quickly smiled again. This silly behavior helped to relax her and she rewarded him with a smile, as she released his hand. "Thanks," she said, as she stepped in ahead of him.

She looked every bit composed and in control. She had pulled her hair up with a silver clip and a tiny strand had escaped to flutter on her neck as she walked to the receptionist desk.

"Hello, I am Koza Kinny. I have an appointment."

"Yes, Miss Kinny. I understand that you are a new client, of Mark Harris. They are waiting for you." She led Koza to a heavy mahogany door and opened it. "Miss Kinny has arrived sir."

"Thank you, show her in."

When Koza stepped past the woman and entered, she knew she was definitely in the inner sanctum of a select few. This was a world of hand rubbed dark woods and leather; of big deals and big money. She felt totally out of place. One wall was lined with rows of matching volumes of law books and in front of them stood Jacob Spencer.

"Jay?"

She felt the butterflies again, but this time they were in her heart. She gave him her most dazzling smile.

"Do you have time to stay?"

"Yes, we have finished with our talk. He is all yours. I was just lingering long enough to see you again. Are you sure you want me to stay?"

She nodded afraid to speak, aware that her voice was showing her emotions. This can't be happening. This whole thing is a fantasy. Pretty soon I'll wake up and everything will have changed back to where it was yesterday morning. If I close my eyes and put out my hand, I will probably be able to hit the snooze button on my alarm clock, she mused.

"Miss Kinny, are you alright? When you didn't respond, you seemed as if you were in deep thought."

"Yes, I'm sorry, but I haven't had a chance to even read the offered contract yet."

"Well to tell you the truth, Jay gave me rather short notice and I haven't had time to go over it yet myself. My secretary made sure we each have a copy so we can go over it together." He handed a copy to John Maxwell and a second was given to her. Jay moved his chair closer to hers, so that he could look on. He breathed in her perfume and had all he could do to keep his hand from touching her loose strand of hair.

As he moved closer, she felt the warmth of his presence and a slight hint of his aftershave drifted past as a gentle breeze from the open window stirred the air. She noted that Maxwell had been right. He has a big corner office with lots of huge windows.

"Most of this is standard. I did notice that on the bottom of page one, the clause about any contract change needs to be submitted and approved within seven days. I think they put that in because you weren't able to be at the meeting yesterday."

He continued reading. Jay stood up and moved even closer, seeming to read the mentioned paragraph. He then sat back down.

"Notice the third paragraph on page four. You will be expected to make appearances for publicity and to attend book signings, both here and abroad, if it comes to that. They pay the travel expenses, lodging, meals etc... That is covered farther down. They are offering you a ten thousand dollar advance and forty percent of the profits after publishing, advertising and distribution expenses. That is an unusually high amount for a first effort. You must have written something they recognize as a very good product. If all this is acceptable to you, I'll need you to sign where I have marked on the pages and my father, Robert, will notarize it. Jay can sign here to stand as witness for your signature." Mark buzzed and a side door clicked open. His father, Robert, had easy access to Mark's office.

John Maxwell stood up abruptly, pushing his chair back and nearly tipped it over. He looked quite disgruntled.

"What about me? I am supposed to get ten percent?"

"It is customary that the writer can choose to have the publisher send you ten percent of her forty percent or she can make other arrangements with you. You are Miss Kinny's agent. The publisher doesn't have to include you at all."

"If I get paid ten percent of her forty percent that is only four percent and quite unacceptable, I want all ten percent right off the top!"

"It doesn't work that way, John; you know that, as well as I do." Mark turned back to Koza. "Koza let the publisher send him his check." She nodded and quickly started to sign all the indicated lines on all four sets. "You will need to send him one thousand as soon as you get your advance. He does get that in addition to the royalty percentage."

Then she turned to John and simply said, "I appreciate your effort in finding me a good publisher. Perhaps we can work together again when I finish my next book."

"It's a case of gross versus net lady. I'm not going to be cheated out of the rest of my commission. You will be talking to my lawyer soon!" He walked out.

"Is he right? Are we cheating him out of his rightful share?"

"I doubt it, but if you want to, you can drop off your copy of the contract you signed with his agency and I'll take a look at it to be sure."

"Thank you, Mr. Harris."

"Now I think my secretary can find an envelope to hold your copy and we can be finished here." He pushed a button and she immediately entered.

She opened a cabinet and removed a slick gray envelope. She slipped the set of papers in it and closed its latch, handing it to Koza.

"I will send copies to your publisher and Mr. Maxwell's office by courier today. The fourth set will always be here in our files, should you need to refer to it for any reason," she said leaving the room as if dismissing them. Koza stood and shook Mark Harris's hand and then turned her beaming smile to his father, Robert.

"Congratulations young lady. I hope you have a long and successful career." She offered her hand to shake his, but instead, he took her hand in both of his, "I would like the pleasure of taking you to dinner to celebrate your first success. Where would you like to go?"

"Unhand her you old gray fox! I reserve that pleasure for myself," said Jay. All three men laughed loudly.

"Well I guess I'll just have to take my lovely wife of forty years," said Robert and they laughed again. Koza stood there with a red face. She was not sure if she had a married man hit on her or if she was the uninformed subject of an inside joke. Jay smiled at her and steered her toward the door.

"I should have warned you. Robert still acts like he is a thirty year old bachelor. I, on the other hand, am! I am looking forward to an evening with you to celebrate. Where would you like to go?"

"I don't know. I don't go out much. Most evenings are spent on my computer."

"You have just published your first book! We are going to have a celebration tonight. I'll pick you up at seven thirty. Can you wear something less businesslike and more like evening attire?"

"That sounds like fun, but I'm not sure that my closet holds anything like you just described."

"That's terrible. A beautiful woman should always have lots of lovely gowns."

"Did you ride here with Mr. Maxwell?"

"Yes, but I can easily get a taxi."

"Nonsense; my car is waiting. My driver circles the block. Although it adds to the traffic congestion and pollution, it is easier than trying to find a place to park. His plain dark blue sedan, pulled up and Jay opened the door for her to slide in and he followed through the same door sliding very near her.

"One of the advantages of being a little person, is I don't require much room," he said smiling.

"Where are we going sir?" the driver inquired.

"Home please." Soft classical music filled the silence. Neither spoke during the short ride home. His hand lay on the seat an inch from hers. She could feel electricity so intense, that it was nearly visible. She could barely breathe. He turned, looking at her and slowly he reached up and removed the clip from her hair, dropping it into her lap. He ran his fingers through the back of her curls and they softly unfolded onto her neck and shoulders. Her body gave a tiny shiver and she was sure if she looked at her arms, that they were covered with goosebumps. She was glad that her jacket had long sleeves to conceal her reaction. She could still feel the spot where his fingers had briefly touched her neck.

"I wanted to do that all through the meeting. A mischievous little chuckle filled the air. He held her hand the rest of the way.

When they reached the courtyard he looked down at her high heeled shoes.

"We better take the sidewalk. Those shoes will sink into the grass. You could trip." She slipped them off and walked beside him barefoot across the well-manicured lawn.

"This is where we part for now. I need to check on Maddie before I go home," he said.

"I'll go with you," she said, putting her shoes back on as they reached the sidewalk.

He looked up and laughed. "I liked it better when the heels were off."

"Wait until you see what I wear on my feet tonight!" It was her turn to laugh.

Briggs was coming out Maddie's door as they arrived.

"Hello, I am glad you are both here. She is in the jungle and refuses to come out. She says she wants to stay there for the rest of her life."

"What brought that on?"

"I'm not sure. She says she prefers her animals to people."

Jay shook his head in bewilderment.

"Koza, will you come with me? Let's go see if we can make sense of her behavior. I usually tell her when I'm coming over, but in this case let's not warn her. I want to see what she is really doing.

As he opened the door, Maddie was on the floor cuddling her animals. All of them had gotten beside or on her.

"Maddie, I hear you have decided to go wild and live in here forever."

"Don't be silly Jay. I am simply acclimating, my new pet to her jungle mates." A tiny black monkey clung to her shoulder and hair as she got up. "Meet Bitsy." She will only get a little bigger. She does bite, so be careful if you touch her. You can hold her like this and she likes it." Maddie cradled the little monkey like a human baby and offered her a miniature baby bottle of milk. The monkey gripped it with all fours sucking greedily. Maddie's face held a tender expression as she looked down at the big round eyes of the baby monkey.

"Why did you deliberately upset Briggs?"

"I like to shake up things once in a while. He always acts like he has to be in total control of everything, including me. Once in a while I remind him in my own way that I am still mistress of this house and that he works for me. He was troublesome earlier and insisted that he wants a raise. He said it would normally take a staff of several, to do all the things he does for me. He can't be serious! "

"Yes Maddie, he can. He is right. He is constantly straightening out the messes you get yourself into. He does all the household managing, scheduling things around your whims and covering for you all while avoiding unpleasant press. Give him a handsome raise and do it graciously."

"Very well, but must you always be so serious? You know I could always have you replace him and let him go work somewhere else."

"Maddie, there isn't anyone else that I would trust. He has skills that others can't learn in a decade. Briggs stays!

"All my poor animal babies have to go in the back room now. Workmen will be here any minute to put a metal grid and mesh across the top of this entire jungle area. I have a few beautiful birds coming and I don't want to lose them out the top. Not to mention that Tonga has been climbing to the top of the trees, venturing up as far as she can. Now that she is full grown she might try to leap out and she could get hurt."

"Maddie, not to change the subject, but do you remember Koza? She walked back with you from the garage. It was her car you struck."

"Yes, well I wouldn't have if she had looked before she backed out."

"Sweet Sister, if she hadn't, you would have run over two little girls playing jacks on the cement. I guess you don't remember that part."

"Why would children be in the garage?"

"That is not the point. This woman saved you from hitting them. Her car was badly damaged."

"You are repairing it, of course and we need to do more than that." Jay said it with a wide smile.

"Maddie I took care of it. You bought her a new car."

"How nice of me," she said with a bitter tone. Koza felt very uncomfortable. She wasn't accustomed to such stinging banter.

"I'm sorry. I just came to make sure you were not injured. Oh and I won't be keeping the new car, but thank you for repairing my old one." She reached for the door with a frown on her face.

"No, Koza, don't go. I really haven't been behaving very well lately. Forgive me. The world doesn't seem to be treating me very well either but I've taken it out on everyone here. I apologize. I do appreciate what you did."

"Maddie, we have just come from Mark Harris's office."

"Oh my dear girl, are you planning on suing me?"

"No of course not," responded Jay instantly. "Mark was checking a contract for her with Garrett Publishing. She has sold her first book! We are going to the Teebes for dinner. Would you like to join us?"

"It will do me good to go out. Yes, I will come if Koza doesn't mind. I promise I will be good." She said. They all laughed at that.

"Jay, what time do you want us to be ready? It will take a while to soak the animal scent off and we need to choose something to wear."

"I won't have that problem, Maddie. I only have a couple gowns. The truth is that they are not really nice enough for "The Teebes"."

"Koza, I would like to treat you to one of the more classic gowns from my last show?"

"Oh, Maddie, I couldn't. They sell for so much money. I would be afraid to eat, wearing it."

"Don't be silly. A gown is only worth the price on it, if it sells. My gowns are like any other, just a piece of cloth." She placed the sleeping baby monkey on a cozy bed with several stuffed animals. "The trainer will move her to the back as soon as we leave." She explained. "Come on; let's go see what I have that looks good on you. We will see you later Jay," she said, as she ushered them out of the jungle and carefully latched the door.

Both women were smiling as they headed into Maddie's private quarters. Once through the door, Maddie pressed a button.

"Yes, Madam," Brigg's voice responded immediately.

"I will not require dinner this evening. We are going out, but we would like a bottle of champagne and two glasses. Please bring it to the gown room."

Jay whistled as he walked across the grass in the direction of his condo. He looked down the court to see the two elderly ladies sitting on a blanket enjoying the kittens. I am a genius! He thought. Two are always better than one.

The women sipped the champagne and sorted through racks of beautiful full length gowns.

"Finally, here is the one I have been looking for."

"Oh, Miss Clay, this is stunning!"

"So will you be in it. Let's just add this." She opened a drawer and removed a large pendant necklace of golden amber with earrings to match.

"The deep chocolate brown satin of the dress will be perfectly accented by these jewels, and there are shoes in the racks in the dressing room. Are you about a size six? There are heels and a few pair of Egyptian sandals. They might be a good choice since Jay will be our escort."

"I like the idea of sandals." Koza was diplomatic and asked the designer, her advice on which pair.

"Since this dress is perfectly simple, you could wear any of them, but we don't want to overdo it. The cream sandals with the crystals will look nice, and carry this matching bag.

"What if this gown doesn't fit? I should try it on."

"I am guessing, but I am sure that you are a small four. It will fit. I will have Briggs deliver these things to you in just a few minutes. Where do you live dear?"

"I live in number "2G".

"Wonderful, that is just down the walk a short way."

Koza was suddenly remembering the condition Maddie had been in the night that she met her. She boldly poured Maddie's glass a little fuller and tucked the bottle under her arm. I hope you don't mind, but champagne will go well with my bubble bath. I am looking forward to a relaxing soak. She smiled at Maddie and hugged her for an instant.

"Thank you Maddie for all the beautiful things. I will take extra care with them."

She raised her glass gaily and left quickly, before Maddie had time to object to her snatching the wine. The trouble is, she can always have Briggs bring more, she thought as she hurried to her front door. Briggs followed almost immediately carrying a large black box, tied with white satin ribbon. He took it in for her and held out a white orchid.

"This is from me. Congratulations." He turned and walked quickly away. Thank you she called as he headed toward Jay's condo. He showed a grin of approval, as he rounded the corner.

Koza closed the front door and moving through the living room to the bedroom, she gently settled the box on her comforter. Jackie was at the side door, eager to go out. Koza watched as Jackie headed for Mrs. Dodge and her sister, rambunctiously greeting each and nuzzling the kittens, then jogging off to water her favorite bushes near the fence to the park. Jackie stood looking through the fence and Koza was sure that Jackie was remembering the encounter with the dogs and the loss of her playmate. Excitedly, Jackie turned and ran full speed the length of the court to reach the condo. When she came in her tongue was dangling out the side of her face and she looked as if she were smiling. Koza gave her the last of the special dog food recipe that Jay had made, along with fresh water.

"Now, it is my turn." She scratched Jackie's ears and gave her a hug.

When Jackie had licked her bowl clean, she pushed open the bathroom door, to find Koza enjoying a hot tub of scented bubble bath. With her two front paws on the edge of the tub, she reached over to lick Koza's face. Koza dabbed a handful of bubbles on Jackie's paws, giggling as Jackie snapped at the bubbles, barking and spinning around bunching the plush bath mat into a heap. Finally she flopped down panting.

"Jackie, I am going out to dinner at "The Teebes," tonight and I will be wearing a designer gown worth thousands of dollars. My book is being published. It's really happening!" Jackie jumped up excitedly cocking her head to the side, responding to the joy in Koza's voice. "Sweet friend, I wish you understood the importance of what I'm telling you. Celebrate with me Jackie!" Koza offered the glass of bubbly champagne to the furry face that sniffed it and then barked. Koza laughed at her and drank the rest of the glass of wine herself. Stepping out of the tub, she went into the shower to rinse away the clinging bubbles. I did use too much of that stuff, but it was fun, she thought.

As soon as I am dry and put on my lotion, I should put the rest of that wine in the refrigerator. I have nothing in my stomach she thought as she pulled her robe on. Maybe I should eat something.

I'll trade this wine for an egg with grated cheese. I don't want to be tipsy. With the pan in one hand and a fork in the other, she scooped the scrambled egg into her mouth, laughing at her own lack of etiquette. She washed it down with a small glass of milk.

In the bathroom again, she removed her polish and scrubbed her nails with a buffer, applying a coat of clear. She arranged makeup and hair products she would use that night. She took her daily vitamin and looked into the eyes of the girl in the mirror. "You are an author. You are going to "The Teebes" with a handsome little man and his famous designer sister and you are going to wear the most beautiful gown you have ever seen!"

Just for a moment, that declaration was followed by a slump in her adrenaline, and she realized how exhausted she was. I need to rest. She set her alarm for six thirty pm and then changed it to six fifteen. With the gown hanging where she could see it, she climbed into bed. Jackie cuddled up next to her, and in spite of the excitement, she drifted off to sleep quickly. Jackie woke her with a lick on her face, because the alarm clock was beeping loudly. She hit the button on the move.

"Thank you, Jackie," she said and took time to scratch the dogs tummy. I don't want to be late. She raced to get dressed.

As the satin dress slipped over her head and settled smoothly on her body, she held her breath. The full length mirror revealed a perfect fit, just as Maddie had predicted. The soft shimmer of the satin clung to her curves showing off her figure to perfection.

Her hot rollers lay in a heap in the sink as she ran her fingers gently through her curls, adjusting them here and there to fall in a casual cascade around her face. Bending far forward she used hair spray and counted slowly to ten waiting for the spray to dry. Doing that gave her hair the professional lift and body that she wanted.

Trying on the heavy jewelry that Maddie had chosen, she decided on a fine gold chain with a small diamond cross that lay at her throat.

As always she used minimal makeup. Her natural coloring needed little enhancement, but as she looked in the mirror she wasn't completely pleased. The neckline plunged enough that it made her feel uncomfortably exposed. A trip to the kitchen solved the problem. The orchid Briggs had given her stood in a tiny vase on the counter. With the orchid's stem wrapped, she tucked the beautiful white bloom between her breasts, covering the exposed cleavage and fastened it there.

"That is what I needed!" She said to Jackie.

"A little perfume goes a long way," she said, repeating what her mother had taught her. The tiny purse held only a few items. She placed it near a rich, soft cream colored lace shawl that lay on the arm of the couch. She paced the room in the sandals. Hoping they would not make a blister before the night was over. I feel like Cinderella waiting for my carriage, she thought, not resisting the urge to look in the long mirror again. "Earrings, I need earrings. My small diamond studs will do nicely."

As she fastened the second one and took a final peek, a light knock at her door drew her attention away from her appearance. She raced to check that the dog door was not latched and handed Jackie a bone she had waiting on the cupboard. Her shawl over her arm and the evening bag in hand, she answered the door with a flutter in her chest but it wasn't Jay. It was Briggs.

CHAPTER FOUR
THE TEEBES

"Mr. Spencer sent me to escort you to the car. Madam is with him. I see that you are wearing the orchid I gave you."

"Thank you, again for it. It is lovely."

"Don't tell Miss Clay, but I picked it in her jungle room." They laughed conspiratorially, as they walked in the direction of the car. "It was a good try, taking the champagne, but I must warn you, she got more. I stayed away hoping she wouldn't. Let's just say she has started the party without you. That's why Mr. Spencer didn't come for you. He was speaking with her."

A long silver-gray limousine waited at the end of the sidewalk. As Jay stepped out, Koza heard a light sniffle from inside the vehicle.

"Good evening, Miss Kozarina Kinny, author," he greeted her spectacularly. "You look ravishing. I have never seen one of Maddie's designs presented in such a lovely manner." He hesitated and then leaned closer saying quietly, "Koza, you are the most beautiful woman I have ever seen. He reached up and stroked the tip of one curl. I'm glad you wore your hair down.

As he helped her into the car, he said, louder than necessary, "I am glad to announce to one and all, that my sister has made a commitment to go on the wagon! In honor of her pledge and your success we have on board, special drinks this evening. All will be served in spill proof cups.

"Really Jay, did you think that was in good taste?"

"Perhaps not Maddie, but unfortunately it is necessary!"

Koza looked at the woman across from her as the buildings and traffic moved outside the darkened windows.

"Thank you for loaning me this beautiful gown. It is so lovely. I feel like Cinderella!"

"You do it justice. No one could wear it and look lovelier in it. I want you to keep it. Where did you get the idea to accessorize with a flower instead of the jewelry?"

"I'm sorry, I hope you aren't offended. The jewels are beautiful, but I am not used to such extravagance."

"I love it. I may steal that look for my next show." They laughed and chatted but the gaiety was superficial. Koza could feel the tension between Maddie and Jay. Maddie accepted her cup with a scowl.

"What is it?"

"Taste it Maddie. It's what we are drinking, with a slight adjustment.

Jay had called ahead and paid handsomely to be sure that his sister was acknowledged and fussed over. He had called the bar and arranged for her to be served no alcohol. Her drinks were to be carefully blended to color match everyone else's.

It was nearly an hour later, when the crisp tuxedoed gentleman opened the door to usher the three of them into "The Teebes," while the limousine was parked. The brightly lit entry and small colored spots played with the beads on the skirt of Maddie's gown, refracting into a thousand colored sparkles as she moved slowly with head held high. She made an entrance like a queen.

As they were settled at the table the waiter said, "Mr. Spencer, your other guest has just arrived."

Maddie's doctor approached the table and kissed her forehead. He slid into the empty chair gracefully after being introduced to Koza.

"Jay, it must be nice having your pick of all the models!"

"Not at all, Koza is a writer. Her first book will be out soon."

"Wonderful, tell us about it."

"No, not about the storyline, but I will tell you that Jay was extremely helpful. I had a small fender bender, when I was supposed to deliver the manuscript and attend a contract signing. He had the manuscript delivered by courier and arranged to have the contract read by his lawyer before I signed it."

"Good going Jay. We have to take good care of our ladies. Madelyn, the music is good tonight." He took her hand. "Dance with me, he said, as he placed her tiny evening bag in his pocket and shook his head to the waiter that had just come up to their table.

He held her close, with his cheek against hers and whispered, "It's like old times Maddie, the same perfume, and the same music. Remember this song? We were at that cabin over-looking the sea. We danced on the patio and drank champagne until dawn."

"We didn't lose our love Michael; our careers pulled us in opposite directions."

"They look good together," said Koza, "She belongs in his arms."

"Yes, I would like it, if they got together. He is good for her. She needs him."

"And Michael, what does he need?"

"He needs the same thing every man needs, a woman at his side that he can't live without. Would you like to dance instead of watching them? We won't look quite as matched as they do, but we will muddle through."

On the dance floor he held her tightly and placed his hand against her waist. Her chin automatically rested near his forehead. Just as they relaxed and got into the rhythm of the music; the band announced a short break.

They returned to their table and she noticed that two place settings had been removed and two simple plates of pasta with beef tips and mushrooms were placed before them. Green salads and red wine completed the offering.

"That was short but sweet. We do seem to fit together rather nicely," commented Jay.

She looked down and her face began to turn red. "Oh no, I'm sorry. I didn't mean... Now I've put my foot in my mouth. I just meant that I appreciated you not wearing high heels."

"Actually it was Maddie who suggested the sandals. Where is she? Have they left?"

"Yes, as a matter of necessity, Dr. Michael Reeves, will be taking her for a much needed rest. Her show is the culmination of an entire year of constant work. The last month is especially grueling. After the new line is revealed, she literally collapses. Her strength is depleted and Michael is the perfect one to get her to rest and rebuild. Now I think I better fill my mouth with food before I say something else that I shouldn't." They both laughed as they tasted the meal.

"This is delicious. I'm starving!" said Koza

"Suddenly, so am I," he said.

They ate quietly for a few moments and then he said, "I brought you a small souvenir of the evening." He pulled a gold bracelet from his pocket and fastened it around her wrist.

"Before you object, these are just little diamonds from a little man.

Koza realized she was holding her breath.

"Oh Jay, this is beautiful, but I can't take this. You have already spent too much money on me."

"I want you to have it. I hope you will think of this evening and smile. Please keep it. Would you like to dance?" He asked, changing the subject. They slid across the floor effortlessly. He is small, but he is a gem. I think I'm falling in love. It's only been two days. How can this be real? How can it be happening? They are wealthy people and my family is working class. People will think I am after his money. They won't see him as I do. Most of the time I don't even notice that he is little. She smiled as she thought, we do fit together well.

"What are you thinking about?" She didn't reply, but instead she snuggled closer, laying her cheek on his hair. Her heart was racing and it wasn't from the slow dance.

As the evening ended, he held her hand and led her out into the cool night air. They headed down the steps but he stopped and turned her around, while he stepped back up one step. He looked directly into her eyes and kissed her gently and then ravenously, and then once again tenderly.

"I love you Koza Kinny. I have never felt like this before." He stroked her hair and kissed her again, lingering, and savoring the moment. Her heart was flying. He moved down the steps holding her hand as they approached the waiting car.

"Thank God, there were no photographers there waiting outside tonight," He said. "I couldn't stop myself." Inside the limousine, he slid close, not saying anything more as the vehicle moved out slowly into traffic. Jay pushed a button and the top opened to reveal the dark sky and the lights of the city above them. "Would you like a cup of coffee?"

"That's a good idea." He pushed a few more buttons and coffee started to trickle into a tall ceramic cup. He pushed another button and a streak of white joined the coffee in the cup. When it finished, he snapped a pretty clear glass lid on it before handing it to her. She noticed another cup filling. "I've never seen anything quite like this. The coffee is ready when you are and it's fresh and tastes wonderful."

"I wish I had met you five years ago," he said. "You could have saved me from the disastrous divorce I am going through now. She has deceived me at every turn and if she has her way, I will be destitute when she gets through. Mark Harris has been attempting to negotiate with her, but she wants my business, my condo and even this car. She had an affair and got pregnant with twins. She asserted the children were mine but DNA proved otherwise. She has convinced a lot of people that I cheated on her. The Social Pages of the papers sometimes run photos of Maddie and me with a group of her models. That's all the judge will need to see. I've had Christmas parties and the models are often there. She has a photo of one of them kissing me under the mistletoe. I didn't hang it; she held it over my head. Koza I just want you to know that I didn't cheat on her ever. I never loved her the way I do you. I thought I had it all. The business, two houses, nice cars and a beautiful wife, but I never really had her. She deceived me. Mark is doing what he can to salvage something of my life. When she went into labor, they had to stop it and do a C section. They had discovered two months earlier that she was having conjoined twins but she didn't tell me. They only lived one day.

"Jay, I am so sorry. This whole thing has to be very painful for you. You don't deserve to go through such a predicament. I want you to know that I feel something for you, but I'm not sure if I'm falling for you or just riding a wave of adrenaline. It has only been two days. I know you are kind and caring and generous. I like you and it is fun being with you. Can that be enough for now?"

"I guess it has to be. It's a beginning."

He leaned over and kissed her cheek as the car stopped in the same place it had picked her up. They walked down the sidewalk and then cut across a strip of lawn. "The grass is wet," she said, holding her dress up until they reached the sidewalk in front of her condo.

He took her key from her hand and unlocked the door. Jackie greeted them with happy barks and wags. Jay knelt and scratched her ears and hugged her. "I'll take her for a walk; I'm not ready to sleep yet." Jackie bounded here and there checking every tree for a new scent. It's time to take you home Jackie. He easily slipped through Maddie's dog door and found the dog food. A couple big scoops should do you. He put an extra scoop in the sack just in case. Come on girl, let's take you home. Jackie paused at the front door and then ran around to the side. He followed her and tapped on the window. Koza answered, wrapped in her yellow robe.

"Here is a little dog food. I know you haven't had time to shop."

"Thank you, Jay; you are such a good friend."

"I want to be much more than a friend, Koza." He smiled and walked away.

She closed the door and as he walked near the first light, she saw a sad expression cover his face.

"Jay," she called after him. "Do you have to get up early in the morning?"

"No, do you?"

"Not really. Do you want to come in and talk for a while?" He stepped in smiling. She made a pot of decaffeinated coffee and they carried their steaming cups into the living room.

"Jay, I want to know everything about you, where you were born, where you grew up, just anything you can think of." They talked for hours without realizing the time.

"I don't understand how you could open a business like you did and train help to be a butler, servant, valet, cook, secretary or companion, sometimes, all in one. Who taught you?"

"I see you have been doing some research. After college, I realized what I wanted to do, so I started gathering people around me that had the knowledge I needed. They became my teachers and training staff. We have expanded into an international company. We have several locations in England, France, Italy and we just opened another one in Germany. I'll be popping in on them someday soon. I would love it if you would go with me."

"I must warn you, the only language I speak is this one," she said. He pushed his shoes off and laid his head on her lap.

"Now it is your turn, he said. I'm all ears."

She smiled at his comfortable behavior.

"I was born in Durand, Michigan. It is just a small town that the train station brought into being. My folks used the same doctor all the years that I lived at home." She looked down. He was smiling, but his eyes were closed. With two fingers, she stroked his forehead, moving his hair back in place. He caught her hand in midair and pressed it to his lips before cuddling it against his chest. She continued her story. "I studied journalism and accounting, carrying a double major in college."

That is when my parents separated and when I went home for Christmas they told me. I was devastated. They stayed friends though and live only two hours apart. My father remarried during my senior year to a woman from his church. Her name is Bethany. She has one daughter, Virginia, a junior in college now. My father adores her. The one time I visited, she was unpleasant to me. I suppose I should excuse her because she is young and just being defensive. My mother hasn't remarried. I don't think she goes out at all. She is active though. She plays golf once a week and works at the library as a volunteer and runs her own books and gift shop. I can't wait to mail her a copy of my book. I think she will carry them in her little shop.

Koza looked down to find Jay sound asleep. She didn't want to disturb him to send him home. She placed a pillow behind her own head and pulled the soft throw over him. She glanced at the clock. It was three thirty.

He has a wonderful face, she thought as she smoothed his dark hair. She was smiling as she leaned her head back and fell asleep.

When she woke, the sun was shining in the window. The drapes were partially opened. Jay had silently let himself out. He went to Maddie's to rest in one of her guest rooms.

Jay hoped that it was going well for Maddie and Michael. He wondered when Michael would contact him to let him know, where they were and if she was cooperating. She never has admitted that she has a drinking problem, he thought, as he closed his eyes. This is a nice room. I think she keeps it simple and neat just for me. It feels like a man's room.

*****

"Madelyn, I should have married you long ago."

"Michael, why would you want me, I am still wrapped up in my designs and you have a patient list a mile long? Our lives are so involved. We have no quality time left for a real relationship."

"You're wrong Madelyn. I have not taken a new patient in 2 years. I have only a dozen and I could transfer them to my partner very easily. I have been thinking of retiring. Can you take a few weeks off without having a fabric fit?" They both laughed as he pulled into the garage and into her space. "Come on, my darling, we are going to pack your bags. Let's go visit our special place, the cabin by the sea."

"Yes, I will do it! That is the most beautiful place in the world."

Jay heard the voices in Maddie's bedroom as Michael helped her pack. Jay made a quick exit. He smiled as he glanced toward Koza's front window. The drapes were wide open now. Jackie came bounding across the lawn to greet him, prancing and wagging.

"I have a secret; Jackie girl. You are not the only one that loves Koza. My furry friend, you heal fast," he said, as he checked her wounds. "I think we can put your collar back on today."

"What do you think of the two kittens that I sent to Mrs. Dodge? Do you approve? I saw you checking them out yesterday. They are small now, but they will grow fast and let me warn you, they have their claws." She had followed him to his door. "Go back girl and find Koza. That's a good girl." He watched as Jackie sped up cutting through the trees.

Inside his door Jay found a pile of mail on the floor. He scooped up the envelopes and dropped them on his desk. He made his way to the shower. With clean clothes and a cup of fresh coffee, he then plowed through the envelopes while his computer downloaded a ton of e-mail. He deleted several before opening one that read, "Jay, we intended to call, but ran out of time. We are using the airport computer, on our way to the cabin by the sea, Love, Maddie and Michael."

That's really welcome news, he thought, as he turned off his computer. I will deal with the rest of that stuff later. Tucking his cell phone in his pocket, he headed for his kitchen. It was his favorite room. It was large enough to work in with custom counters just the right height. His table and chairs were also custom made to accommodate his four foot tall body. Here he didn't feel like a little person, he felt average and normal. In his home everything was comfortable. The colors of the Mediterranean echoed from room to room in a soothing and coordinated manner.

I wonder if Koza will like it here. I hope she will be comfortable, but we wouldn't need to live here at all. We could live anywhere. She is a writer. As long as she has her computer with her, she can write. I'll get her a new one. A good laptop she can take with her wherever we go. I'm getting ahead of myself. She hasn't said she loves me, yet…. He thought, but she will.

With his cell phone in hand, he headed to the garage. "Yes, two dozen long stemmed pure white, at five o'clock sharp. The card should read, "You are pure joy." "Love Jay"

Shopping at the food market took an hour. He stocked his pantry in good fashion. His freezer received steaks, lobster, chicken, fish and French lime ice. All of his selections were delivered to his back door just a few minutes after he arrived. He was busy planning and cooking all afternoon.

*****

Madelyn looked around the little cabin. "It is exactly as I remembered it. We are lucky that it was available on such short notice."

"Maddie, it will always be available. I own it. I bought it right after we were here." He poured her a drink in a tall glass and one for himself. The liquid reflected the setting sun, creating tiny red beams on the stone floor of the patio. "This is cranberry juice and citrus soda with a vitamin concentrate and just a twist of lime. Try it. Do you like it?"

"I would like it better with some vodka in it!"

"Darling, I like you just as you are. The alcohol changes you. Do I dare just say that you are not as lovely when you are drinking? I want our true feelings and true words while we are here. Don't you?"

"Of course I do. Look Michael at the last glimmers of the sun on the sea."

They stood hand in hand near the patio railing. He slipped his arms around her and kissed her tenderly. They watched the beautiful golden light subside and the early evening darkness allowed the millions of stars to twinkle through.

*****

The doorbell rang and Koza received the white bouquet of roses, right at five as ordered. She had never received roses before. She caught her breath as she read the card. "You are pure joy, love Jay." What a lovely sentiment, she thought; I will keep this card always. She put it in her jewelry box, under the bracelet he had given her.

After arranging the flowers in her biggest vase, she slid her coffee table against the bottom of the window and placed them in the center for the world outside to see. She sat on the couch enjoying them, when Jay's face appeared above them through the glass. She opened the front door laughing.

"Thank you for the lovely roses."

"You are welcome. You should always have fresh roses and be surrounded with exquisite things, but for now all I can offer you, is mere sustenance. Will you join me for an evening meal in my kitchen?"

"Have you been cooking again?"

"I have. Guilty as charged."

Koza fed Jackie before leaving, pouring a generous amount of dog food into her bowl.

"There you are girl," she said as she set down her bowl of clean water. Jackie crunched a mouthful while wagging as she ate. He stroked her back and she wagged faster looking up at him. "She loves you. She remembers that you helped her when she was hurt and cooked her some special food."

"Jackie, I am going to borrow Koza for a while. We will see you later girl." He took Koza's hand. "Let's go eat, pretty lady." His home was filled with wonderful aromas.

Koza didn't show it, when she noticed the custom sizes in the kitchen. She found that she was glad that she was not tall. Usually furniture seemed a bit too high for her, too. This, although a bit lower than she was used to, seemed quite comfortable. He poured glasses of iced tea and served a colorful salad of fruit. On the top was a slice of star fruit drizzled with a special sweet sauce.

"This is beautiful! I have never eaten a pleasing salad like this before. It is delicious. Jay, you are charming and clever. He smiled as he popped his entire slice of star fruit into his mouth."

They enjoyed the meal he had so carefully prepared. They talked and laughed taking pleasure in each other's company. Just as they finished their tangy bowls of French lime ice, his phone rang. He paced the room, running his fingers through his hair. She couldn't make sense of the short replies from Jay, but it was obvious that it was good news. "I will as soon as possible. Yes, I'll ask her." He said and hung up. "Koza, Maddie and Michael are getting married. They want us to fly over and be witnesses this weekend. Will you do it? This is the best thing that could transpire. Will you go with me Koza?"

"Why would they want me?"

"I talked to them last night and told them, you are the finest thing that has ever happened to me."

"Jay, I told you that we need to move slowly. I'm not sure what I feel for you yet and I am new in my job. I don't know if they will let me have time off."

"They will. Don't worry. I know Bennington. He owes me more than one favor and maybe you can figure out your feelings while we are on the trip. You can rest and enjoy the coast of Greece. Jackie can join Maddie's bunch and she will love it. By the way, I don't think you realize it but Briggs has already been inviting her to come in when you have been gone. She is an accepted part of their group.

Please say you will go with me," he coaxed with his most persuasive smile. We can fly out on the first flight tomorrow."

"Greece? I may regret this, but alright, I'll go with you, but you need to know that I am doing this for Maddie, because she was so generous. I owe her big time and I like her in spite of our traumatic start."

"I promise, you won't regret it and all you need to do is pack casual clothes for warm weather and don't forget to give your boss a courtesy call. Koza, I am so glad that you are coming with me. I'll make all the arrangements and call you with the time we will pick you up."

"Jay, slow down. I know you are a take charge type but you haven't given me time to really wrap my head around this! Greece?"

*****

As the huge intercontinental jet waited on the tarmac, for its turn to take off, Koza felt overwhelmed. She was sure that she had forgotten something. She had packed two large cases and a carryon. Everything is so rushed. The last few days have been a whirlwind. I can barely catch my breath before something else unexpected comes along.

Jay gently took her hand and pressed it to his lips.

"Relax Koza, from here on its all fun. Here we go we are rolling." She gripped his hand tightly as they turned onto the runway. The big bird vibrated slightly and made a loud whining, roaring, whooshing sound as the jet gobbled up the runway.

"Please God keep us safe." She murmured as the plane left the cement, climbing at an angle that was disconcerting but at the same time reassuring and thrilling. Koza had never been in a plane so large and powerful.

"You can open your eyes now," he whispered in her ear as he kissed her cheek. "You do a good imitation of Snow White." She smiled and admitted that she was glad she wasn't alone.

"I like being with you Jay, but I think you are casting a spell on me. I can't allow myself to fall in love with you. You are a married man."

"Not for long Snow White. Mark called me last night after I walked you home. Evelyn has finally agreed to the conditions of the divorce, if I let her have the villa in the south of France. I never really liked that place anyway. It is too big, and she always managed to fill it with her friends when I was there. I didn't like them either. They just hung with her for the free ride but she couldn't see it. She just thought they loved being around her. Well she can have them and the place. In addition, she gets the profit from the branches of "Spencer's People" in France and England, plus five million a year for five years. She can't touch the structure of my staffs in France or England and has no authority, but she gets all the profits for those years."

"That is an extremely large amount of money to give someone for being your wife for a few years."

"She did more than just be my wife. She lost twins. I was ready to have those babies and love them even though I knew they weren't mine. She can't have any more children. Evelyn blamed me when they were born as they were. She said if I was normal, then they would have been. They died twenty hours after they were born. She has hated me ever since. The doctor told her they were not mine but somehow she had convinced herself that they were."

"Oh, Jay, what a terrible thing for her to say, I'm so sorry." She leaned over and placed her head on his shoulder, cuddling close to comfort him.

"I wanted children as much as she did." he continued, "She never considered how I felt. When she left the hospital she went to her precious villa and has not lived with me since. Her family is good. They were kind to me and tried to get her to come back. It was no use. Her own mother told me to accept that Evelyn would rip my heart out and tear it into pieces. She said for me to prepare to lose everything and that Evelyn will never have enough. I think her mind was affected when the twins were lost. With that thought in mind, I guess Mark Harris has done a good job for me. It will be wonderful to be free and able to move on with my life."

"Let's change the subject," she said with a gentle smile.

"You are right. I don't want to think about her anymore. Come on let's go up to the lounge."

He led her to a circular stair case that seemed to wrap its padded railings around them as they ascended.

At the top Koza found herself in a fairly large room with soft music and plush carpeting. The small tables and dim lighting gave an intimate feeling as they selected two pearl gray velvet chairs in the corner. The swivel chairs and tiny table were bolted to the floor. The waiter brought their coffee in heavy mugs and placed them on rubber coasters that looked like lace. A dinner plate sized tray of fruit, cheese and tiny sweet rolls nearly covered the table top.

"We may run into some turbulence soon. It will be more comfortable for you if you fasten your seat belts," the waiter suggested. Koza smiled. She hadn't noticed the belts hanging on the sides of the lounge chairs.

A dark cloud bank slid past the windows, and suddenly the big plane moved in an up and down motion leaving them feeling as if their stomachs were above and then below them for an instant. Koza noticed that the waiter had seated himself and was also buckled in. One other couple near the stairs had carefully returned to their seats below. Jay and Koza sipped their coffee and ate from the tray as the storm was left behind. The plane entered a beautiful blue sky.

When Jay and Koza returned to their seats, they found that the movie was about to begin. Jay seldom watched television and never went to the movie theatre.

"No time." He explained as he adjusted his headset. Her head found his shoulder and soon she was asleep. Koza had been up most of the night, first talking to her father and then her mother. They each rejoiced with her about publishing her first book and agreed that a week's vacation with a friend was just what she needed.

Neither suspected that her friend was a man, and they would have been shocked if she had explained how she had met him and that she felt she was falling in love with everything about him, even his small stature seemed special and unique to her.

As he laughed at the silly movie, he felt her shift and sit up.

"Welcome back Snow White," he said, as he touched her cheek with his finger. You have a line on your cheek from my collar. You slept through the entire movie."

"I'm sorry. I am not very good company when I am tired. I was up most of the night making calls and then packing. I was dreaming about Jackie. Do you think Jackie will be safe there at Madelyn's? She seemed a little intimidated when we dropped her off."

"When I looked back, the trainer was rubbing her belly," said Jay. "She will be fine."

The night had gone slowly providing time for them to talk and think. By the time the plane began to descend Koza knew that she had lost her heart and was sure she had also lost her good sense. This man beside her was still married and she really didn't know very much about his life or the real person beneath the professional veneer that he so expertly used to dazzle her.

Inside the terminal Jay and Koza were met by a driver in uniform. He took a cart and gathered their luggage, leading the way to the limousine.

As they swept past quaint store fronts and inviting lovely restaurants, Koza longed to get out and walk along the sidewalk. Jay seemed to read her mind when he told the driver to pull over to the curb.

They were out strolling along when a young olive skinned lad with black shiny hair had stopped and offered her a seat on his bicycle handlebars. Jay interpreted the offer and she giggled with delight shaking her head "no". Flower boxes spilled sunny colors down the stone walls, beneath open windows. Jay pointed to a structure that looked like it had stood the test of time. Made of stone and heavy beams its doors stood wide open to welcome guests. A time worn sign hung above their heads, peeking through a vine, announcing the establishment's name. Koza pointed at it and said "it's Greek to me." They laughed as Jay told her what it said.

"This is where we will stay. Tomorrow we will drive to Michael's cabin by the sea.

The Inn was cool inside, and felt almost chilly to Koza's sun warmed skin.

"How far is it to Michael's?"

"I think it is less than a hundred kilometers, but it will seem much more. The roads are narrow, and with a lot of twists and hills. I am glad we have a very good driver. Let's settle in our rooms and rest. I will pick you up at six, Grecian time. We can come down to their dining room and enjoy the music, fine food and wine."

"Sounds like a good plan to me." She said with a happy smile that melted his heart and left him wanting to wrap her in his arms. Seeming to sense his intent, she went up the stairs, feeling as light as a feather, and behaving like a little girl.

Koza didn't want to waste a moment resting. She was energized and full of butterflies. I need to be more dignified. She scolded herself. I need to remember that I am just a friend that has been invited to witness a wedding, she thought, not act like a flirt, as father would say.

"Take a deep breath and cool your jets!" She laughed at her own excited state as she stepped into the wonderfully deep, claw foot tub, with her favorite scented bubbles. The last time I did this I was drinking champagne and Jackie was putting her feet up curious about the bubbles. I miss her. "Please father, watch over her and keep her happy and safe. Thank you again for everything you are doing in my life. So many wonderful things have happened recently that I can't imagine what events you have in store for me. Please give Jay and me your blessings. Help him to work things out so that I can in good conscience feel free to open my heart to him. Please help Maddie and Michael to work through her problem and let them have a good life together. Thank you for this, the tub, the Inn, the trip, and thanks for Greece. I never thought I would come here. This is like a dream, a wonderful, superlative dream with a little man in it! I love you Father and I love Your Son. Please watch over my parents and continue to bless them. Amen."

The double doors in the bedroom opened to a small balcony with a pair of lounge chairs and a table. Several clay pots of bright red geraniums sat on the wide railing overlooking the vibrant red tile roofs of the many nearby buildings. I can't see the ocean from here but this is a beautiful view, she thought, as she wrapped herself in a light blue cotton robe and walked out. She looked back at the heavy doors with small square windows all the way to the floor. Everything is so lovely, she thought. I can smell the ocean.

Being thrilled with the sight, she used her phone-camera and snapped several photos, and then she included the bathroom and its tub and the comfortable bed. Mother will love these, she thought. I'll send them to her later. She returned to the sunshine to give her hair a good brushing, and then stepped in closing the double doors and drapes. She slipped into a long turquoise skirt and matching strapless top with silver sandals and a silver chain of tiny stars that circled close to her throat. I'll just scoop my hair back on both sides with these small clips and let the rest flow down my back. He will probably pull them out before the evening is over. She smiled as she touched up a few curls with the curling iron. I am glad they provided this for me. I guess their electricity is different than ours in the states. Jay said not to bring mine.

She looked at the clock. It read exactly 6 o'clock. She wasn't sure what she should do next. She wondered if she should call his room to say she was ready. Gently she opened her door partway and nervously peeked into the hall. There sitting on the carpet a few feet from her door was Jay. His head was tipped back against the wall and his eyes were closed. She wondered how long he had been there. "Jay?" she said softly.

His eyes sprang open and a smile spread across his face as he saw her standing in her doorway. You are lovely and ready on time. Yum, you smell good, too," he said, leaning toward her for a kiss. She smiled and gave him a small peck, before saying, you smell pretty good yourself."

At the bottom of the stairs, he held her hand tightly and spun her around.

"This will be our only evening alone, until after their wedding. We should make the most of it. Dance with me, I want to hold you," he said, cuddling closely, as they entered the floor filled with couples of all ages. The music was vibrant and lively. Koza felt a happiness that filled a void she hadn't known existed.

Suddenly, she giggled. "What is it?" he asked as he smiled up at her.

"I was just thinking, we do fit together pretty well," she said, bringing an explosion of unchecked laughter from both of them.

CHAPTER FIVE
GREECE

When they finally left the dance floor, the waitress had a table ready for them on the patio. She wore a crisp white, gathered skirt that covered beyond her knees and a white peasant blouse. A small brightly embroidered apron added the only color to her unique uniform. She beamed a wide smile for Jay.

"You are Mr. Spencer, yes?"

"Yes."

"I am Iona. Were the rooms satisfactory, sir?"

"Yes, we are happy. You may serve the meal Iona. I called the chef earlier and he has it ready by now, I am sure."

She scurried away, returning with plates and bowls full of food that smelled delicious, but most of it was not familiar to Koza. She sampled each, finding it all very flavorful. She thought it interesting that they had cooked and served food in grape leaves. The chicken had an herbal glaze quite different from anything she had ever tasted. Desert was a filling of honey and nuts between layers of flakey pastry. He said it was called baklava. The coffee was dark and strong, requiring a second splash of cream to make it palatable for Koza.

When the meal was over, Jay ordered two light peppermint drinks, that Koza enjoyed sipping. They took their glasses and wandered away from the patio, drawn by music and laughter down the street. A noisy bunch of patrons were at their usual tavern. As the beautiful woman and little man passed, the loud voices seemed to ebb as they observed the interesting couple. Koza could feel the eyes focused on them. She felt the need to talk.

"Jay, I have never seen such trees before. They look like they have been here for a very long time. They are beautiful the way they twist and the trunks are deeply gnarled and knotted."

"These are olive trees. Greece is known for its olives. I believe that Renoir had them in his garden. He too, thought they were beautiful." It was then that Koza noticed that lights had been placed to shine on the trunks to reveal the marvelous texture of each one.

When they got back to the patio, it was quiet.

60

"It is late but it is so lovely here. I don't want to end this evening. Do you think we will have time to explore in the morning before we leave?" she asked.

"If you can get up early, we will have time."

"What do you consider early?"

"I know a little cove within walking distance that is truly spectacular when the sun rises. Can you be up and dressed by five?"

"I can if you can." She laughed. He knew that the air and excitement of the day would lull Koza into a deep sleep as soon as she slipped between the polished sheets.

The ring of the phone startled Koza awake. Her windup clock was buzzing its alarm. She pushed the button on the clock and picked up the receiver. It was Jay.

"Are you ready, Snow White?"

"Give me five minutes. I will meet you in the hall." She pulled on jeans, her blue sweater and brushed her hair into a pony tail. She splashed her face with ice cold water to help her wake and applied a bit of mascara and soft rose lipstick. Her feet were half in the white sandals as she rushed out the door.

Once again Jay sat against the wall next to her door. He jumped up, grabbed a hold of her hand and quickly led her down the dark hall, across a creaking balcony and slowed as they went down the warped wooden steps with his flashlight beam showing the way.

"Come on Sweetheart, we don't want to miss the first rays." They were both panting when they saw the water ahead. He raced with her hand in his until they stood beneath a stone arch at the water's edge. Silently watching and waiting as the sky grew lighter and then suddenly, the sun spread a golden blanket across the water all the way to their feet.

"This is like being in an awesome cathedral," she said softly. "It is breath-taking. Even the craggy rocks above us look like they are made of gold." Jay reached down and picked up a tiny shell.

"Look, Koza, a gift from the sea, so you will remember this moment."

"Jay, you always say and do the right things." She tenderly held the shell in her palm. "You are like this shell. Little, but perfect in every way, if only...."

"If only what?"

"If only Evelyn were not in your life."

"She won't be. Mark is working hard to get her to sign the papers."

"Jay, after we fly back, I don't want to see you, until your divorce is final."

"Why? I have been a gentleman! Have I said something that I shouldn't?"

"No Jay, you have been wonderful. That's the problem. I am falling in love with you and I don't want to, not now, not while you are still married."

"I wish you had waited to tell me until we were on the plane back. Koza, how am I supposed to act around you?"

"I don't know Jay. I am trying to do the right thing."

"I know you are and I respect that, but Koza, you don't understand. Evelyn hasn't been in the same place with me for one night, for over three years!"

As they headed back, they continued their talk, but Koza was wishing, too, that she had waited until the flight back. Jay seemed like a different person. His shoulders slumped and the sparkle had left his eyes. For the first time she saw a frown line between his brows.

"Jay, you know that soon you will be free and if you still want to see me and pick up our relationship, then just come to my door. You know where I live."

"Koza, I need you in my life now. I am not saying in my bed!"

"Jay," she stopped at the bottom of the stairs. "We better change our clothes and get ready for the drive to Michael's cabin.

They didn't notice the fresh flowers on all the tables as they passed through the patio area. Just as Koza, was about to climb the stairs to her room a taller version of Jay stepped into the lobby to greet them. Jay's father was graying at the temples and his smile wrinkles were a bit deeper. He was wearing crisp dark blue slacks and a pinstriped shirt with the sleeves rolled up. It is easy to see why Jay used him for all the "Spencer's People" photos, she thought.

Jay had been wearing a serious face until he spotted his father. His face brightened and they hugged.

"Dad, I didn't know Maddie had called you. I am so glad you are here. Where's Mother?"

"She is coming. We arrived late last night. She is a little tired and cranky this morning, be warned." He said it laughing.

"James, are you spreading stories about me again?" The voice came from a three foot tall woman so perfect in dimensions that she looked like an animated porcelain doll. Her dark hair and dark eyes matched Jay's. She hugged her son, not wanting to let go until she noticed Koza standing off to the side. Then she hurried over to hug her too. Her arms wrapped around Koza's hips as she looked up.

"I am Rosie, Jay's Mother."

"You must be Koza. We are all happy to meet you. Jay has told us all about you." She looked back at the doorway and spotted Adam her younger son just entering. He was at least two inches shorter than Jay and walked with a rolling gate that suggested he had a serious hip or leg problem. Koza felt he was not as good looking although he had a family resemblance. His face had creases from constantly scowling. He held his lips in a straight thin line. It was as if he begrudged the gaiety of the moment and that was as near a smile as he would allow himself. Rosie introduced him to Koza as if showing her a special treasure. Koza politely shook his hand and found herself swept into a strong bear hug by James, Jay's father.

"Let's go inside. All these flowers are giving me a headache," complained Adam. They filed into a smaller area filled with tables inside.

They helped themselves to a scrumptious breakfast buffet and were served juice and coffee. Jay suggested they all eat up and hit the road as soon as everyone could get ready. Koza immediately excused herself and hurried to her room to change. After a quick rinse, she put on a skirt and slid into summer shoes, with two inch heels. My legs are so white, she thought. I'll brush on a little of my bronzing powder. There that looks better. She ran a comb through her hair and put it up in a high pony tail. A fresh touch of makeup and she was ready to zip her case shut. A tap on the door told her that someone was there to pick up her luggage. Just as they started out of the room, she remembered the little shell in her slacks pocket.

"Please put that case down for a moment. I must get something out." She searched the pockets and down in a corner she found the shell nestled in the seam. "Thank you so much," she said as she handed the young man a generous tip.

She ran down the stairs and climbed into the limousine, followed by Adam. She was seated beside Jay's mother. I am sorry, but I don't remember your name from the introductions earlier."

"Call me Rosie, everyone does. Isn't this a beautiful day for a drive? We will be near the coast soon. Oh and I want to warn you, that I may fall asleep along the way. Riding always makes me sleepy, and we did arrive very late last night. Please don't think me rude."

"Of course you should rest if you can. I doubt if I will. Everything is so beautiful. I don't want to miss a thing." Koza smoothed her skirt and crossed her legs. She felt nervous sitting across from the three Spencer men. James had closed his eyes and leaned his head back against the seat as soon as the vehicle started to move. Soon Adam did the same. Rosie was sound asleep before they had gone five miles.

She pulled her purse to her lap and searched for a pen and pad of paper. She could feel Jay's eyes on her as she wrote.

"It will only be a few months. Please try to understand." He reached for the pad and started writing.

"I do understand, but I hate the thought of not seeing you!" She took the pen.

"We will survive this. Jacob Spencer, I love you!" He leaned forward as if he wanted to whisper. She slid forward crossing the space that separated them. He gently placed his hand on the back of her head, drawing her even closer, but he didn't whisper in her ear. He kissed her softly. I love you too, he mouthed, as they slid back in their seats. His eyes were shining and he was wearing his impish grin as he tipped his head back and closed his eyes.

She does love me! She even put it in writing! He felt such joy that he couldn't possibly rest, but it was easier to fast forward to the months and years ahead, if he didn't look at her.

Koza was staring out the window not really seeing the beautiful coastline of Greece as the driver cautiously maneuvered the long car around the curves and hills.

Sunshine bounced from one sleeping face to another as the trip continued. She closed her eyes too, leaning back against the seat and flipping her ponytail up so it didn't cause an uncomfortable bump behind her head. She lifted her lids just enough to see Jay's eyes looking at her.

The next thing she knew he was sitting beside her with her purse on his lap. He plunged his hand in and pulled out her note pad. Very slowly and quietly, he removed the page she had last written.

"I will keep this forever. It will help me through the next months of waiting. You are right Koza," he whispered, "but for an additional reason. If her lawyer gets any idea that we are seeing each other he would drag your name into the mess somehow. You don't need that and neither do I."

He touched her hair and her cheek.

"Koza, not being with you is going to be the hardest thing I have ever done."

As he moved back onto his seat, Adam opened his eyes. "Aren't we there yet? This trip is unbearable!"

"Adam, who did you leave in charge? It isn't often that the whole family is gone at the same time"

"Actually, I took it upon myself to bring the top man from Paris and London branches a week ago. I know Evelyn will not miss them. She seems to think she can run the offices herself. She as much as said so the day she called my office. She thinks that you and I do nothing. That Poor woman hasn't got a clue! Peter and Andrew will stay if we want to use them here. In the mean time they are observing the staff and will recommend any changes they feel necessary when we get back."

"Well done brother, you surprise me with your wily ways." Jay gave him a high five, and Adam grimaced.

"What?"

"No one does that anymore!"

"I do."

The driver pulled the car into the shade of an ancient tree. "This little restaurant has a place to refresh. If you want, you can get something to snack on," he said.

Jay slipped his hand into Koza's as they walked up the path to the pretty patio. A canopy blocked the late morning sun and the breeze from the sea was cool and salty. The waitress smiled as they walked near, but the smile didn't reach her eyes. Koza and Rosie headed for the ladies restroom. Inside, Koza noticed that Rosie could not possibly reach the sink without getting the front of her dress wet.

"Would you like me to wet a finger towel for you?"

"Yes, dear, that would be nice. You are thoughtful. Most regular people pretend that they don't notice when I can't reach things. I think they are afraid they will embarrass themselves or me. You are different. I like you Koza. I hope that we will become good friends."

"Thank you, I hope so too."

After a snack of fresh wheat rolls dipped in olive oil and herbs and nibbles of several kinds of cheese, they took their sodas and headed back on the road.

"Why do I feel that we have just had a stage coach stop," asked Adam, actually managing a smile?

Jay sat beside Koza, but talked business with Adam and his father nearly all the rest of the way.

"I think after we go back, I may head to England and then to France and prepare them for the change. I want to see the properties there too, before I hand its profits over to her. Mother would you like to come with me? You are always a good travel companion."

Thank you, my darling, I would be delighted. It has been a while since I went to Paris. I could stop in that lovely little dress shop and order some new clothes."

"We can do anything you want Mother. For the next few months I may need you at my side more than ever before."

66

"It is wonderful that you consider me a comfort Jay. I would love to see a lot more of you than I usually do."

"Look everyone, we are almost there." Jay was smiling at Koza as the car pulled into the driveway totally filling it.

Madelyn peeked through the window and quickly opened the front door. "You have all arrived together, how wonderful!" She said, hugging each one in turn. Michael shook hands with the men, receiving congratulations but gave Rosie a quick hug. "Koza I had very little time to get to speak to you the night we were at the Teebes. It was rude of us to leave so soon, that night. I hope we will have time to have a nice talk this week." He gave her a quick hug too.

"That's all the mushy stuff I can take," said Adam. "I'm going to go for a swim as soon as I can change. Jay, are you coming?"

"No I don't think so. I never was a good swimmer like you are."

Adam seemed to be in the house for only a moment and he was back, dropping a beach towel and his watch and cellphone on a chair on the patio. He ran down the path to the water's edge. "Be careful," Maddie called, "The currents are treacherous out there." Adam's face wore a grin as he turned back to the water and waded into the first wave. In his bright red suit, he headed straight out, stroking strongly.

"He has been a fish since the day he was born. His favorite time of day was bath time. He always loved the pool. Do you swim Koza?" Rosie was talking to Koza, but her eyes were drawn to the sea. "That's the first real smile I have seen on his face since we left New York," she said sighing. "I can tell that something is troubling him. He isn't usually moody."

"I can swim, but I am not as enthusiastic about it as he was," she said smiling. Madelyn placed a tray on the patio table, where chairs surrounded its heavy plank top. Striped canvas moved overhead as the breeze played with the blue and white fringe.

"There is plenty, but don't spoil your lunch. Maria is making us a lovely meal. Say Hello everyone. This is Maria." The servant placed a heavy pitcher of lemonade on the table with one hand and a large bottle of red wine with the other. "Hello," she said, nodding her head as she left quickly to return with another tray of glasses and ice.

Rosie took charge and managed to pour lemonade in several glasses. "Koza, would you prefer wine?"

"No, the lemonade looks refreshing. Thank you."

James took the pitcher and filled another glass handing it to Madelyn. "I'm going down and ask Adam to come join us. James walked the beach hollering for Adam, but he couldn't see him.

Rosie suddenly jumped up from her chair.

"Something is wrong! James can't find him!"

Jay held his mother's hand and helped her down the steep path to the beach. She was starting to cry. Michael hurried along the edge of the water, shielding his eyes from the glare. He ran scanning the waves rolling in. A huge jagged rock that rose from the water a few yards out had snagged something red. James held his breath in fear as he and Michael both waded in. Under the water, held by the rock's sharp edges, was Adam's body. Together they lifted the little man from the waves as they crashed against the rock. Quickly he was rolled over on the sand of the beach. "He has no pulse." Michael took over, forcing the water from his lungs. Jay took the role of compressing his brother's chest, counting one, two, three, four, as Michael tried to breathe life into Adam. James called for emergency help, even though he feared it was too late. There was no way to know how long Adam had been under the water. Jay was sweating from his frantic effort to continue his steady rhythm.

"Let me take over now," Michael said. "Help will arrive soon."

Jay looked around for his mother. She sat on the sand, with Koza's arms wrapped around her. As Rosie wept, Koza rocked her and prayed for Adam to cough and breathe. She hoped to bring a feeling of security and peace to the emotionally shattered mother. Madelyn knelt near Adam's body. Tears streamed down her face.

"I told him the current was treacherous. Why didn't he listen? Why wasn't he more careful? His poor body is cut and bruised," said Maddie. Michael was examining the deep fracture on the back of Adam's skull.

"It looks like his head must have slammed into the rocks really hard. It may have knocked him out," said Michael.

The medics hit the beach running. They strapped on oxygen, while searching for a pulse. When electrical stimulation didn't work, they tried again and again. The police arrived with sirens blaring at nearly the same time as the medical emergency team. They walked the beach searching for any indication of foul play, with shaded eyes they searched the water looking for any sign that something was unusual but it all appeared normal. One officer walked back into the water with James so he could show him where they found his body trapped beneath the water. He took several pictures before wading out of the water.

"The waves are strong here. This is not where I would ever swim," he said as he made notes in his computer. "They should have a warning sign on this beach."

"I told him the currents were really bad out there, but he didn't even slow down. He just dashed to the water." Maddie sobbed and moved away from Adam's body and knelt beside their mother.

Lord I don't know this family very well. I don't know if Adam was saved. Please use this opportunity to bring them all closer to you, Lord. Use me if I can be of use. Give me the words to say. Koza prayed silently.

Finally the oxygen mask was removed and the time of death noted. His body was placed on a stretcher and taken slowly up the path. The family followed it all the way into town. Koza continued to pray.

Later, Adam's body was taken from the morgue to a mortuary and prepared for the long trip home. Adam's death was declared an accident.

Madelyn and Michael postponed their wedding. It was the only thing to do. She and Michael flew back with the family.

Maddie packed a large trunk that Maria brought from the attic, collecting Michael's personal things. She asked Maria for a screwdriver and with help, she removed a small round stained glass window, placing it in the middle of the trunk, after wrapping it well.

"Michael, I doubt very much if we will ever come back here. I took the little window to remind us of happier times. The glass repairman will be here soon to replace it. You may want to call the real estate agent that sold you this place." She moved gracefully to the bedroom and closed the door. Jay was on the phone with the airlines making arrangements. It took him nearly an hour before he had everything settled satisfactorily. The police were kind and had helped to expedite things. Michael did call his realtor but at the last moment instead of placing the cabin on the market, he asked him to come and carefully seal the place and to oversee the replacement of the window. The beautiful cabin on the shore of Greece would remain in the family, at least for now.

The family was allowed to stand beside the waiting plane while the casket was loaded on board. They boarded last and could feel the eyes of the other passengers as they took their seats. Jay had manipulated the seating to give each couple privacy. Madelyn and Michael were across the aisle and up one row. His parents sat two rows ahead of them.

Koza had a strange feeling that things were changing in Jay that she didn't like. When she looked at his face, it was stern and grim as if the lines from Adam's face had transferred to Jay's. She looked at his hand holding hers tightly.

"Jay, I am so sorry about your brother." She lifted his hand to her cheek.

"Thank you, Koza," he said very softly. "I am very worried. The fact that I will miss him terribly has nothing to do with it. His holdings in the corporation revert back to me. Evelyn may have a right to take half of his shares, too. I need to talk to Mark Harris as soon as I get back." He had released her hand from his without noticing. Producing a small notebook and pen, he kept himself engrossed for the next two hours without saying a word.

Finally he looked at her as if he had just discovered she was there.

"I have been ignoring you. Would you like to go up to the lounge?"

"Yes, that would be nice." Maddie and Michael were there having a light meal. Jay and Koza joined them. The waiter gave them a moment to settle and then asked if they wanted to eat now. Koza chose a chicken salad and cup of green tea. Jay took just a black coffee. He immediately turned the conversation to business.

"Michael, do you know any talented accountants that I can steal?"

"No I don't Jay."

"What about you Maddie? Do you know a good accountant that might change jobs with the right incentives?"

"Yes I think I do. Koza didn't you tell me that you carried two majors in college? One was journalism and literature, and wasn't the other business accounting?"

"Yes, that's true, but I already have a good job in accounting at Bennington International."

"Are you saying you would rather stay there, than work with Jay?"

"No I just think I need to keep a distance between us until Jay's divorce is final."

"Jay, did you know that Koza is an accountant?"

"Actually, no I didn't. We never discussed it."

"It's not my favorite thing to do but it's a living and it isn't something that fills my mind when I get home. That leaves me free to write." She remembered telling Jay the night that he had fallen asleep in her living room with his head on her lap. I think he missed more of what I said than I thought.

"Are you eager to start another book?" Madelyn's interest was piqued.

"I have been writing stories for a long time. I just need to put them in the proper format and polish them up a bit."

"What is your first book about?"

"I'd rather have you read it instead of telling you about it. May I drop off a copy for you when they are ready?"

"I'd love that. Be sure to sign it, so I can show my people that I know you."

"Maddie, it is not as if I were famous."

"I think you will be soon Koza, with all your brains and beauty."

"Wow, Thank you Maddie for the compliment and vote of confidence."

When they all returned to their seats, Jay settled back with a pillow. Koza decided she should rest too. Her eyes were closed but her mind was busy. He is building a wall between us. That is his way of dealing with everything that is happening, the divorce, losing Adam and the impact on the corporation and me not wanting to see him until the divorce is final. I will tell him that he can call me if he needs to talk. That will help a little. The last two weeks have been the most exciting, frightening, wonderful, sorrowful days, I have ever had. I will never forget a single moment of them.

CHAPTER SIX
THE PROMISE

She felt Jay cuddle closer. When she peeked at him, she saw tears on his cheeks. He needed time to grieve for his brother. She wanted so much to hold him in her arms, but instead she gently sought his hand and held it tenderly.

"Koza?"

"Yes Jay."

"We had a terrible argument before I left. I called Adam names and told him that if I could I would fire him. When I left, the office I told him he was stupid and incompetent. He had a fifty thousand dollar shortage in one of the accounts. I didn't mean it Koza. He was brilliant with mathematics. I never told him I was sorry. I was still angry with him when he asked me to swim with him. That's why I didn't go. Maybe if I had, he would still be alive!" Jay choked back a sob as more tears slid down his cheeks.

"This isn't your fault, brothers do argue. If he was caught in the currents, you could not have saved him." He pushed the arm rest up so he could lay his head on her lap. He lay on his back with his face up and knees bent.

"Koza, will God ever forgive me for what I have done?"

"God already has, the question is when are you going to forgive yourself?"

"Koza I need you near me. I can't stand the thought of not seeing you."

"Jay, you will see me, just not alone, not out socially. We can't give Evelyn any reason to extend the proceedings. Take your mother to Europe as you planned, as soon as Adam has been buried, open a new branch office somewhere. The work will keep your mind occupied and the new business will help you to replace some of the revenue that you are losing to Evelyn. Jay you do need a top accountant. I work for a man named Alexander Everett. He can do anything with figures. If you can get him to go to work for you, it would be the deal of the year."

He sat up suddenly, smoothing his hair and clothes. "Darling I am going to freshen up a bit and I would like you to go up to the lounge and have a drink with me. Would you meet me up there in a few minutes?"

"That sounds like a good idea." She followed him to the stairway and continued up to a lady's room she had noticed at the top of the stairs. After a quick comb, a dab of perfume and some new lipstick, she stepped out to find Jay sitting on the floor against the wall, waiting for her. "Jay, you don't have to do that. You could have chosen a table for us."

"I wanted to wait for you. You don't mind do you?"

"Of course I don't mind. It makes me feel special and taken care of."

"You are special and I will always take good care of you, if you will let me." He placed his hand on her waist and steered her to the same table in the corner.

"Hello again," said the waiter, "What can I get for you?"

"Get us a bottle of your best champagne," said Jay. His eyes twinkled with excitement as the waiter placed the wine and glasses on the table. Koza's fingers sought the bracelet covered in tiny diamonds. She had worn it daily since he had fastened it on her wrist. She didn't see him as a little man. He seemed bigger than life and her heart ached to hold him. She knew the pain he endured. Somehow, some way she longed to ease it.

Jay had poured two glasses of the champagne and was looking at her intensely.

"Koza, will you wear my ring? Will you marry me when I am free?"

"Jay I am not sure of what I should answer. My head tells me that I have known you just a short time, that I should wait to give our relationship some time, but my heart says, I already know that I love you." She paused, taking a deep breath. "Yes, Jay, I will marry you."

He sprang from his seat and knelt on one knee beside her. "Kozarina Kinny, will you marry me?"

"Yes, Jay, I will marry you!"

"Until I can get you a proper ring, please wear mine." He slipped his wide hammered gold band with a single large diamond in the center from his finger and onto hers. She noticed the extra warmth of his hands as he transferred the ring. It was loose on her ring finger, but fit well on her middle finger.

"One day, I will marry you," she replied softly, her voice muffled and husky, holding back tears, "We will have a beautiful child and I will never leave you."

He covered her lips with a tender kiss. The waiter had witnessed the love scene. He smiled knowingly as they sipped their wine, holding hands and talking quietly.

"Jay, we have to keep this a secret until you are free. We can't tell anyone, for the same reason we can't be public about dating."

"Koza, I will see you, even if I have to crawl through that little dog door in the middle of the night." She laughed as she removed her cross and chain and slipped the heavy ring on to it. After it was fastened, again, she tucked it inside her sweater. "In the eyes of the Catholic Church I was never married. Evelyn and I had a civil ceremony. We were not married by a priest.

"Jay, I didn't know that you are a Catholic."

"I was raised to be, but I don't know if I am now. We used to all go to Mass every Sunday. Now I don't go."

"Jay, maybe it is time to talk to a priest. He can help you figure out a few things."

"You are right Koza. That is good advice." Soon they returned to the main part of the plane.

Back in her seat, Koza could not wrap her mind completely around the promise she had given. What will my parents say? They don't even know about him. She mused. The first meeting we have with them will be an interesting one. Nothing they can say will dissuade me but I have a strong feeling that they will try.

"Jay, will you trade seats with me for a few minutes?" Rosie stood in the aisle next to him. "Your father wants to talk to you." Jay smiled at Koza and hugged his mother as he moved past her. "Hello, Koza, I just wanted to talk to you before we land. There are some things that you need to know." She reached over and patted the lump that the ring caused beneath Koza's sweater. The waiter told me. We all know and are very happy for both of you. First, Jay snores, he talks and walks in his sleep. He constantly has women throwing themselves at him for the novelty of being seen in the company of a little person and for his money. You probably have already noticed that when his mind is absorbed in solving problems, he shuts down on everything else. Don't ever take it personally. Usually, his biggest meal of the day is breakfast. Some days it's his only meal. He loves animals but won't have one of his own, because he is gone so much. His favorite place is the Mediterranean. He hates it when it gets hot in New York, and loves the snow and cold. He has been known to go for long walks in the rain or snow and returns soaked or frozen, but happy and mentally refreshed. That's about it, except I am glad that he found you."

"Thank you, Rosie. It sounds like you know your son very well. I am glad that you approve of him asking me to marry him when he is free."

"Yes Koza, I am so happy for him. I know that you are a good person and you are good for him. As sad as he is over Adam, you still have been able to return the sparkle to his eyes and a smile to his face. Thank you for that but Koza, do you love him enough? Do you love him enough to accept that you may have a shorter life together, because little people don't live as long as regular people? At least that's been my experience in our family. You may have a child that turns out to be a little person. Ask yourself how you really feel about that. I'm not trying to throw up road blocks. James and I are delighted that Jay found you. I just wanted to make sure that you go into this with your eyes open. Does your family know about Jay?"

"No not yet."

"When they get to know Jay they will slowly come around, but it will take time."

"Thank you Rosie, for telling me these things, and thank you for being happy for us. Oh, just so you know, we won't be going around together until he is free."

"That's good, no use complicating his legal mess."

"That's what I thought."

"Here, I brought you a little treat. It is chocolate that I bought at the airport. When I get angry or upset, I always crave chocolate. Here please try one."

"This is delicious."

"Keep the rest of the sack; I have eaten more than I should."

"Rosie, I am so glad you came back to talk to me. I feel like I have a good friend."

"I am your friend dear, and I want you to know that we all love you and consider you part of our family already." With that, she stood and walked back up the aisle. The flight attendant followed her to be sure she wouldn't fall. People perceived Rosie as fragile but in reality she was strong in body and spirit.

"Everyone knows. They approve." Jay returned wearing a big smile.

"Yes, your mother told me the same thing."

They sat quietly for a time until others around them started to stir and look out the windows. The plane was descending. Buildings looked like pieces of a Monopoly game, as the plane cut through a bank of puffy white clouds.

On the ground they were respectfully escorted to the ramp where a waiting hearse received Adam's coffin for the trip to the mortuary.

"I will call you when the arrangements are made for the funeral," said Rosie holding Koza's hand. It seemed she was drawing strength from the younger woman. Koza felt her small hand tremble as the coffin was removed from the plane. With dignity it was placed in the waiting hearse and the family was escorted to a waiting limousine. Their luggage would be promptly delivered, as an accommodation of the airline.

As the big automobile maneuvered through the New York traffic Jay seemed to be wearing a gray mask. The Jay of earlier had disappeared. Once again the sad reality of the here and now prevailed.

Briggs met the car and escorted Koza to her door.

"I will bring your luggage to you when it arrives and Jackie will be freed to come as soon as possible.

The animals were let out and Jackie came bounding home.

Koza sat on the floor, petting, scratching and loving on the animal until suddenly tears began to flow. She held Jackie in her arms and felt the comfort the animal offered as she wet her fur with tears. All the tension of the many recent events spilled over and when she stopped crying, she felt drained, and exhausted.

"Jackie, you are the only constant in my life. I love you girl. I am sorry I had to leave you." She reached into the pantry and found treats for her friend and then filled her water bowl with fresh water. "You didn't come in to check on things while I was gone. Did you? Your bowl was still full of water. The trainer must have kept a close eye on you." Jackie crunched her treats and wagged.

"Now that I am calmer, I think I will call my publisher," she talked to Jackie as if she were a human sometimes.

"Hello Joanne, this is Koza Kinny. I am back in town and will be available now for whatever you might need."

"That's wonderful Miss Kinny. We were hoping you could be here for a photo shoot as your first book comes off the press. From now on publicity is in direct ratio to sales."

"Yes, I understand that. You have the schedule for my job at Bennington haven't you? Just give me drive time."

"Yes, we did talk about that. Did you note your advance? I deposited it in your account as you suggested."

"Thanks Joanne."

"See you soon, Miss Kinny."

Koza turned on her computer and checked the balance in her checking. She admired the larger amount with pride. It is wonderful to finally be paid for the long hours of work that I have put into my stories.

A light knock at the door caused Jackie to bark more than usual, because of her excited state. Koza opened it to find Madelyn looking quite agitated.

"What is it Maddie?"

"It's my Bitsy. She has gone in her nest and doesn't want anyone to touch her. The trainer says that she and Jackie have bonded and that they have played and slept together all week. Bitsy has been riding around on Jackie's back like a little jockey. I know it is an imposition, when you have just gotten home, but would you come over and bring Jackie with you so I can lure her out to feed her?"

"Of course I will. Come on Jackie, your baby Bitsy needs you."

"Thank you so much, Koza."

"I would like to see Jackie give a monkey a ride on her back." The women were smiling when they entered the Jungle room with Jackie.

As soon as Bitsy saw Jackie she came out of her nest and climbed on Jackie's back, clinging as tightly to her neck as she could.

"She stays like that for hours. Hello, I am Tom," he said to Koza smiling. "The only way I have been able to feed Bitsy is to offer her the bottle while she is on Jackie's back or curled up with Jackie in her nest. She screeches at the other dogs and Tonga. It is unusual but understandable. She has accepted Jackie as a surrogate mother. Jackie seems to take pleasure in the role."

"This is amazing," said Koza. "As long as she is happy and serving a purpose here she can stay, but please give her access to a way to come home when she wants to."

"We certainly don't want to take your dog away from you, Koza."

"I know that," acknowledged Koza. Maddie sat down beside Jackie, on the dirt floor in her good clothes. She patted Jackie and talked to Bitsy at the same time. Slowly the baby monkey released her tight grip on Jackie's fur and hopped onto Maddie's lap, crawling up and wrapping her tiny arms around Maddie's neck while burying her face in her hair.

"She does remember me! Thank you, Jackie, for taking care of Bitsy. You are such a good girl." Koza made a quiet exit while Maddie enjoyed being covered in bundles of furry affection from all her pets that had converged on her.

After finishing her unpacking, Koza made a pot of coffee and fixed herself a slice of toast. She felt the ring on her chain, still amazed that she had been swept up in the moment and jumped into a commitment of love.

It was past midnight, when Jackie came through the dog door and joined Koza on her bed, snuggling closely. Now I feel like I am home, thought Koza.

"Hello girl, I love you," she said as she scratched her ears and belly. "Don't ever forget to come home. Remember I need you too."

Jackie hopped out of bed as the alarm clock went off. She headed out the dog door to Maddie's and her new responsibilities. Everything has changed thought Koza. Nothing will ever be the same again.

CHAPTER SEVEN
CHANGES

The beautiful new car waited for her in her space. She was going to enjoy driving to work, for the first time in a long time. Her old car had lumbered along and its appearance embarrassed her.

At work she gave the security desk the information it needed about her new car. She couldn't help letting a small moan escape her lips when she saw her buried desk. No one had made an attempt to do any of the usual reports. Her coffee cup sat abandoned with a disgusting brown layer in the bottom.

After scrubbing it, she returned with a clean cup full of fresh coffee and began to prioritize the mounds of paper. Her phone rang. It was her boss, Mr. Everett.

"Welcome back Koza. Can you come into my office for a few minutes, before you get involved in your work?"

"I'll be right there Sir." Koza hung up the phone, picked up her cup and walked the few steps to his office. It was an accepted custom to take coffee with you at Bennington. He was sipping his as she entered.

"Koza, something wonderful has happened and if I don't share it with someone, I will burst! You are the only one here that I know will not break my confidence."

"What is it?"

"I just had a call from Jacob Spencer, of "Spencer's People." He wants me to come to work for him. He said he will pay me double what I make here and I will start by traveling with him to set up a new branch in Europe, and get this! He asked me if I had anyone I would like to bring with me. Same deal, at twice the current salary. I recommended you. What do you think Koza? Should we bail out together and go to work for Spencer?"

"Mr. Everett, I don't know. This is so sudden. What do you know about that company? How stable is it?"

"He said he is going through a shake up and splitting some of the branches from his corporation. He is getting a divorce. Those big corporation guys are always divorcing. He wants me to make sure that the branches allocated to his wife, remain successful. That's pretty decent of him, if you ask me."

"Sounds like a heavy responsibility."

"We can pull it off, Koza. We are a good team. You have always helped me with seeing the big picture. I can burn through reviewing their books like a wild fire. You know if anyone can do it, we can. He said he lost his head accountant recently. He needs our decisions right away!"

"Give me twenty four hours to pray and think about this. I will let you know before I leave work tomorrow. Are you going to take it whether I go or not?"

"It never occurred to me that you might turn down an offer like this one, Koza. Think about it; a new challenge, new surroundings and twice the salary."

I promise I will let you know as soon as I have made my decision. Now I better go see if I can find the top of my desk. I won't say a word to anyone about this. Thanks for picking me. Why did you choose me over Tom or Bob?"

"That's easy to answer. You are a lot prettier!" She laughed as she left his office, knowing that he was teasing. He had a strong marriage. She already knew the real answer.

Her smile faded as she saw her desk again. She plowed through the report requests and spread sheets stacked on her desk. Her inner office e-mail had still more work to be done.

It was two o'clock when she finally stopped to take a break. The cafeteria was quiet when she entered. She chose a large salad and a glass of milk and carried the tray to a corner booth.

"Father, things are moving fast. The last two weeks have turned my life upside down. Please stay very close to me and help me to bring Jay and his family back to you. Bless them and bless me. Help me to make the right choices in the days ahead. Give me wisdom. Thank you for all the wonderful things you have brought into my life, like Jay and my publisher. Thank you for Jackie and this food, and my new car. Amen" she said it softly.

When she opened her eyes Alex Everett was standing beside her table. His tray was loaded with food.

"Is it alright if I sit with you?" He had never sought her as a lunch companion before. She could instantly feel the pressure. She was sure he would push her to take the offered position. Finally she nodded yes.

"I thought you were never going to lunch. I waited until now so we could talk some more."

"You talk, I need to eat this salad and get back to work. I am very behind from being gone."

"Bennington appreciates your dedication but we have something more important to be thinking about."

"Mr. Everett, I will give it some thought tonight. Is there anything else in the offer that you haven't told me?"

"No. I am sure you can call your own shots."

"What does that mean?"

"It means you can decorate your office the way you want. You could buy any equipment that you might want for starters. It means you would have a company car. You would have the works. This guy is loaded!"

"That's interesting. I'm heading back now. I have two reports to finish that were due while I was off."

She didn't even tell me where she went on her time off, he thought as she hurried away to place her tray on the slide that disappeared the tray and dishes into the clean-up area of the kitchen. She is a very private girl, I like that about her. She is certainly the best and brightest worker in the whole department. He mused as he pushed a huge bite of hamburger in his mouth.

Koza left work a half hour later than usual, but she had managed to get a handle on the backlog of work. First I need to go to a mailbox to drop off these envelopes, and then to the market to get some groceries. Less than a block from the market was a small dress shop she liked. She quickly looked for a new dress.

"Koza, we just got this one in. Isn't it beautiful? It is the color of the sea."

"I don't think it is what I need just now."

"We have the same design in a soft gold. Would that work better for you?" Koza liked it well enough to buy it and a simple black suit.

Rosie will probably call me tonight, so I don't want to be gone longer than I need. She was right. The phone rang just as she was putting away the last of her groceries.

"Tomorrow at seven p.m. at Saint Andrew. Yes, I know where it is. Thank you for remembering to call me Rosie. I will meet all of you there. Yes, I'm sure. Thanks again and you can call me anytime if you need something or just want to talk. Yes, thank you Rosie. Goodbye."

As she hung up the phone and turned around, she found herself enfolded in a strong hug. Jay was smiling from ear to ear. "Come sit down with me." He poured two glasses of red wine, and uncovered two beautiful plates of old fashioned pot roast.

"Jay, that smells delicious. I forgot to eat tonight. I had so much to do. I only got home about half an hour ago."

"I have been busy today, too," he said. "I put this in the oven then I went shopping."

"I went to the market too. Funny we didn't see each other."

"That isn't the kind of shopping I was doing. Let's eat. Our food is getting cold."

She reached for Jay's hand and lowered her head. "Bless us dear Lord, bless Jay and his family. Tomorrow will be a difficult day for them. Bless our decisions in the coming months. Give us wisdom and bless this food that you have given us, in Jesus holy name. Amen."

"Amen," said Jay. They sipped the wine and ate enjoying the flavor of Jay's cooking. Jay, true to his mother's description, had not stopped to eat all day.

"Jay you ate so fast! I hope you don't get a stomachache," she said laughing.

"I'm eager to finish so we can talk." She slid her plate away. "I can't eat another bite. You gave me too much, but it was wonderful. Let's take our wine into the living room. I can clear up later."

Jay closed the drapes and then switched on a lamp by the couch. "I got some news today that caused more shocking sadness and then peace at the same time."

"What is it, Jay?"

"While we were in the plane flying to Greece, Evelyn's family left an urgent message on my home phone for me to call as soon as I got their message. I called them when I heard the recording. They said that Evelyn killed herself! Mark Harris contacted them almost immediately. He identified himself as my lawyer and he called right after the French police did. He told them that because she was out of the country that they should have her cremated. They thought it would simplify things to take his advice. They said to expect this, by special messenger. It arrived this morning. France is certainly more efficient about this stuff than the US."

"What is it Jay?" He opened the black velvet box, much like a ring box. Inside, the plush lining was shaped to hold its precious contents.

"It is a delicate porcelain rose. Inside is a small portion of her ashes."

"It is quite beautiful. I have never seen anything like it. I am so sorry, Jay. That had to be a terrible shock. I know you still loved her and always will."

"Yes, I will but I never loved her the way I love you. It is over Koza. Do you see? It is over. No more legal struggle. No more waiting to be free."

He wrapped his arms around her and held her tightly, letting a deep sigh escape his lips as he fully began to realize the great weight that was lifted from him. Then slowly he drew a small blue velvet box from his jacket pocket.

"This is what I was shopping for this afternoon." He lifted the lid to display a large perfect blue white diamond surrounded by rose baguettes in a platinum band. "This is a one of a kind ring, a Tiffany's original." It fit her finger just right. Her hands shook as she pulled his heavy ring from her chain. She placed it in his palm and then still shaking she slipped the magnificent ring from her finger, putting it back in the blue Tiffany's box.

"What are you doing?"

"It is too soon Jay. I can't deal with so much at one time. I want you to go now. I have a lot to think about. I'll see you at St Andrew's tomorrow night. Koza kissed him softly and said, "I love you with all my heart," as she forced the ring box back into his hand. "It is just too soon. Keep it for me." She closed the side door behind him and slid the lock. She made sure the release on the dog door would allow Jackie to come in.

The morning was so bright and sunny that it seemed to mock all the serious issues she had pressing in on her mind. She had worn the black suit, to work, but chose a pale pink blouse and left her jacket in the car.

"Mr. Everett, Good morning." She was surprised to find him sitting at her desk. He jumped up, taking her cup to fill it with coffee.

"Don't sit down, come in my office," he said over his shoulder as he headed to the coffeemaker. She knew he wanted her to say she would take the offered job. He had no idea that she had recommended him and that she had no intention of going to "Spencer's People" to work for Jay.

She stalled at her desk for a moment, collecting her thoughts, deciding how she wanted to handle his insistence.

When she entered his office, he sprang to his feet. "Well? Did you decide to come with me?"

"No, I decided that I want to stay here. You should offer the chance to Bob. He is honest and bright and has a large family. This would be a big break for him. We both know he can produce twice the work that Brian does. His work is accurate and he deserves to have a chance to better himself."

"Koza, what are you afraid of? Are you positive that this is the route you want to take?" You came here from Michigan and left your family behind and live alone. That was a big step! This is just a taxi ride in the opposite part of town. You know you will regret this."

"No, I think I know what I am doing. Besides with the two of you gone, they will have to promote me to head accountant and hire some good help for me. I'm comfortable here. I know the work and what they expect. Who knows what that company will require?"

"You are making a big mistake Koza. I thought you were smarter than that! I will ask Bob. I think you are right about him, but by tomorrow night you will regret your decision!"

"I don't think so, but thank you for asking me first." She walked out with her full cup of coffee. It was cold now. She poured it down the drain and filled it with fresh.

She knocked on his door and stuck her head back in. "I will be leaving an hour early. I have a friend's funeral to attend tonight."

"Sure, no problem," he growled.

*****

She deliberately waited until the private mass was starting before she entered the side door and slid into the heavy wooden bench beside Rosie. She tried hard to keep her mind off the small body in the coffin. She studied the grain of the wood, picked at her nails, noting to get a manicure as soon as possible.

The priest droned on during his homily, something about an honest and hardworking man. I can't see Jay. I wonder how he is. Rosie reached for her hand and held it tightly. Rosie had given in to tears as soon as she had seen the bronze casket, near the altar.

It is strange that there is no one else here, not even Mark Harris, she thought. Madelyn Clay sat next to Michael, wearing an opaque black veil. Always the drama queen, thought Koza. That was not nice of me, but why is she afraid to show emotion. It was her brother. She is allowed to cry. This is a strange family, but I like every one of them. They sure are characters. Suddenly it was over. The priest blessed the family with holy water. He spoke privately to James. She didn't hear the question, but she heard the answer he gave. He had answered that they would not be going to the cemetery. As they walked down the main aisle toward the doors to the front lobby, Jay appeared beside her, taking her hand firmly and leading her down a row of seats to the very end at the side aisle. The stained glass windows towered above them filling the area with tones of color that appeared as fragile as the antique glass that produced them. The street lights were on.

"Koza, I understand why you wouldn't wear my engagement ring yet, but I need to know that nothing has changed between us. Do you really love me, Koza?"

"Yes Jay, I love you. I miss you when we are apart, but respect is something built into me. Your wife died just days ago, and I feel that we should wait. Wearing a showy ring is out of the question. Right now, you have just lost two people you loved. You can't push on as if everything is fine. Give yourself time to mourn and time to heal."

"You are right, of course, but I just fear that I might lose you, too."

"Jay, I am not going anywhere and I'm not going to work for you, either"

"It was worth a try," he grinned. "Thanks for the lead on Alexander Everett. He gave his two-week notice today. We may include him in our visit to the branches in Europe. It would let him get an idea of what the company really is."

"Jay, I think the priest is waiting for us to leave so he can turn the rest of the lights off."

"Let's go somewhere and get something to eat."

"What about your mother, father, Maddie and Michael, you should be with them."

"They are all going back to Maddie's."

"You should go, too."

"I am heading home," she said softly.

"They have all left. Jay do you need a ride?"

"No, I came on my own." He started to walk away and then came back to her side. "I found this here on the steps when I came in," he said. "This is just what you need." He cracked the little plastic bubble and handed her an adjustable smiley ring.

"Jay, this is precious. She gave him one of her most beautiful smiles as she put it on her middle finger of her right hand. He reached for her to kiss her, but she pulled away.

"No kissing, not here in front of God and everyone going by! That would make some picture for the paper. I can see the caption now. Not what we need right now Jay!"

She handed him a key. "No more using the dog door either, I had this made for you.

"Thanks, I will see you after I stop at Maddie's."

The streets were busy with cars. It may as well be noon, she thought, as she carefully joined the moving multitude of cars. I am going to splurge with two steaks, two baking potatoes and salad. This should be a quick stop if I can find a parking spot.

Once home she had to carry her sack past Maddie's door. The lights were on and she could hear the sound of muffled voices inside.

"Jackie, Jackie" she called, but she was gone again. She likes it there. I liked it better when she was home to greet me, she thought.

As soon as she put the groceries in the kitchen, she got out of her suit, showered and put on a velour outfit with slacks and a cozy long sleeved top. She dropped her sandals by the back door, just in case she had to retrieve Jackie before she went to bed.

I hope Jay won't be much later. I am hungry. With the table set and coffee brewing she heard a gentle tap on the side door as Jay came in.

"This is a lot better," he said as he smiled and slid the key into his pocket. "I have ruined the toes on two pair of shoes since I met you." They both were still laughing when he smothered her lips with a soft lingering kiss.

"Did you eat at Maddie's?" she asked, looking at him while he held her close.

"No, they ate a little earlier before they went to church. They weren't hungry but Briggs insisted they have something." Jay wandered into the living room and then back into the kitchen as he slipped his suit coat off and hung it on the back of a chair.

"Mark Harris called me. He wants to see me first thing in the morning. He said it had to do with Adam's will and a small insurance policy, that goes to mother. He says he needs to talk to me in private. He wouldn't say anything further on the phone."

"That reminds me Jay. I will pay for the time he spent on my contracts. He checked the one that I had signed with Maxwell's agency and said that it read as we had thought. Maxwell gets a percentage of my royalty only."

"You don't need to do that. Mark is on a retainer. He gets paid handsomely every month, whether he does anything for us or not."

"Jay got up, checked the potatoes and turned them back on. I feel right at home in this kitchen," he said.

They ate in warm companionable silence. Both were tired and emotionally spent.

As they finished, Jackie came to the side door and barked to be let in. Koza released the latch and instantly was busy with furry-faced kisses and enthusiastic greetings.

"She loves you a lot," he said. Jackie trotted to the table and greeted Jay with friendly wags and a lick. Koza put down a bowl of food and some fresh water before returning to the table to refill their cups and suggested they go into the living room. Jay tried to hide a yawn as he set his cup on a coaster beside the lamp.

"You must be very tired. This was a difficult day for your family." He nodded and leaned his head back against the couch; with his eyes closed he sought her hand and held it in his lap. His breathing steadied and she realized that he had fallen asleep.

How could he fall asleep so quickly? Is he all right? She worried. I will just sit here and drink my coffee and quietly watch the news. If he wakes, I will send him home, if not; I will cover him and leave him here to sleep. I feel exhausted myself. There has been so much going on.

Koza carefully adjusted the sound as she turned on the television. Jackie came near and snuggled against Koza's feet. She loved Koza and wanted the closeness.

Just as the news ended, Koza could sense Jay's eyes looking at her.

"Hello, sleeping beauty," she teased.

"Koza, I am so sorry. I guess I was so relieved to be here where I could finally relax that I dropped off."

"There is no need to apologize. I am glad that you can relax when you are near me."

Just then a loud noise outside startled all of them. Jackie started barking and Jay hurried to the front door. A man was limping away across the grass and a large broken tree branch lay on the lawn opposite the front window of Koza's condo.

"He was trying to get photos. I guess I am glad that I went to sleep. He must have been bored watching me sleep. At least he couldn't get anything else. We must remember to close the drapes when I come over. I don't want your picture in the paper."

"Yes, I can imagine the top line. "New author finds short love." She was laughing so hard that she had tears in her eyes and didn't see the overwhelming look of joy on Jay's face.

"I love you so much Koza, it could never be a short love. Reporters never get the story right." They both started to laugh again until Jay glanced at the clock.

"It is really late, I better go home." With a quick peck on the cheek, he was up and headed out the side door grabbing his jacket on the way. "I'll call you tomorrow after I finish with Harris. Thanks for the nice meal." Just like that, he was gone. She peeked out her drapes to see him running in the direction the photographer had gone. I wonder why he is doing that. He can't possibly catch him.

The last thing that Jay did that evening was to call his old friend, detective Joe Downing, at the local precinct, and asked him to meet him for coffee at seven a.m.

"That little coffee shop on 5th will be fine. I know that you work late hours Joe and I wouldn't ask you to be up and out so early unless it was very important." Joe said he would be there.

The morning was gray and a steady rain fell as Jay jumped out of the car and walked into the little café. Joe sat as far from the other patrons as he could, offering privacy to Jay's conversation with him. The waitress immediately brought steaming coffee and plates of fresh scrambled eggs and toast. Joe had ordered for both of them, trying to expedite their meeting.

"Have you got any of that wonderful marmalade today, Betty?" Joe asked as she turned to leave their table.

"I'll be right back with it." They waited sipping the coffee until she had brought it and left the area. Immediately Joe seemed to change his demeanor.

"Jay, I sensed a tone of emergency in your voice last night. What's up?"

"I am going to dump a lot on you in one sentence, Joe. I suspect two murders."

"Who was murdered? What are you talking about?"

"You probably read about my wife's suicide recently in the papers. I don't think it was a suicide. Joe, they said she killed herself with a gun. She was petrified of guns. She wouldn't allow one in the house. The second one was Adam. He was the best swimmer I have ever known. He wouldn't drown taking a pleasure swim when he was fresh and rested. He had been warned about the currents. Something is very fishy about that, too."

"I don't know Jay. You are distraught, and you have lost two people recently. It is natural to question how it is possible. Do you have any evidence at all?"

"Not now, just a gut feeling, but I have money and I will hire investigators to help you. If you are willing and can look into things for me, and direct the investigation then I will accept the outcome whatever it is."

"I wouldn't worry too much about Adam's death. I will check things out, but I do think that if there were anything suspicious about Adam's death, the officials in Greece would not have released his body. But let's start by sending a good man to check out that villa in the south of France and see what he turns up. If all else fails we can exhume her body and have it checked by a different M.E."

"No, that's not possible. Her family had her cremated."

"Joe I would appreciate anything you can do but in the meantime, I have a suspicion that Mark Harris is up to something very shady. If I was a woman, I'd call it intuition, but it's a very strong feeling. Can you spend the morning with me?

"If you need me, I will come with you."

"Thanks Joe, you are one of the few people that I trust." Jay tossed a large bill on the table as the two men finished their coffee and left hurriedly. Jay's eggs were untouched.

Jay's driver had been circling the block again, and came around the corner soon after they stepped to the curb.

"Nick, take us to Harris's office," he said, as the car entered the surging morning traffic. "Joe I want you to be able to listen to my meeting this morning with Mark, I will do my best to get him to admit what he has been up to."

Just as they entered the empty elevator and pushed the button for the tenth floor, Jay called Joe's cell phone.

"I will leave my phone on and in my front pocket. You should be able to hear everything that is said. Attach this to your phone and it will record my conversation." They stood in the hall until Joe was ready.

"Nothing I record will be admissible in court. You know that don't you?"

"Yes I do but I thought this way you will know which way to head to catch him in whatever he is doing."

"Jay, I don't know if we should do this. I don't think it is legal without a warrant."

"It's too late now."

"You sound certain that he is up to something."

"I am."

When they entered the heavy glass doors to Mark's outer office, Jane, his secretary was just leaving.

"Hello, Mr. Spencer. Mr. Harris is expecting you." She turned politely to Joe and asked if there was something she could do for him.

"No thanks, I will just wait out here for Jay, if that is all right."

"Yes, of course, be seated. I have to take these papers to the courthouse, and then I will be right back. Help yourself to a cup of coffee if you want some," she said as she left with a polite smile.

"Nice girl," said Joe, as he headed for the small coffee area. Jay entered Mark's office feeling lucky that she had left. He wasn't sure how far the sound of the conversation on the cellphone could be heard. "Good morning Jay," Mark was wearing his official lawyer demeanor. Jay was wondering why Mark had insisted on a face-to-face meeting and wouldn't tell him what he needed to talk about over the phone.

"Hi, Mark. Why all the secrecy. What is it that you couldn't tell me on the phone?"

"Wait just a minute." Mark clicked on his intercom and said into it. "Hold all my calls, and don't come in here for any reason. I do not want to be interrupted." He clicked the machine again, turning it completely off. "Nosey woman, I think she listens to everything that goes on in here."

"She is not out there. She said she had to take some papers to the courthouse and then she would be right back."

"Yes, I remember now, I did send her on an errand. Good, let's get started. Jay, sit down, you must be very tired. These have not been easy days for you. They haven't been easy for me either. I am sorry about Adam, more than you know. He was smart and listened to reason."

"Thank you, Mark."

"I need to tell you what I have done for you, and what Adam has taken care of. We solved your divorce problem. We couldn't let her split up the company, now could we? That crazy fat cow wanted more than she could get her hands on. She was planning on ruining you and your company name. I called someone and he took care of the problem. It cost you a mere fifty thousand dollars. That is peanuts compared to what she would have taken from you in court."

"What are you saying? You killed Evelyn?"

"Of course not, Jay, she killed herself. That's what the papers said.

"I don't appreciate you calling her names, and I don't understand what you are talking about."

"I am talking about you being a little appreciative of the fact that you won't be going to divorce court. Adam was smart enough to see that my solution was better. He helped by transferring the funds to an off shore account. Now that he is gone you will need to instruct your new person to do the same. I expect fifty thousand on the first of each month. You can call it a gift of gratitude."

"I can't take all of this in. This is impossible to believe. I don't think that Adam would take part in something like this. What did you do to force him?"

"He did participate quite efficiently as soon as I explained that I would have you framed for her murder if he didn't cooperate!"

"How could you do such a thing? I didn't hate Evelyn. She was a disturbed woman. She didn't deserve to die."

"She was what she was. Now she can't hurt you. I made the decision to help you out. It is done. She isn't the first person that I have had eliminated. I go all out for my clients. I am a problem solver, Jay. It gets easier after the first time. Do you remember the Russell scandal? She drove her car off the road and the fishing accident of Horace Mendel? That was my man's work too. Sometimes we have to be realistic and creative. Some people aren't worth having around. That's when I expedite an easy solution." Robert Harris had opened the side door when Mark had proclaimed himself a problem solver. He stood behind his son, a look of agony and horror on his face. He had heard enough to know that his son had orchestrated several deaths.

"Mark, how could you become such a monster? I always told you that the best way to practice law was to be honest and morally exemplary. When did you decide to play God?"

"Dad, I didn't know that you were there! I never intended for you to know." Silence filled the room for a long moment. Three police officers entered the room through the mahogany door and Jay watched as his friend handcuffed Mark Harris. One of the officers read him his rights and led him from the room.

"Miss, you are not to touch the files in Mark's office. They will be removed for evidence and all the computers will be taken also, including those in his father's office. Jane sat at her desk crying. Robert Harris was not arrested but later after a long investigation, he would be a vital witness against his son. Robert, Jay and Joe had heard it all. It was obvious that greed had become the catalyst and that Mark would be proven guilty of many crimes before this investigation was over.

"Jane, I'm sorry you had to see all this. You will continue to work for me, won't you? I will need you more than ever." Robert said. "I give you my word. I was not involved in any of this."

"Yes, of course, sir. I will be here to help you. Should I call his clients that are scheduled and see if I can work them into your schedule?"

"Yes please do. Also, check when his next client was scheduled in court. It will be necessary for me to cover that, for sure. See what you can do to keep things running as smoothly as possible. I am not sure what that entails. Jane, I am so sorry."

"If the officer hadn't let me print out your schedule and his before he took my computer, I don't know what I would have done."

"Jane, I am going to follow them down to the station, I think you should clear all the office appointments for the rest of this week. I will call you from there. Let's just do our best to cover the court sessions. They are not easily postponed or rescheduled.

Also, call somebody and get us two new laptops so we don't feel quite so ill equipped to handle our work. Get whatever programs on them you know we will need. You are in charge, Jane, and thank you for not running out and leaving me stranded."

"Yes Sir, Thank you, Sir. I will be fine, really. We will be alright. I know you were not involved."

"After you manage all that, take a walk around the block and get some lunch. You can put a sign on the door that we are closed for lunch. You'll need to take a break."

"Thank you sir and should I call Georgina to come in tomorrow? We will probably need her."

"Yes, good thinking. Do whatever you think is necessary to keep this place afloat until we can pause and see where we are. I am leaving now and I will call you later."

As he walked to the door, her eyes had followed him. She noticed that his crisp step and straight shoulders were gone. He suddenly appeared very old.

When the elevator opened officers swarmed both offices, removing all the files. Cabinets stood open and empty. Mark's desk was nearly empty when they finished. They did the same to Robert's office. Jane began to cry again. She couldn't believe what she knew to be true.

When she had returned from her brief errand, Joe had showed her his badge and signaled for her to be silent. He had called his precinct from her desk and requested back up. She had heard some of the conversation through the open cell phone. She too, had heard his confession.

"His wife will be devastated. I know she is a good woman. She couldn't have known anything about all this." Joe indicated again that she be silent. He had used the office phone system to call, after placing his cell under a pile of cushions. She felt devastated and knew that Robert Harris would probably never totally recover from the shock of finding out that his only son was nothing that he had wanted him to be. He had been betrayed.

As she sorted things out in her mind, she shuddered to think that he had actually had people killed, for financial gain. I wonder if they will be able to catch the man he was paying to do all that. He should be in jail forever! How can people be so evil? She rubbed her forehead, realizing that her head was throbbing. She rummaged in her purse and found two pills and washed them down with cold coffee. I need a fresh cup of strong coffee before I start calling clients, she thought. The smell of the brewing pot filled the office. Mark's first appointment walked through the door.

"Good morning, Mrs. Langley. I have a message for you from Mr. Harris. He won't be able to see you this morning, he had a family emergency, but if you like I can call you later this week and we could set up a new appointment."

"That is really not convenient. I will be going out of town. I'll call you when I come back." She turned and mumbled something about someone getting too big to be of use as she left. Jane found that the next two on her list didn't answer, but she left messages, hoping they would get them so she wouldn't have to deal with them in person. Without her computer she couldn't pull up their files and find a backup number. As she worked her way down the schedules of both lawyers, she realized that it would take quite a bit of clever juggling to get things somewhat back on track.

Getting the laptops ordered was easy. She called a local office supply store and told them what she needed and who they were for. They delivered them within an hour. She had including a scanner copier and printer for Robert's office as well as for hers and the supplies to go with them. They hooked them up and got them working on her desk and on Robert's.

When she looked at the clock, it was nearly six o'clock. She had not spoken to Robert. She wondered what was happening. She had not eaten all day and her headache was still there making itself known. She turned off the coffee and closed the office, making sure the door was locked.

Then she thought there is not much in there to steal. I dread tomorrow.

CHAPTER EIGHT
JOE'S FRIENDSHIP

Robert had found Jay and they waited together on a rather uncomfortable bench that the desk officer had suggested.

Finally Joe came out and said because of the nature of the crime, he doubted that Mark Harris would be released on bail. It won't take us forty eight hours to collect enough evidence to keep him, now that we know what we are looking for.

"His hearing will be tomorrow."

"I'm going home. I can't do anything further here," said Jay. "I'm sorry Robert but this is going to affect you, your practice and your family. I'm not sure what tipped me off. I was already feeling suspicious that Evelyn had been killed by someone, but I didn't think it was him right away. There was something in his manner on the phone. He acted like he had just put his hand on the gavel and he was the judge in charge!"

"What do you mean?"

"In all the times that we have discussed business and contracts, he has never told me what to do. He always politely asked me to call or come in. This time he just told me to be here!" His whole demeanor had changed." Jay turned to Joe and asked if he would like to come with him. I'll drop you off after we have something to eat. "

As they rode through the traffic Jay noticed Joe's head bobbing. He wondered how few hours of rest his friend had actually had.

"I am pretty tired, Joe. Will you come over to my place some other night soon? I want to thank you properly for being there for me when you were off your shift. I want to make you a steak."

"Yes of course I will, and no thanks needed. It was fun to nail a guy like him. Just drop me on third and I will walk home from there. It is only a block and a half." Jay didn't respond but he was thinking that it hadn't been fun to find out that someone he had really trusted had betrayed him and killed Evelyn and who knows how many others. Jay shook his head in anger and bewilderment. His emotions were in turmoil.

"Joe, I still can't wrap my head around the thought that Mark had Evelyn killed. How could he do such a thing?

"Many people aren't what they seem. I see it all too often in my line of work."

Jay's driver pulled the car up near the door of the big apartment building, knowing that Joe would appreciate not having to walk from the corner.

As Joe turned to climb the steps to enter, he stopped and returned to the car and opened the door.

"You know Jay that you can always count on me. I am what I seem and I will always do my best to be there for you. I don't want your money or anything else from you. I am your friend." He closed the door firmly and stepped heavily up the stairs as Jay's big car pulled away.

In spite of the circumstances Jay was smiling. Joe's declaration of true friendship had touched his heart. It was something that he needed to hear just then.

At home, Jay's mind wandered to the comforting image of Koza. He poured himself a glass of wine and folded a piece of French bread around a large spiced sausage, placing it on a plate with a wedge of sharp cheese. "Dinner is served." He said out loud with a slight laugh. I am too tired to cook or do anything. He carried his wine and plate to the beautiful Mediterranean room with the automatic sliding glass walls. With a push of a button he opened the glass doors and could feel the cool air from the courtyard as the drapes stirred sliding open slowly. He set the lights low. The soft glow allowed him just enough visibility to sink comfortably into his favorite chair. He sipped his wine and stuffed the end of his makeshift sandwich in his mouth chewing slowly, savoring both the flavor and the silence.

This has been a terrible day, he thought. It couldn't have been any worse. At least now I can relax.

Just as he swallowed, he felt something sting his shoulder. Another pain seared his temple and side of his head. A third "pop" filled his chest with such pain that he found breathing nearly impossible. He dropped the wine glass and tipped over swiftly, deliberately sliding to the floor. The hand held control for everything, lay beside him. He managed to touch the correct button before passing out. The glass walls slid shut and locked, the lights grew bright and then dimmed, bright and then dimmed, over and over from the weight of his arm against the control. The silent alarm button clicked on and stayed on as his weight pressed against it. He was unconscious.

The police arrived with lights flashing and sirens blaring. While paramedics struggled to stabilize Jay's vital signs, Jackie's barks woke Koza. She could tell by the direction of the lights and sounds that the trouble had to be at Jay's place. She jumped into her sweats, grabbed her purse, hugged Jackie and unlatched the dog door. She hastily locked her front door as she left. The grass was still wet from the sprinklers but she ran full out taking a chance on falling. "Oh God, whatever it is, please watch over Jay, and let him be all right."

The stretcher was being placed in the ambulance as she arrived.

"Oh no!" she wailed. "Please God! Is that Jay?" A paramedic nodded. She couldn't tell if it was. They had an oxygen mask on him and a sheet pulled up over his chest. She saw the blood seeping into the sheet that covered his chest wound. "I have to go with him. We are engaged to be married." She jumped in beside him as the door was pulled shut. Kneeling beside his feet she prayed silently, with her hands touching his legs and tears spilling down her cheeks. It was then that she became aware of the soaked bandage that had been swiftly wrapped around his head.

At the hospital he was lifted to a gurney and whisked away to the emergency room. She was not allowed in. Koza had seen the deep pool of blood where Jay's head had rested. She sat and dialed her cell phone. Rosie answered.

Next she called Maddie. It seemed ages before they arrived, but in reality it was less than a half hour.

Huddled, they waited together to hear news. Time passed and they were told that he had been prepared for surgery. The hospital's head surgeon came out to talk to them. He sat down beside Rosie and spoke more to her than the others gathered there.

"He was shot three times, Mrs. Spencer. One bullet to the left side of his head, one is lodged in his left shoulder and the other is in his chest. We won't know how much damage was done until we get in there. I did a body scan and they are doing some more tests right now," the surgeon explained. "I will be back when we are finished. I will send out news as the team's work progresses. I have called in my top surgical team. Please know that we will all do our best work. Relax if you can. It is going to be a long night."

Hours stretched by. Rosie and James paced the length of the small waiting room. Koza slipped out and sought comfort in the chapel. As she sat on a bench praying she felt someone slide in beside her. It was Joe.

"How is he doing?" he asked.

"I don't know. He is still in surgery. It has been two hours. Shouldn't they be done by now?" A tear meandered down her face as she weakly asked the question.

"These things take time. We don't know what they ran into when they opened his chest. With him being smaller but an adult, seems to me that could complicate things. They are working in tight quarters. Let's go get some coffee and take it to his family."

When Koza stood she suddenly felt embarrassed by her appearance. Her sweats that she had pulled on over her pajamas were rumpled and Jay's chest wound had stained her shirt when she had leaned down to kiss him in the ambulance.

"I look terrible. Jay was all I thought about when I saw the commotion near his condo. As soon as they tell us he is out of danger I will go home and clean up. If he sees me like this it will scare him." Joe chuckled and nodded.

"You look like you were dragged out of bed by an emergency. Jay is all anyone cares about right now."

The cafeteria was closed but a small sign indicated they could help themselves to the donuts and coffee for a small donation.

"I probably should take a donut because people think they are the main nourishment of the police. It is expected of me." His kidding eased Koza's pain for a moment, as they returned to the waiting room with five coffees.

Rosie and James sat near each other on a worn leather couch that offered little relief from the agony of waiting. No one said more than a murmured thank you as they accepted the coffee.

"Spencer family, I have good news," came the cheerful voice of Dr. Roberts, as he entered the room. "Jay is in recovery. Let's start at the top and work our way down. His head wound was the least serious. The bullet grazed his temple and slid just under his scalp to the back of his head where it exited. It only required a few stitches. The shoulder shot was several inches above his heart. It did muscle damage and shattered the edge of his collar bone. We cleaned up the fragments and that should be fine. The chest wound was our main concern. The bullet damaged the vena cava and lodged against his spine. We have repaired the artery. He lost a lot of blood. The bullet has been removed successfully. He is very weak. We plan to keep him sedated for a couple days so he doesn't move around. Someone was watching over him. Just a fraction of an inch to the left and he would have been paralyzed. It didn't touch the spinal cord."

"Doctor, is he going to be alright?" Rosie was frightened to hear the answer.

"Mrs. Spencer, I have done all I can. Now he needs to rest and your prayers will help. I must tell you that he is a tough man. His signs are steady. You will be able to peek in on him after he is taken to the intensive care unit. There is a waiting room over there if you all want to shift. I believe it is a little more comfortable and there is more room."

"Thank you Dr. Roberts." James had stood up as the Doctor entered the room. Now he was anxious to move and walk. He had a lot of pent up nervous energy.

Tears of relief spilled down Koza's face and she wrapped her arms around Rosie, who was also crying.

"Dear Jesus, please heal my son," she said. The others in the room answered "Amen" as they gathered their belongings to walk down the hall.

The critical care unit wasn't far away and soon they were once again seated, looking at each other with exhaustion showing in their faces.

"I'm going home and take a shower and get into some clean clothes. He said that it will be two days or more before Jay even knows we are here. I thank God that he is alive and in recovery."

"I am going to get the bullets they extracted and take them to ballistics." said Joe as he left the room hastily.

Outside the hospital Koza hailed a cab that had just dropped off someone. The cab driver pulled in as directed, commenting on the police presence. From the sidewalk at Koza's front entrance and she could still see police outside Jay's condo. Jackie greeted her with happy barks and bounced beside her as she opened her door. An envelope lay on the kitchen tile. Koza felt strange as she slid the note out of the envelope.

"Next time," was printed in the middle, nothing else. She instantly knew that it was a threat to Jay. This note was from the person that shot Jay! She called the hospital and tried to reach Joe, but he had left. She called his precinct. The policeman on the phone said he was off duty.

"Please officer; I have a note under my door that says that someone is going to try again to kill Jay Spencer! I don't know what to do."

"Miss, you have just done it. We already have a guard on him and an officer will be there soon to pick up that note. Don't handle it any more than you have." He took her address and thanked her for calling.

She took a very short shower, not more than a splash. Then as she tied her yellow terry cloth robe around her, the front door bell rang. Her soggy hair trailed down her back as she crossed the living room carpet on bare feet and answered the door. Two officers came in, identifying themselves. They placed the note and envelope in separate evidence bags and then one of them asked her if she could think of anything else that might have changed while she was gone.

"Well, this will sound silly but I did pick up several small pieces of thread on the kitchen floor. I don't know where they could have come from. The house was clean when I left. The thread is dark and the floor is light or I may not have noticed them."

"Where are they?" She lifted the kitchen basket showing the officer the threads resting in the bottom of the clean liner. They put those in an evidence bag too. They dusted her entire back door, mail slot and handle for prints and hurried across the grass court to the group of police still working at Jay's taking the evidence bags with them.

"I want to get back to the hospital to be with Jay, as soon as I can. Jackie your friend is hurt. I can't stay here with you today." I'll call work from the hospital and let them know that I won't be coming in today or tomorrow, she planned. She filled Jackie's biggest bowl with as much dry food as it would hold and did the same with her water. She had no idea that Jackie had provided important evidence. She hugged her dog's neck and scratched her ears while fighting back tears.

Quickly she pulled on a beige pantsuit with a soft yellow sweater under the jacket. She brushed her hair back and put it in a ponytail pulling a few wispy bangs forward, a touch of makeup and mascara with a soft rust colored lipstick and she was heading toward the door when she realized that she didn't have shoes on. The brown flats were the first pair she spotted that would go with her suit and she put them on. This is no time to wear heels. She had her Bible under her arm, she took her purse and left by the side door leaving Jackie's dog door unlocked.

"You can go visit your friends if you want to," she said. "Jackie, go see Bitsy." The dog wagged and bounded in the direction of Maddie's Condo and barked at the side door. She was immediately allowed inside. Koza rushed to her car. It still has that wonderful new car smell. Funny that I would even notice that with all that is going on. The car gave her pleasure because it was something that Jay had chosen for her.

*****

The bullets removed from Jay, had been sent directly to ballistics and forensics would work on the letter, envelope and the dark threads. CSI had removed a third bullet from the back of the chair where Jay had been sitting.

The cell phone taken from Jay's lawyer, Mark Harris, had been scrutinized and the last number he had called went to a phone that was later found in a trash can, two blocks from Jay's condo, wiped clean of prints.

The man Mark had called was temporarily living in a large apartment only two blocks from Jay's condo. Mark had promised him a generous bonus if he would take care of this problem tonight.

"Sure I can do it. What do you want, an accident or something quick and clean?"

"The latter," Mark answered and hung up as an officer entered the small office.

"That's your one call, Harris!" The officer took the phone and slid it across the table to a second officer that took it and headed down the hall with it.

Within a half hour Mark's problem solver, had walked the two blocks and concealed himself in a patch of shadow behind a bush outside Jay's patio. He waited there for over an hour before a light finally went on in Jay's condo. He had planned to simply knock on the door and do the job when Jay answered, but when he saw the big glass doors of Jay's patio slide open and Jay now sitting in his chair. It all seemed perfectly easy. The silencer on the gun stifled the sound of three quiet thuds, a smile crossed his face as he saw the lights grow brighter and then dim over and over, as he strolled to the fence that separated the courtyard from the park. He went through the gate and simply walked slowly away in the deep shadows of the trees in the park. He circled around and spent a few minutes in his apartment meticulously wiping his fingerprints from the gun and placed it back in his bedroom in the vent. Each unused bullet had been wiped and placed back in the box. The spent cartridges he had tossed in the big dumpster behind his apartment. The urge to watch overcame him and he walked back toward the flashing lights and sirens. He arrived just in time to see a young woman run from her condo, and jump into the ambulance just before it hurried away.

"What happened?" he asked one of the many policemen.

"Jay Spencer was shot!"

"Is he dead?"

"No, but he is pretty bad off."

"Hey, I thought this was a good neighborhood! It seems like nobody is safe anymore," he offered backing up. He left soon after, to once again walk the two blocks to his apartment, where he prepared the envelope. He returned with it and slipped it through the dog door in Koza's side door, taking care so he wouldn't be noticed. He panicked when Jackie came rushing out her dog door growling and barking. He ran as fast as he could to the busy street behind her condo and dashed across between cars, hoping she would be hit.

Still holding a tiny shredded piece of his trouser leg, Jackie stopped at the curb. Koza had trained her well.

The ragged bits of cloth lay on the kitchen floor. She picked up the envelope and shook it but dropped it leaving teeth marks. Poor Jackie was filled with anxiety too, from the strange happenings of the night. She sensed that this man had no good reason to be in their area.

*****

Dr. Roberts had permitted Koza and Jay's parents to peek in from time to time, but Jay continued to sleep soundly. The guards changed shifts and one was always at the door to his private room on the fourth floor. He was given a full time nurse and Jay's family requested the room with no easy access. They paid for additional guards to be placed at the elevator and the stairs. Money had its privilege.

As days passed, Jay began to lose weight. He slept on. This no longer was the induced sleep of medication. It was a coma. Koza sat beside his bed and claimed the healing passages in her Bible and prayed for hours in the evenings after work. Often she forgot to eat. She grew thin, too and looked exhausted.

The police worked hard on the case, and forensics matched the bullets taken from Jay, and one from the back of his chair, to one found inside the front tire of the little red convertible driven by Mrs.

Randall. That case had never been closed. Now they had linked it to the person that had tried to kill Jay. The tiny bits of fabric yielded skin cells, and DNA that led directly to the killer.

The nurse checked Jay's vital signs often as the many machines and tubes connected to Jay did their job. They monitored his every breath and heartbeat.

Jay's father looked after the business as well as he could. He followed his instincts, taking comfort in the knowledge that the top accountant that Jay had hired was capable of doing a good job. The new man he had brought with him was also proving himself very capable. James had been working in the New York office for several years and understood what was needed.

When he thought about it he realized that it was possible that he might lose his second son. His heart still hadn't healed from the loss of Adam and now the suspicion that Mark Harris may have had a part in that; made James grind his teeth with anger.

Finally on the fifth day, Jay opened his eyes and asked for Koza. Immediately the nurse sprang into action with a smile on her face. The doctor checked him and with joy allowed Koza to come in the room. Rosie and James slipped in too, just for a minute to see that their son was awake and suddenly looked so much better.

Two more days passed before Jay was taken off the critical list but remained under guard. He was allowed visitors. Joe came with his big smile and brought the best news possible.

"They got him Jay! They got the shooter! They arrested him this morning. He was staying just two blocks from your place. They have enough evidence to put him away for life and there is plenty to connect him to Mark Harris too. I saw Mark's dad, Robert, this morning and he says that he will not represent Mark at his trial. He will be a witness against him. He is sickened by this whole thing. They found the convenience store that sold the burner phone. He was on the surveillance tape. It is the same phone that Harris called. We have lots of evidence. His shoes still had the mulch in the grooves of the soles from the place he hid by the rose bushes in the court outside your place. His footprints were there and the men made a cast of them. We are tracking some leads on the gun that was used on your wife. This guy bought it there on the street. It is a small pearl handled derringer. I guess he thought that something small would make it more believable.

Jay held Koza's hand constantly and seemed to draw strength from her. His wounds healed rapidly. Now that he was getting stronger he was allowed to go home. A staff of nurses would share the responsibility of taking care of him around the clock.

During his absence, James had made sure that Jay's condo was not as vulnerable. He reduced the size of the windows and all of them were replaced with bulletproof glass. No longer did they slide wide open. Jay fussed when he saw the changes but he knew that his father had acted out of love. He felt that he was living in a fort and he resented that it was necessary.

*****

Maddie and Michael announced their engagement in the paper and their picture appeared often in the society pages, attending functions with other high profile couples.

Jay and Koza managed to keep their intentions quiet.

After a surprise visit to Michigan where Koza was able to put together a small party for her family and friends, the couple officially announced their engagement. Many calls and long conversations had prepared her parents to accept Jay. Teri and Keith actually found him quite pleasant and since he was famous and wealthy, they decided for now to support her decision. They could easily see that she was in love with this little man.

Back in New York, Koza and Maddie decided that it would be fun to have a double wedding. That spring Koza had taken instructions and been baptized in the Catholic Church. Joe stood proudly beside Jay and was his best man. Michael surprised everyone when he asked Briggs to be his best man.

"He has been taking care of Maddie and knows her better than I do," he said laughing. "I am hoping that he will continue to do so after we are married."

"This really is taking advantage of our friendship, Jay! You look great in a tuxedo but this thing makes me look like a store mannequin," said Joe.

Jay laughed at his remark.

"You wore a uniform for years until you became a detective. This isn't that different."

Maddie had taken inspiration from the occasion and was planning an entire line of wedding gowns for the coming year. Surprisingly, neither bride chose an elaborate gown. Maddie had deliberately worn a simple off the shoulder, cream colored dress with no train and no veil. Instead she had secured a crown of white cymbidium orchids and tufts of gold lace, on her hair. Her bouquet was matching white orchids and ivy with long, trailing, cream colored ribbons. Maddie was very excited. Her first wedding to Carl Clay had been a quick civil ceremony and had ended badly. This was the wedding she had always dreamed of with a man she had loved for years.

Koza smiled at Jay as she walked down the aisle of St. Andrew Catholic Church on the arm of her father. He too, had objected to the tuxedo until he saw his daughter in her floor-length gown of white silk with a modest train. A thin gold ribbon circled her tiny waist and several trailed from her bouquet of pure white roses accented with seashells and gold tuffs of lace.

Koza had designed the dress and bouquet with Maddie's help. It was reminiscent of the occasions that had brought Jay and Koza together. On her neck she wore her simple cross, but in the middle of it a jeweler had fasten the tiny shell that Jay had found that early morning on the beach in Greece. The gold ribbons were to remind him of that beautiful golden sunrise and the white roses were the kind that he had first given her.

"Father, you look very handsome," Koza whispered.

"Maddie, are you ready?"

"As ready as I will ever be," she replied with a stunning smile. James stepped beside Maddie and extended his arm. "Thank you father," she said quietly. "Thank you for everything."

Close friends of Jay and associates of Michael and assistant designers from Maddie's company flowed slowly down the aisle, ahead of them, in every shade of blue imaginable. Twenty couples moved slowly down the aisle preceding the brides. The end of every pew was adorned with bouquets of white flowers. The altar they slowly approached was ornamented with huge circles of white orchids, and several shades of blue flowers mixed with soft ferns and trailing ivy. The seats were filled with family and friends. Each had been given an embellished memento of the occasion as they entered. This wedding was quite unlike any they had ever attended. It was extravagant but at the same time it was elegant and in good taste. Every detail had been checked and double checked to assure perfection.

Finally the double wedding ceremony took place and all without one photo being taken. The press was allowed in after the couples had said their vows and the long, High Mass was ended.

The reception was the high point of the social calendar. The news coverage seemed to drag the event on for days as some small token of private thoughts or spoken impressions were examined. The sparkle of gold and blue filled the tables as the guests found the cuisine unusual, delicious and beautiful. The salads were all topped with Jay's favorite star fruit and special sweet dressing. The platters that lined the buffet were piled high with every imaginable tasty treat. The wedding cake actually towered above all of the wedding party as the two couples simultaneously cut a small slice from the bottom layer.

Much later, Koza hugged her mother and asked if it had gotten any easier, dealing with Dad's new wife and daughter.

"I worried for you, when I knew they would be here."

"Actually, it has. Because of your engagement, we have gotten together several times. She doesn't feel threatened by me anymore and Virginia is in total awe of you and Jay. Your father and I are so proud of you Koza. Your book is hard to keep in stock and I have had to increase my order!"

Their pictures appeared in the society pages of the paper in full color. Koza's white silk gown was lovely and fitted and his tuxedo in pearl grey with a gold cummerbund set off the white rose in his lapel.

*****

Jackie approved when Koza and Jay left both condos and moved to an old farmhouse with ten acres. It came with two very old sway back horses and a goat that was mischievous and took a bit of getting used to. Soon she had made friends with the three residents and enjoyed walking in the field to visit them.

The old barn leaned dangerously and Jay decided to restore it. The contractor shook his head and said it would be cheaper to tear it down and just build a new one but Jay held his ground and by late fall the newly repaired antique barn stood straight, strong and tall again.

Jay hired a plumbing contractor and had new plumbing installed throughout the house, with a fresh kitchen and two bathrooms. He added on three bedrooms and another bath as soon as they moved in.

Koza became pregnant and their third visit to the doctor confirmed what she already suspected with concern. She was having twins. The news frightened Jay. The ultrasound on the next visit predicted that it was a boy and a girl. Everyone was delighted. This was a happy balance to the headlines that shouted the news of the ongoing murder trial.

They avoided it as much as possible. Jay had to spend three days in court to give his testimony. After that they tried to enjoy the peace of being in the country. Koza took walks in the field with an apple in each pocket and one in her hand. The greedy goat always managed to gobble the first one, but soon the horses had learned that she was their friend with good treats and they would amble over to greet her. The vet had checked them all and said they were healthy, just very old. Jay left the big door to the barn open so they could go in for shelter as the nights grew colder. They made a point of coaxing the animals in for their evening meal so they could close the door. Koza insisted that they not be tied to a stall area and that two small lights be left on, "so they can see each other," she said. "It is friendlier that way. I don't want to force them to stay anywhere.

The first snowfall of the season was beginning to coat the ground when the call came. It was a reporter wanting a statement from Jay. He informed him that the trial was suspended while another investigation took place. This would drag everything on into the New Year.

"What are they investigating now," Jay asked the reporter.

"Mark Harris was the last one to see or hear from Allen Quinn. His disappearance seems now to point in Harris's direction."

"Are they going to add that to the cases already listed?" Jay asked.

"Could be, I don't really know what they can do, but I was hoping you would give me an opinion on it."

"All I know is what has been on the television."

"Would you give us a comment for tomorrow's paper?"

"I just wish the whole thing was over and both men were found guilty. That's all I have to say."

"Goodbye sir and thank you for your time."

"Just say that I will be very glad when it is over."

Jay placed the phone back on its cradle.

As he crossed the large living room, his frown disappeared and his heart was filled with wonder at the beautiful woman smiling up at him. He thought of the children that would soon fill their lives with the fullness of a family. This will be a good place to raise them, he thought as he lowered himself next to her on the loveseat. The fire crackled and smelled of pine and oak. Almost instantly he popped back to his feet.

"I'm going to get us a drink. You can have juice, some of that nice tea you have been enjoying or decaffeinated coffee. What will it be?"

"I'll take the juice. Thank you, Jay."

"Good girl. You are a good mother already. I am going to follow your example and have the same."

When he came back from the kitchen, he carried a tray with the juice and a few snacks. He placed it on the coffee table in front of Koza and walked over to the window and drew open the drapes. When he flicked on the floodlight, the scene before them could have easily been on a Christmas card. The horses and goat stood just inside the barn peering out at the late November snow scene in front of them. Framed by the red barn they stood as if they too, enjoyed the first snow of winter.

"I am going out to close the door and make sure they are comfortable. I will be right back dear." He returned with a smile on his face.

"We have a white cat! She is curled up in the hay in the corner."

"How do you know it is a she?"

"I know because she has four tiny kittens that she is cuddling."

"Oh Jay, that's wonderful. We need to feed her!"

"I think she is fine for tonight, but when I go to town tomorrow to get feed for the others I will get her something too. This is her first night there, so I don't want to disturb her but we can take out something for her to eat in the morning."

CHAPTER NINE
COUNTRY NEIGHBORS

I need to check with our neighbors for advice on how much hay and grain that I will need to order to stock up for winter. I'll order them some too, if it looks like they need it."

After Jay's visit to the neighboring farms on his road, he discovered that he had been too busy to get to know the folks nearby. They had been pleasant and helpful. He did notice that the couple two miles down lived in a small house with little land. Their pile of wood for the fire was very small. She had answered the door in a thick sweater and her children were bundled against the chill. The hearth was their only source of heat and it held no flames. Before he left he had a lengthy mental list of the necessities they were lacking.

"Could your husband stop down this evening after work? I sure could use his advice on a few things."

"I'll send him down, after he has had his supper."

"Thank you, Mrs. Calder. I will look forward to talking to him."

*****

In spite of the absentee owner in the main office, Spencer's People continued to grow. The income increased and Jay was delighted to be able to help people anonymously. He told Koza about the couple with the three children in the small cold house and asked her advice on how to help them without embarrassing them.

"Jay you could suggest that they all come down to dinner here. Tell Mr. Calder that because I am pregnant, it would be good to have a woman near here that I could talk to. That would be a way of meeting them and seeing what size clothes the children need."

"That's a good idea, Honey."

Mr. Calder did stop down after his evening meal and Jay talked with him about the farm and about maybe buying more land.

"I need someone here that knows horses. I plan on adding a couple of yearlings in the spring so I think it would be a good investment to add on any land that becomes available. My wife and I are city folks, but she says she wants a big garden. That means finding someone that can teach us about that, too. We admit we are

115

green horns but I have been blessed and can pay well if I can find someone who is willing to help us."

"Well Mr. Spencer, my wife and I would be happy to do whatever we can for you but we don't need your money. We will be glad to help. Now I am sorry to cut this short but it is late so I'll just get on home. I can ask around if you like about anyone wanting to sell you a few acres."

"Mr. Calder, would you be willing to bring your wife and kids down for supper some night so we can get acquainted?"

"Well, that's real nice of you to ask but I don't want you to go to a lot of bother for us."

"Please come. How does Friday evening at five thirty sound? I know that children get hungry early."

"Yes they do, and that sounds fine. I'll tell Sally and we will come down Friday night. Please don't go to a lot of fuss for us. We do just fine with a simple meal."

A pleased expression was on Jay's face as he stepped in from the cold night.

"Good night Harold. This may be tougher than we thought. He says he doesn't want pay for helping us."

"Well I thought of a way to get them free firewood. We have two dead oak trees behind the barn, Friday you can suggest that Harold could have the wood if he would help you cut it and hall it away. I thought I could tell Sally that she could have half the produce from the garden if she will help me with it. It is more than likely that she would be able to can it. I'll ask her if she knows how. I haven't figured out extra food for this winter yet or extra clothes for them, but I will."

"Koza you are good at this! Maybe we should ask the priest. He might have some ideas that would help us."

As Jay and Koza worked to help their neighbors anonymously they became part of the community.

The grocery store on the edge of town had a big empty box near the door with a sign on it explaining that food placed inside would be given to needy families at Thanksgiving. Koza inquired if she could add a family to the list. They said sure, but explained that the area had many families in need and that they were just one small store. Koza told Jay about the box that evening. The next day he drove to the store and when he left the store owner was scratching his head and looking at a check that would buy every item in his store many times over. All of the items were to be delivered to the families on the list.

"Well I'll be! You never know about folks, do you Hon?" He said, as he showed the check to his wife. "Do you think this Spencer is related to the one in the news? He sure has a lot of money!"

"I don't know, but it looks like we have a lot of work to do and I don't think we should wait a minute to start ordering stock. Delivering, will take a week or so to get the stuff brought here and then more to sort it out and get it out to the folks that need it."

"This is wonderful. I don't mind the extra work and I know of a couple men that will volunteer to help if I ask them. This will be fun! I feel like Santa Claus! Remember Abby that Mr. Spencer doesn't want anyone knowing where the money came from. He said that it would take his blessing away if folks start thanking him."

"What do you think about this idea? I want to get on the phone and tell certain folks that this year we want to add warm blankets and clothes to the deliveries. Maybe they will donate some and we can get them out there where they are needed most."

"Funny but we could have done this before. It took that little city man to inspire us to be good country neighbors."

"That's a good idea, Abby, but could you just put it on the phone chains at the churches here in town? They know who to call. Besides you are going to need your time to work here with the sorting and ordering. When you call, ask them to say we need baskets and boxes, too and tell them we can use help."

Trucks brought cases of the ordered supplies, but soon the small store could not accommodate all of it. The crates and boxes began to collect outside.

"What are we going to do Dear? When the people start bringing their donations we will have no place to put them."

"I think that we need to ask our pastors to let us use the churches."

The next day people came with pickup trucks and helped move the operation to the Catholic Church. All denominations were helping in any way that they could. Soon a steady, organized stream of goods entered the back and packed boxes were stacked and labeled for specific locations. The front doors stood wide open as crates, boxes and baskets filled the pickup trucks of volunteers. Mountains of coats, boots, hats and gloves were sorted by ladies who tried to guess the sizes for children. If they weren't sure they chose a larger size.

"We all know that kids do grow rapidly," said one of the volunteers. Blankets were allocated, one for each member of the families. The list grew as work continued.

"Let's take some to the orphanage in Bedford," Suggested Pastor Dave. "I will be driving over there tomorrow. They can use clothes in any sizes left and blankets too. If we have provided for the folks on the list, let's take the rest of the food to them."

It was a good idea they all agreed. Slowly the church returned to normal as the last loaded trucks pulled away for their destination just two days before the holiday. The pastor's little black pickup was mounded and covered with a tarp to keep its contents safe on his trip to the Bedford Orphanage the next morning.

Jay had no idea the affect his check would have on the town of Merritt. He had asked Paul and Abby to keep his donation anonymous and they had honored his request.

When they took the check to the bank, they asked the bank teller to promise to not tell anyone. The town continued through Christmas without knowing who had donated the money for all the food deliveries.

The New Year was a good time for the town to start a fund to provide food for their next effort. It would be a yearly drive. In the weeks and months that followed, the people of Merritt found they had made new friends while working at the church. They seemed to become more aware of other's needs and worked hard to help. Loads of firewood appeared in the dark near houses where it was in short supply.

Koza had made friends with several ladies and had found a new skill in quilting. By the time spring came she had finished one lovely pink and white crib blanket and was working on one in shades of blue.

"I spoke to my mother this morning and she wants us to come and stay with her until the babies come. I told her I would talk to you about it."

"What would we do there? It would be better if she could come here. She hasn't seen our place. I think she could use the peace and quiet."

"You don't mind Jay? There are lots of jokes about mother-in-law visits."

"Call her tonight and see if she will come."

"Thank you Jay. I would like to have her here to visit and see our home. Should I call my father, too?"

"Maybe we should wait to call him until you are in labor. I know they get along well but there is no sense in making it hard on them. Oh I forgot to tell you, Koza that Maddie called. She said they have set a date for Michael retiring from his practice and she is going to turn most of the design and creation for her line over to her people. She said that they plan to travel and send the inspirational themes back for her crew to create."

"Good for them, I am so glad."

"She said she will leave it up to you because she wants to have a party here with just close family to make it official."

"Here? Are you kidding me? How could we have a party here?"

"She said she wants a farm theme and no fancy gowns or anything. She said that she is planning on wearing work clothes and a cowboy hat! That's if you agree of course."

"Jay, I hope she will wait until the babies come. Right now I feel as big as a barn! Is that considered a farm theme?" Koza and Jay laughed together and then he suggested that she call Maddie and have a nice talk.

Days passed and Koza became more uncomfortable as her time drew near. Jay tried not to hover but he was apprehensive and urged her to sit or rest often. He feared that another disastrous delivery would be more than he could stand after his last experience.

Her mother arrived two days before they left for the maternity wing of the hospital. Finally the date arrived and Jay drove slowly and carefully to the hospital.

Rosie and James were already there and met them with smiles and hugs. The doctor assured Jay again that an induced labor was a safe way to have Koza there surrounded by care and her family. Jay introduced his parents to Koza's mother, forgetting that they had all met at the wedding. He was quite distraught.

When the medicine began to work and Koza became aware of the strong contractions the nurse took her from the waiting room and placed her in a labor room where she would monitor Koza and the babies.

"Pat is my name. I see from your chart that your name is Koza. That's unusual. Is there a story that goes with that name?" The nurse chatted trying to distract Koza from the increasing pain.

"My mother was reading a novel about a Russian ballerina when she was pregnant for me and named me after the main character. My name is Kozarina. I never wanted to be a dancer. I don't know if that was a disappointment to her." The nurse laughed and Koza grimaced as another pain came.

"Those are getting closer together. I will ask the doctor to come in here to check you."

The rest of the morning was a blur for Koza. Jay didn't want to be in there for the birth. He just wanted it to be over and to know they were all healthy.

As hours passed Jay paced becoming more troubled, until finally the doctor stepped out to the waiting room and asked for Jay to come in.

"Mr. Spencer your wife is asking for you."

"Is she alright? Are the babies alright?" He ran down the hall to the doorway where a nurse stood smiling.

"Yes, Jay, I am alright and your two sons are fine, too," said Koza as he entered.

Jay hopped up on the bed beside her and kissed her and then each baby in turn.

"Koza, I love you so much! I was petrified all the time you were in labor. I have been praying the whole time that you would be alright and that the babies would be healthy and normal." Jay unashamedly let his tears spill onto his cheeks. He picked up first one and then the other, assuring himself that they were in fact healthy normal babies.

"Which one is the boy?"

"They both are. I guess we will have to try again for a girl."

"My sons," he said tenderly. "I have two sons!" It was finally sinking in. "They are big boys, Koza, and handsome too."

"Jay, they look like you." The nurse came in and interrupted their conversation by saying that the babies should go to the nursery now and that their mother needed to rest. "Jay you can have the pleasure of telling our family about the boys and they will be able to see them through the nursery window in a little while." The nurse nodded agreement as she tucked the boys together in one crib on wheels and headed out the door with them.

Jay wiped away his tears and blew his nose in the hall, taking a deep breath before entering the waiting room. Koza's father had arrived by taxi while Jay had been in with Koza.

"She is fine!" Jay announced, "Our family now has two more growing men! They are healthy and big for twins." Everyone started talking at once and laughing. "I have two boys!"

"What are you going to name them, Jay?" Koza's father asked. Jay had not intentionally ignored him. He was just overwhelmed with joy at the moment. Jay walked to him and shook his hand.

"I'm not sure, Grandpa. We have been reading lists of names and none of them seemed right to us at the time." They all laughed again at the first use of the name Grandpa. "We thought it was a boy and a girl. The nurse has taken the babies to the nursery and I think we can go see them through the window." The nurse directed them and they took the elevator. Stairs were difficult for Rosie. The nurse held the babies up where they could see them and take lots of pictures.

After the usual comments of how perfectly handsome they are, James and Rosie said they were treating and that they should all go to a restaurant for lunch.

"Well, this isn't New York, but we do have one nice place here in Merritt. It's right on Main Street on the left, about three blocks from here. I hope you all can find something on the menu. I usually get the T-bone and a salad."

Jay said he would be there in just a few minutes. He headed for the nurse's station. After a short conversation he was satisfied and headed out of the hospital to meet his family at the restaurant.

When Jay arrived, he was surprised to see Maddie and Michael just being seated. The small restaurant was doing its best to accommodate the growing group by sliding tables together.

"Does everyone want coffee?" The question was asked by a middle aged woman with a wide smile. She was pleased to hear the happy banter of her customers. She felt that she was being included in this happy occasion.

"So your wife just had twins? That's wonderful! Two boys are going to keep you both plenty busy."

"Yes, but I am already busy. She gave me the job of coming up with names that she likes." Everyone laughed and said that was an easy job.

"It could be"... Jay said with a grin. The first born will be James for my father and Adam for his middle name and the second one we will call Keith for you, Grandpa, he said smiling at Koza's dad and Jacob for his middle name. If Koza agrees then my work is finished!"

"Silly man," the waitress said, "Your work has only just begun." Everyone burst out laughing again.

Michael and Maddie added to the joy by announcing that they too were going to be adding to the family, but not for several more months. Maddie turned her coffee cup over on the saucer and asked for a glass of milk.

"That is wonderful! I think it is time you two settled down someplace permanently. You can't keep traveling the world with a baby," said Rosie.

"Yes, you are right, and we don't want to live in New York. I have started to find homes for some of my animals. The birds were easy to place. The aviary they are in is huge and they look beautiful and happy there, and Tom has agreed to keep Tonga, Congo and Chase together and he will live there in my Condo. Briggs will be coming with us as long as we make room for him to have a wife. He has been seeing a young woman for several months and I think he plans on proposing soon. Michael found a lovely home for us in California. It has a pool and a guest house that we will enlarge. I have only seen it on line, but it looks amazing."

"So much is changing for all of us. Maddie, you didn't say what you will do about Bitsy."

"Yes, that is a dilemma. I want her to stay with Tom in the jungle, but he isn't sure that he wants to keep her. She has taken to biting him and you can't blame him for resenting that."

"Maddie she should go to the zoo. They said they would take her and there she will be with others of her kind. We could go see her there and someday she might even have a baby of her own. Unless of course Jay wants to take her home with him and let her ride around the farm on Jackie." Michael was laughing as he said it.

"No thank you," said Jay. "That farmhouse is going to have enough activity without adding Bitsy to the mix!"

"I have a great idea! Why don't you all go out to the farm and paint the two pink walls in the nursery, to match the rest of the room? I will go back and see Koza and ask her about the names for the boys."

"There is room out there for all of you to stay. Just pick any room but mine," he said it in a kidding manner but was hoping that they might actually put their hands to work and make the changes in the nursery before Koza came home.

Just then Jay's phone rang. It was John Maxwell, Koza's agent.

"I have been trying to get ahold of Koza for two days. I was wondering when she will have another book ready for publication."

"Hold on please." Jay looked at the people gathered at the table and decided to share his thoughts with all of them. "This is Koza's agent. He wants to know when her next book will be ready!" He paused another moment and then said," I will have her call you back as soon as possible." He ended the call. "His timing isn't great. Here she is having twins and he wants her to get her manuscript to final edit."

Keith smiled broadly and looked at the others.

"Jay, I have an idea. Did you ever fix Koza a little office where she could write?"

"No, I intended to do it, but it just never happened. We added on rooms and did a lot of remodeling. She could have picked any of the new bedrooms but she didn't. When she worked, she usually did it in the dining room at the table."

"How hard would it be to have one of those prefab offices put out under the trees at your place and run a little juice to it and a sidewalk before she comes home?" Keith was grinning as he shared his idea. "I will be glad to pay for it."

"No, we should all pitch in so that it is from all of us," said James. "I want to help, too."

"Jay, it would be fun to surprise her. She will need a place that's quiet. Have you got a nanny lined up?" Jay's father was eager to know that everything was in order. He was a lot like Jay in many ways.

"Yes, of course, have you forgotten what we do for a living? I found a nice nurse. She is the right person for us."

"Good, that's comforting to know. Well, what do you all think? Can we pull this off? "

Teri, Koza's mother, was smiling broadly.

"We girls can plan the inside while the men do the outside."

Michael signaled for the waitress to come over and he made two quick requests. She returned with hot coffee and a phone book. The men sat in a huddle each making calls until they had lined up responses for the following morning. Michael called the head of the hospital and when he had finished, he had convinced the man that Mrs. Spencer and the two baby boys should stay in the hospital an extra day.

The little town of Merritt had not experienced such a flurry of activity since Christmas. Trucks headed out to the farm with gravel to create a base. One poured concrete for the slab and several men were still pounding stakes in the ground to support the forms as the cement sidewalk was started.

When the building arrived, it was nestled between the trunk of an old oak and a perfect clump of birch trees. They hadn't planned it that way, but the trees would be outside her windows each creating a lovely foreground in the natural beauty of the farm.

In keeping with the tradition of Koza's conservative color palette the ladies decided to change it up just a bit. They had the ceiling painted a very beautiful pale blue and the walls a warm cream. The carpet was tan and made to last a lifetime. Over the horizontal shades, filmy curtains were covered with thick insulated drapes in a warm brown. She could use none, one or all depending on the weather. Her desk faced the north window that looked out at the base of the oak tree and the open fields. The front room was her office with overhead lighting and a good directional lamp on her desk. In the back were a half bath and a kitchenette.

"All the comforts of home, "said Teri.

"I don't want her to get too comfortable," said Jay. "We will want her to come visit us inside the house once in a while." He was kidding, but at the same time he felt bad that he had not done this for her sooner.

"All that is missing is a dog door," said Maddie.

"You are right! Jay waved at the carpenter who was just now loading his truck to return to town. "We forgot one important thing! We need a dog door!"

"It's too late tonight, but I can come back in the morning and install one. Where would you like it?"

"Could you put it in the bottom of the front door?"

"Certainly, I can have it installed before noon. I am guessing that it has to be big enough for her to use." Jackie was standing beside him wagging.

"Yes and it wouldn't hurt to make it a bit bigger."

The carpenter was smiling as he left. He was wondering if Jay realized that his dog was pregnant. She will need a bigger door, he thought. Jackie had become a friend to all the animals on the farm.

She was very fond of the old mare and would occasionally go in the field and walk with her. She shared her food with a stray once in a while but none had stayed with her.

CHAPTER TEN
BABY BOYS

"Jay, the names are fine, but shouldn't the first born have your name as his first name?"

"No, honey, I think it gets confusing when you have two guys in the same house with the same name."

A nurse stepped in at the right moment, bringing forms for them to fill out for the boy's birth certificates.

When they had finished she took the papers and said that she would make name cards for the baby's cribs in the nursery.

"That way when you look through the glass you will be able to see their names. "

"It would be easy to mix them up. They look so much alike. Koza, do you think they will be regular people or little like me?"

"Jay, is it important to you to know?"

"No I guess not, but there is a test they can do and then we would know. You wouldn't have to tell anyone if you didn't want to."

"Jay, you said that as if there would be something wrong with them being little. Don't think that way. Let's just wait and see what God has planned for them. I will love them no matter how big or how small they are. I fell in love with you, didn't I?"

He chuckled and then said seriously, "How are we going to keep the right name on the right boy?"

"Permanent markers work well!" Koza said laughing. "When are they going to let me take the boys home? I am ready to get out of here."

"I think it will depend on the doctor releasing them. They have to weigh a certain amount, you know."

"The nurse told me that yesterday."

"Koza you know I am eager to get my family home but not until it is safe. We have to be patient. I should go back to the farm now. Your folks and mine are there and so are Maddie and Michael. I don't want them to all think I am ignoring them."

"They wouldn't think that. They know you are here with me." He gently kissed her forehead and gave her the thumbs up sign. As he left the room he whispered.

"Rest now, while you can. I love you Koza. I'll see you tomorrow."

Jay felt conspiratorial as he stopped at the nursery window to enjoy the sight of his sons. He was eager to tell her about the writing studio they were creating for her, but he managed to keep it a secret.

On the way to his car he thought of the smiley face ring he had given her on the steps of the church. He walked to the flower shop in the opposite direction.

"Oh, I am so glad that you are still open. I want to order some flowers for my wife I would like two dozen pure white roses and then put in two blue flowers. We just had twin boys!" He said it with laughter. "I need something with a big yellow smiley face on it, too."

"We have something very special. These blue flowers are called Blue Cajun Hibiscus. I can cut them from the plant and put them in a pick filled with water. They are beautiful and rare. Aren't they lovely?"

"Yes, they certainly are different. I don't think I have seen them before."

"We have these balloons with a big smiley face on them. Would one of them do?"

"Yes, that is perfect, and on the card could you put this?" He jotted down the note in stiffly printed letters.

"My writing is terrible. She probably wouldn't be able to read it. I know you will do a much better job."

She carefully wrote the message and handed the card to Jay for approval.

"That's nice. Thank you. They need to go to room 211 for Koza Spencer. Will they be delivered yet tonight?"

"Yes, I can take them myself as soon as I lock up. I will drop them off on my way home."

"Thank you. I appreciate it." He whistled his way to his car and smiled when he thought of her reading the card.

"To our Mommy: Daddy says you are still pure joy. You make him smile.

We Love you, James and Keith."

I will keep this card with the first one always, thought Koza when she read it.

*****

Everyone had been too busy to bother picking up the newspaper from the lawn. As the last truck pulled away, Jay looked back at the little office tucked into the trees. It looks settled, as if it has been there for a long time, he thought as he bent and picked up the Daily Star and carried it inside. The headline stopped him in his tracks.

"Juror causes mistrial!"

Jay's hand shook as he finished the article and placed the newspaper on the coffee table.

"I saw that on the television at noon. That juror should have told the truth before he was seated! How can people be so dumb? He said he was scared to tell it then. He was blabbing in the jury room that he had heard a phone conversation that Harris had in his office at least two weeks before he was arrested. This guy is actually a client of Harris's. He heard him talking to someone about a small hand gun and the smaller the better. He should have been on the witness list, not a juror! I am so sorry son. Now they will have to drag that all up again," said James.

"It seems like we are never going to have peace."

"Mr. Spencer, the new cook wants to know who eats first, you or your animals."

"Thank you Susan. Tell her the animals do and I am going out there right now. I nearly forgot! Some farmer I am," he mumbled as he made a dash to the barn.

Well at least I don't have cows to milk or chicken eggs to gather, he thought as he patted the aged rumps and poured the grain and water in the containers. He looked in the corner where little Lulu had been keeping her kittens, but they were not there. He called her as he set her bowl of food and one of fresh water against the wall.

He heard a sound above his head and looked up as a single piece of hay drifted down in front of him. Standing on the very edge of the hay loft was Lulu and her four kittens. "Be careful there. I guess all the trucks and extra people caused you to take the babies up where you thought they would be safer. I am not climbing that ladder to deliver this. You need to come down here. He said it laughing. He knew she would probably jump down as soon as he left. Leaving two small lights on, he closed the big door.

The next day was both fun and exhilarating. Jay managed to slow down the process of releasing his family at the hospital until the carpenter called and said that the dog door was finished. Now with the baby boys in their new car seats in back, Jay drove his family home.

Koza was excited and talked most of the way home about what they would need to change in the nursery and saying that she hoped that she would like Susan, the new nanny.

"I only met her once at our interview with her, Jay. What if she isn't the right one?"

"Koza, she has been there for two days and has really been helpful with us having your folks, mine and Maddie and Michael there. I can always find another nanny if Susan doesn't work out. Just relax dear."

"Jay, you didn't need to get us a cook. I am not that spoiled! I could have managed."

"Yes, I know you are capable of doing it all but you shouldn't have to. Anyway there are other things that are more rewarding. You should spend quality time with the boys and maybe when a few weeks pass you will feel like getting back to writing."

"There are many things I could do, Jay, but taking care of my family is first on the list right now."

"Well if you feel that way about it, I will tell Mrs. Calder that she isn't needed. She was delighted when I suggested it. She was just going to come down at three and leave as soon as the kitchen was back in order. I am sure they could use the money."

"Oh Jay, you didn't say it was Mrs. Calder. Who will watch her kids?"

"Their oldest will and I offered a small babysitting fee so that things would go smoothly."

"Jay that was a great idea, you are always thinking." As he pulled up the driveway everyone in the house converged on their vehicle. Teri and Rosie each started unbuckling the babies and talking baby talk to them. Rosie surprised everyone with how efficiently she removed James from the car and carried him cuddled close to her heart. Teri pulled Keith into her arms and her eyes filled with tears.

"Look, dear, you have a grandson with your name. He is so beautiful."

"Yes, Teri, I saw him at the hospital. Why are you crying?

"I don't know. It is just all so overwhelming. Koza has twin boys. It is so special." He chuckled at her sentimentality and then said quite loudly that Jay had a surprise for Koza and that the two of them should go ahead.

"Koza, are you feeling well enough to walk down this new little sidewalk?"

"Jay, what is this? How could you do this in the short time I have been gone?"

"I didn't do it alone. Everyone helped. It was your dad's idea and we used the phone book and got the professionals involved." Jackie was barking and wagging joyfully. Koza stopped long enough to give her some attention and then watched as she darted through the dog door just ahead.

As each person stepped inside they had to move toward the back so that others could enter. Michael and Maddie were already inside and had prepared a welcome home party in the little kitchen. Juice and cookies were sampled as Koza eased herself into the new desk chair. This is heaven! She looked through the window and back at the people gathered there to greet her.

"Thank you, all of you must have been working very hard. This is perfect. I am sure that it will get lots of use. I like the colors and where it sits. The windows have a nice view. You are all so thoughtful. Thank you Daddy for thinking of it and all of you for helping."

"You are welcome Koza. I should have done this for you sooner. Now I think we should take our sons in the house and introduce them to their new nanny." Susan had been prepared for this moment and took both the boys, one on each arm.

"Koza, we took the liberty of painting the pink walls a shade of blue just a bit darker than you used. We didn't find your paint can and we thought it best not to make a poor match." Maddie smiled as Koza turned slowly around absorbing the lovely room with cribs ready to receive her sons.

"Your mom thought it was good to do it before you came home so it would dry and there would not be any fumes."

"I am impressed with all that was accomplished so beautifully, Maddie. Thank you for being here. You were in Europe last I heard."

"That is what planes are for. Michael and I were thinking of buying a home in California, but now just being here for a few days and doing hands on work has given me second thoughts. I think we may look for a farmhouse out here in your area. It would be nice to live close so our children can grow up together."

"Oh, Maddie, are you pregnant?"

"Yes, I think that we will have our baby in late summer. I haven't chosen a doctor yet. I want to find a home first and then a doctor that I can stay with through all the years that the baby's growing up."

"I am so happy for you," said Koza. While the women had been talking, Susan had changed the diapers on both boys, checked the names on their feet and placed them in the appropriate crib. It was then that they each noticed the little signs above the cribs.

"I will soon be able to tell them apart, but in the meantime I put the signs up so I will use the correct names with them. I hope you don't mind."

"I don't mind at all, Susan. It will be helpful for all of us."

"They are tired from their first ride, but after a little nap they will be hungry. I have sterilized their bottles and the formula is ready to be warmed when they want it. I will take it from here. Mrs. Spencer, you need to rest now. You have been through a lot. I am sure you are very tired."

"Yes, I am. I think I want to change into my pajamas and take a long nap, too."

Jay peeked in the nursery door and Susan met him halfway in with an anti-bacterial wipe.

"I will keep these here near the door on this table. Please use one every time you come in here near the babies. Their systems are still developing and they could easily get sick from germs."

"Thank you, Susan; I will try to develop a habit of doing that. There is nothing wrong with being careful." He looked with awe at the sleeping boys in their cribs.

"I can see that you have taken charge already. Thank you for being here. Koza will need you for a long time. She is a writer you know and will need some time out in her studio to work. I am sure that she will rely on you heavily now and when she is stronger."

"That's why I am here." He was smiling as he came down the hall. He was glad that Teri and Rosie had tucked Koza in for a nap. The house wasn't quiet exactly, but peaceful. It seemed to have a fullness of life feeling that Jay couldn't quite explain. The men had gathered in the living room and were watching a ballgame. The women were sitting around a small table in the kitchen with a cup of tea and enjoying a conversation when Jackie came in and flopped on the cool tile.

"Is she allowed in here?" Mrs. Calder asked.

"She owns the place!" said Teri. Jackie wagged and then stretched out with a deep sigh. She was happy that Koza was back.

"I am going to fix a tray for Koza and then she should rest again after she eats."

"We won't have to worry about her with you here. I am so glad that you could make the time to help out here. I have to leave first thing in the morning, said Teri. "I have a woman running my shop that has to go to her son's wedding in two days. I think Keith will be leaving tomorrow afternoon. This has been so nice getting to spend time here with all of you and to work together to make things even nicer for Koza."

"She is a good girl, Teri. We all love Koza very much. Maybe you will be able to come back for the baptism. Catholics do that when they are still babies you know. "

"Well, yes I have heard of that. I don't know if I can make it or not, but I will try."

CHAPTER ELEVEN
EMPTY CRIBS

Things went well at the Spencer residence until one day Jay was notified that he would have to appear in court that following Monday. He had managed to push things into the back of his mind and concentrate on his wonderful baby sons and Koza.

She had settled into a routine of breakfast with the babies, helping with their bath time and then Susan would put the boys down for a nap and do some light housework while Koza spent the next several hours out in her peaceful office. She had sent her manuscript to the publisher via the internet and this time John Maxwell would not be involved at all. She had developed a dislike for the man. He was too self-concerned and pushy.

Her contract was basically the same and she was surprised that her second book revived interest in the first.

*****

Susan had finished vacuuming the living room. She washed her hands and went in to check on the babies. The cribs were empty! The window was wide open and the screen lay on the grass outside. Susan's scream could be heard in Koza's office and in the barn where Jay was brushing a new brown and white yearling.

They both ran to the house afraid of what they would find. Susan was crying and shaking so badly that she could barely explain what had happened.

"I cleaned the living room and put the sweeper away and then I noticed it was near noon so I checked the boys. That's when I screamed. They are gone! Both boys are gone!"

"Jay how could they do this? We are here! It is daytime. Why didn't Jackie bark? Who would take our boys?" He was on the phone to Joe Downing instantly.

"Joe, someone took our twins! They pulled the screen off the window and just opened the window and took them."

"Was it locked?"

"Yes Joe, we had it locked. They must have pried it or something."

"Jay, get ahold of the local sheriff and report this right away. I will be out as soon as I can. You need to be sure you tell everyone to

134

stay out of the nursery. Maybe we can get prints. I have to get my other line, but I will be there as soon as I can."

Joe picked up the ringing line and heard sobbing. It was his wife.

"Joe, they took Cody! Someone grabbed him while he was waiting for the bus out front. I saw it Joe! It was a big gray van-truck thing with no windows in the back. A man just picked him up and tossed him in the back and they drove away fast. You know I always stand and watch out the window until the bus picks him up. Joe what are we going to do?"

"I'm coming home honey, don't cry. We will get him back! Where is Michelle? Is she alright?"

"Yes, she has a bad tummy and she didn't want to go to school today so I let her stay home. If I had made her go, maybe she would be gone, too! Oh Joe, I am scared. Please tell me what we should do."

"Don't do anything! Lock the doors and windows and sit down in the living room and wait for me. I am on my way!" Joe called an instant meeting in the office. He briefed the officers on the missing children and explained that he was sure that the kidnappings were connected to the Harris case.

"Jay and I were heavily involved in getting him arrested!" Two crews were assigned and left immediately. Joe was not allowed to work the case. He was instructed to go home and stay with his wife. He had with him recording devices that were quickly attached to his phone and Darla's. She clung to him and didn't want him to move.

Jay spent only a couple of minutes on the phone informing the local sheriff of the missing babies. Ten minutes later, the flashing lights of the responding officer's cars filled their driveway and part of the lawn.

They quickly questioned the family, and Susan. No one had seen or heard anything unusual. Yellow crime scene tape was fastened to the trees on the side of the house and no one dared step inside the rectangle that they had created. They were preserving the evidence for the detectives coming out from New York City.

Jay's phone rang just as he feared it would.

"This is the only call you will get. Your sons are fine, and will stay that way so long as you don't testify." Silence followed. Tears streamed down Susan's face as she repeated what had happened to a detective. Koza was shaking. Jay considered giving her a sedative, but called her doctor instead.

When he arrived, he did give Koza a mild sedative and told her to rest.

"Even if you don't sleep, it will help you to cope. There is nothing that you can do right now." Jay held her close as he walked her down the hall to their room.

*****

Joe Downing and Darla were sitting together with Michelle between them on the couch. They had experienced a similar incursion of officers and detectives. They answered questions over and over.

"He has on his red hoodie and jeans and a ball cap, black or dark blue. I can't remember." They showed Darla pictures of vans and SUVs until they came to the conclusion that it was a delivery truck that had been painted gray.

"It was Cody's black one with the check mark on the side."

"What miss? What did you say?"

"I saw Cody in the hall and he had his black cap with the check mark and his back pack. He said it was too heavy. He had a lot of homework last night and he doesn't like to do it on the computer. He does it the old way."

"I thought all kids liked computers!"

"Not Cody." The questioning continued.

"Can you remember anything else Mrs. Downing? What was the abductor wearing?"

"He was wearing jeans and a black hoodie with the hood up. I never saw his face. It all happened so fast." Joe paced the length of the house and back.

"They haven't called. They should have called by now." He wrung his hands and paced some more.

"Joe, all that nervous energy isn't doing any good. Sit down with your wife. We are working every angle. We will find Cody, Joe. I promise we will find Cody."

"You can't promise that! No one can promise that!" Joe's phone rang in his pocket. It was barely audible. He had bumped the volume button as he moved.

"Hello, hello?" It was a dead line. "Someone is toying with us." He turned the phone to full volume and placed it slowly on the coffee table before him. It rang again.

"Hello?

"Do you hear that? That's your boy. You better lose your memory or he will lose his life. Got it?"

"Yes, I understand."

"Click." They played the recorded conversation and Darla burst into sobs.

"That's Cody. Cody is crying. They are hurting him! Oh God please help us!"

Mrs. Downing, I doubt if they have hurt your boy. He is probably frightened. They may have scared him to make him cry so he could be heard on the phone."

*****

The kidnappers had planned well and the house they had entered for their purpose was far enough from neighbors that no one would notice their activities. Cody was placed on the floor in the bathroom and told to stay in there. He could hear a baby crying nearby and wondered why no one was picking the baby up or taking care of it. Its cries were joined by a second baby fussing and then getting louder.

"Hey guys, there is a reason I don't have kids. You hear that? That's it!"

"Smalley, get in there and shut them up. Change their diapers and give them a bottle. That's all you have to do"

"You didn't tell me there would be two of them." Cody peeked around the corner and saw the two babies on a blanket and on the floor of an empty room.

"I will help you," he said. Coming out slowly he moved toward the babies. Do you think they are hungry? I hold our neighbor's baby and feed it sometimes. She lets me play with him. He is bigger than your babies, but not much."

"They're not my kids. I am just watching them." She pulled two bottles from a big bag in the corner and then pulled out an unopened package of diapers.

"Here," she said. "You change them while I go warm the milk."

"I never changed a baby before, but I'll try." Cody had been taught to always help anyone who seemed to need it. He knew these people were not like his parents. They spoke to each other rudely and seemed angry. Cody was afraid of them, and the woman seemed like someone not interested in the babies' care.

Cody had struggled with the onesie but managed to get one diaper changed before she returned. It was hard to do with the baby kicking and crying.

"He has his name written on the bottom of his foot. This is James. Hi little Jimmy. Are you hungry?" Cody talked soothingly to the infant. "

"That's good Cody. Here you can feed him and I'll do this one." With his back against the wall, he cuddled baby James and fed him.

"We need to bang their backs halfway through so they don't get a tummy ache."

A loud burp announced that his patting had been successful. Cody helped him finish the bottle then patted again for a similar result.

"Your baby is going to have a tummy ache if you don't sit him up and pat him. He thinks his tummy is full but there is air in there. That's why he is sleeping and he didn't finish his milk."

"Alright kid, put yours down and do this one."

Cody gently placed the sleeping baby on the blanket and folded the corner over him. As he took Keith, the baby fussed a little and gave a big burp.

"See there kid, you have the touch. Here's his bottle, I am going out and see if those deadheads thought to put any food for us in the kitchen. I'm starving! Are you hungry kid?"

"No but I think I better get my books and study for a while. I have a social science test Friday. Is it alright if I bring my books in here and sit with the babies?"

"Sure kid, just keep them quiet and stay down below the windows."

Cody put Keith next to his brother and covered him. He quickly retrieved his book bag and placed it against the wall out of sight from the doorway. He pulled out two heavy books and put them on the floor in the doorway. His hand searched the bottom of the bag for a smaller book that his father had told him to always carry. He lifted the cover, pushed the snowman's belly and heard a click. Quickly he replaced the special book in his bag. It would send a signal to the nearest phone tower. Within minutes of detecting the signal, they would have an area to search for the missing children.

The woman returned with a peanut butter sandwich and a glass of milk for him and she was having the same.

"They knew we would need to eat."

"Sorry kid, that's all there is."

"That is good. Thank you, I like peanut butter." He was hungry, but had said that he wasn't because he had finally remembered to do what his father had taught him when he gave him the special book. I have got to get my book bag and turn on the special book, he thought.

In the beginning in the van, he was crying and frightened. He had no idea why the two men had taken him.

Soon he realized that he needed to listen to their conversations. When they arrived at the house in the suburbs, the woman was already there with the two babies. He thought it odd that there was no furniture at all in any of the rooms. The men sat down on the living room carpet. The phone, near the man with the deep voice, rang.

"Yes, we are being careful. The van is in the shed. We parked the car behind the house. Yes, the babies are fine. The kid is a good babysitter! He fed them and got them to sleep. How long are we going to have to stay here? My back hurts. Did you know that this place doesn't even have a chair in it? Who picked this house? What? Why?"

"Smalley, take a look at the kids. It's too quiet in there."

"They are all sleeping. The boy is on the edge of the blanket, just inside the door. You guys keep it down. I don't want to have two bawling brats again."

"You are a piece of work! There isn't a maternal bone in your body!"

"Why should there be? I don't want any kids!" Cody had pulled his book bag as close to the doorway as possible. Not only did his special book send out a signal, but it recorded sounds and sent them to a recorder in his father's office.

"Smalley is a strange name. I never heard it before," said Cody to the woman. "My name is Cody. "

"You can call me Patty. Let's pretend that we are camping, ok Cody?"

"Sure if you want to."

"Do you like hot dogs? I am going to tell one of the guys to go to the store and get us some food. What do you like to eat?"

"I'm not hungry now. That sandwich was enough."

"I mean for later tonight. What kind of cereal do you like?"

"Mostly I like the ones with the little marshmallows in it or chocolate Flakes," said Cody.

"Yum, I like those too."

"Hey, I was wondering why you don't have a phone or a computer. Most kids now days are loaded with electronic gadgets." One of the men had searched his bag as soon as the gray van had gotten underway with him inside.

"I can't have a phone yet. Dad said when I am ten he will get one for my birthday. I don't like computers much. Seems like they get in your head and you keep doing stuff on them and all the playtime is gone and you haven't got time for any of the really good stuff outside."

"What's outside that you like so well. I have friends and we go to the park and play. We play ball a lot. I want to be a ball player when I grow up."

*****

Joe Downing jumped to his feet with a big grin.

"I hear the beep. Cody is using his book. If we tune in on the signal, we will be able to find him." Joe ran to his office and stood over the tiny unit that continued to beep. The officers gathered around watching as the small screen pinpointed the location of the sender. "His unit is recording the sounds near him. We can't tap into that now, but we can head for that beep location."

"Oh Joe, I am so glad that you got that device for him," said Darla. "It could be the thing that saves his life."

"You guys need to go right away because the battery will run down and the beep will stop," said Joe. The officers surged toward the door.

"You two stay here. The rest of us will head out. It will take us at least an hour to get to the bridge. Will it last that long?"

"Joe you should stay here and let us know if the location moves. It looks like he is just on the other side of the William's Road Bridge." I am leaving two men here at the house, just in case they call again." While the rest of the men headed north of town as fast as they could with sirens screaming through the New York City traffic.

Joe called Jay to apologize for not coming and to explain the current situation.

"I think the same people that took Cody may have your boys, Jay. We have officers on their way there right now. Cody has a device in his backpack that he was finally able to turn on. They are following the signal."

"There are several old houses out in that area. We get calls on break-ins all the time." The heavy traffic slowed their progress and it was closer to two hours before the sirens were silenced and the police cars crossed the bridge.

"Sergeant, the signal is getting weak. Where are you guys?"

"We just crossed the bridge and have stopped on Waldo Rd. I have an idea. We are going to use a Trojan horse. I called and they are bringing us a moving van. I will put my men inside as soon as we are sure which place it is. They will think it is furniture coming and open the door up. There is a place up ahead with a shed out back that is big enough to hold that van. I have men in the trees watching the place and a mile from here with a similar set up at a second possible location. Both these places are sold to a developer and this will all be commercial soon."

"Sergeant, I can see people moving around in there. There is no sign of the kid yet."

"How many can you see?"

"Someone just got in a car out back and is leaving. There is a woman yelling to him "

"Can you see anyone else?"

"Yes, there is at least one other man. I am sure that the kid is in there. I saw the top of a blond child's head. They must be making him stay on the floor. I can't see any furniture at all, not even a lamp. The scope on my rifle acts like binoculars. I wonder how long that guy in the car will be gone. "

*****

"Thank you Riley. Is it just as I ordered? Great, don't forget the two in the cab have to have moving company uniforms. Good. Thanks." He turned to his fellow officers and explained. "The local precinct is bringing a moving truck and two uniformed men are putting on moving company uniforms. They won't get here for at least an hour."

"Sergeant, the signal will be dead by then."

"That's alright Joe. It has done its job. We know this is the house."

The time passed slowly with the men keeping out of sight with their cars parked behind the trees on the side road.

The car that had left the house returned and they observed him carry in several sacks.

*****

"Smalley, you want a beer?"

"You know I do! Did you get the stuff I said? "

"It's all there. I bought a pan too. You didn't say to get one but this place is bare. I figured we would need it."

"Cody, he got you a candy bar. Do you want it now?"

"Sure, thanks." Cody noticed a small red light glowing from his book bag. He casually dropped the candy wrapper in the bag and at the same time turned off the special book. He knew the red light meant its battery was dying. Now they won't be able to find me, he thought. The babies were awake and starting to fuss again. "I think they want to eat again. It has been a long time. "

Cody crawled over between them and patted and talked to them while he started to change the first one's diaper. Patty, they are hungry again. "

"That's ok kid; we have two packs of formula. At least we have electricity so we can warm their bottles."

Suddenly, one of the men looked out the window and spoke loudly.

"A truck is backing in the driveway!"

"Rob, check it out. We are getting furniture!"

"We can't let them in here!"

"Why can't we? We will tell them we have been waiting for them. Ask them what took them so long."

The truck continued backing until it approached the back door and swerved wide putting the large back door of the truck out of the view from the windows. The officer driving opened the door and jumped down holding a clipboard. He wore a slightly rumpled tan shirt and trousers and a tan ball cap. The logo on the shirt matched the large one on the side of the truck. It read, "Gibson Moving and Storage." He tapped lightly on the back door and waited. Patty opened the door with a big smile.

"It's about time. I thought I'd be sleeping on the floor tonight. What took you so long?"

"I am sorry Ma'am, but we had a flat on the highway. Are you Carol Owen?"

"Yes, I am."

"If you will sign right here, we can start bringing in your stuff." He walked casually to the back of the truck and another officer, also wearing moving company clothes, got out of the truck cab on the other side. He pulled up the big door and noisily proceeded to let down a ramp. "We have a couch first and a couple of living room chairs. Is it alright if we bring them right in through here?"

"Sure, we will be glad to have them." They carefully brought the couch up the back steps, completely blocking the view of anyone looking out the back windows of the house.

"I am glad that your door is wide enough. " He spoke and moved efficiently filling the doorway as six men moved into position at the front door. Four followed the couch up the steps and inside. As the signal was given they all came in crashing the front door open. Immediately, the men were taken into custody and the children were secured. Patty screamed and started to cry as she was hand cuffed. Cody was glad to see the police uniforms flooding into the rooms.

"Are you Cody Downing?"

"Yes Sir I am."

"Are you alright? Have they harmed you in any way?"

"No and the babies are fine, too, but they are hungry. That's why they are crying. I changed their diapers and Patty was warming bottles for them. "

"What about you? Did they give you any food? Are you sure you are ok Cody? Did they hurt you?"

"No, I am alright, but I was scared when they shoved me in the van. They tied my hands and made me sit on the floor of the van. It didn't have seats in the back part. Can I talk to my mom now?"

The officer immediately dialed Agent Downing." Joe put the call on the speaker.

"Mom, don't cry. I am not hurt. Patty made me a sandwich and the babies are fine, too. Dad, oh Dad I am sorry that I couldn't put the beeper on right away. They had my hands tied and then when we got here my book bag was on the floor in the other room. I clicked his tummy as soon as I could Dad."

"You did a good job Cody. We are proud of you! You saved yourself and the babies."

"I just want to come home now. I want to come home." Cody had not shed a tear since he arrived at the house in the suburbs. Now he started to sob.

"It's going to be soon Cody. The officers will bring you to us right away. We love you Cody. You were a brave boy."

"I love you Mom and Dad. I am going to come home now. Don't cry Momma, I am coming now." The Sergeant took the phone back and gave them instructions where they could meet Cody.

"Joe you are near New York General. That's where we will take the kids. The Spencer babies are fine. Yes, we are taking them there, too. We will meet you there." Many police cars had converged onto the property by then and the men were handcuffed and placed in the back seat of separate cars. Patty was also arrested. Cody tried to stay near her, thinking she had been his friend. He watched as the babies were carefully loaded into a helicopter.

The babies were both crying.

"They need their bottles. They are hungry," he said. One of the officers took the bottles and sat between them holding a bottle for each as the police helicopter waited for Cody to be secured inside. A woman officer rode beside him. Slowly it lifted out of the yard circling and then headed to the hospital. He would also be thoroughly checked before being returned to his parents.

The media had been kept away by using only cell phones for their police communications. Now they converged in hordes just in time to see the helicopter lift and swing away. Reporters were setting up on the edge of the road as the entire area was being cordoned off with yellow police tape.

CHAPTER TWELVE
A GOOD BABYSITTER

The phone rang in Jay's hand. He had been holding it for over an hour.

"We have them Jay! The babies are fine. We are taking them to New York General to be checked, but they are fine. They are flying in a closed helicopter right now. One is on its way to get you and Koza. You will meet us there. Tell Koza that they had a good babysitter. Joe Downing's son was taking care of them. He insisted that they be fed on the way in. He is quite a boy!"

"We owe that youngster a lot," replied Jay. "The copter is here. They just set it down on the road out front. We will see you soon, Joe." Koza, Jay and Susan, boarded quickly. Susan was just as upset as they were. She wanted to see the babies and be sure they were unharmed. She had invested her heart as well as her work during the few days that she had cared for them.

Later, Jay and Joe Downing stood together in the hall of the pediatric wing of the hospital, watching through the doorway as the doctors made sure that the boys were in good health.

"This has to end Joe. We both know that Harris was behind this. I will go to the ends of the earth to see that man behind bars for the rest of his life. You know as well as I do that he arranged the kidnappings to keep us quiet. Well, it is not going to work!"

A police guard was posted near their homes and in the hospital the hall was active, with important people doing their jobs. Jay noticed a woman coming toward him that didn't seem to belong there. She stopped in front of Joe and asked if he would like to give a statement for the news.

"No, I would not. How did you get in here?"

"I just walked right in. I am trying to do my job!" Mr. Spencer, will you give us a statement for the evening news?"

"Yes, I will say a few words. The professionalism of the police department has made it possible for us to get our children back unharmed. It is certain that in the days to come, you will see that their kidnappings were orchestrated by the same man that had my wife and others murdered for his financial gain. Everything that I testified at the first trial of Mark Harris was true and I will not be deterred from repeating it!"

*****

Maddie and Michael were waiting for them when they arrived home. Their yard was still populated with police cars and fluttering yellow tape.

As soon as the family entered the front door the police presence subsided to a lower level. Jay made it clear that he wanted his house back and that he was sure that they had taken enough evidence to solve the case. The babies were not taken to the nursery. Koza and Susan made pallets for them on the floor of Koza and Jay's bedroom. They were bathed and fed and cuddled long into the night. Koza didn't want them out of her sight and neither did Jay or Susan. They ended up eating on trays, sitting on the edge of their bed. Maddie and Michael sat on the loveseat at the end of the bed and the adults talked of all the frightening moments until the subject had been exhausted.

Mrs. Calder served with swollen eyes, and feet. She too had been crying and worried sick over the missing children. Now she gladly brought food and chamomile tea. Slowly as she walked around the room pouring the tea, she took the liberty of softly touching the hair of each sleeping baby as she moved near.

"Thank God they weren't hurt," she said as she left the room.

"Thank you Mrs. Calder for the food and your prayers. You are tired and your children have missed you, I am sure. Please go home now and rest. We appreciate all that you have done for us. Take the weekend off and don't come back until Monday. We will be fine until then," said Koza.

Susan sat at the foot of the temporary bed they had made for the children. She looked at Jay and voiced what she was thinking.

"Why didn't Jackie bark? She always barks when a car or truck comes in the yard. I don't think I would have heard her when I was vacuuming but one of you would have."

"She was in the office with me, sleeping in her bed. She gets tired easily now that she is near delivering her pups. Where is she? She didn't come in the house when we came home?" Jay and Michael left the house saying they were going to check the animals in the barn, and find Jackie.

Jay opened the door to the office and turned on the light inside."

"There you are girl. Well I guess you have been busy taking care of your own babies! Thank God she is alright. I was afraid they had done something to silence her. Look Michael, she has four pups!" Jay knelt beside her and stroked her head. Michael carefully checked each pup to be sure they looked healthy and discovered that they were three females and one male.

"I am no vet but they look fine to me. She looks happy."

Jay went to the cupboard and filled Jackie's bowl with good food they kept there. He washed her water bowl and filled it with fresh water.

"There you are girl. I think this is the best place for you until the police all leave." He switched on a small light beneath the cupboard that lit the counter and turned off the overhead light. "Goodnight Jackie, sleep well. This place will calm down soon, I hope."

The two men walked to the barn smiling. The animals were in and comfortable. Jay checked their stalls and made a mental note to clean them in the morning.

Koza and Maddie were delighted to hear that Jackie had four puppies during their time of trial.

"She may have had them a little early due to all the commotion. They are quite small, "said Michael. "I have never seen newborn pups before."

"Jay, what color are the pups? Poor Jackie, I wasn't even with her to give her comfort," said Koza.

"One is tan and the rest are black and white like she is."

"Koza, if you want to go out there to visit her and see her new family, I will be glad to walk out there with you."

"Thank you Jay, but I think she is best left in the quiet. This has been a disturbing day for all of us. I will go see them tomorrow."

*****

The Downing residence was also energy charged and still filled with officers from Joe's precinct. Each wanted to be sure that every possible step had been taken to assure a conviction on the kidnapping. They were definitely working this case by the book.

When Joe finally arrived with his wife, Darla and son, Cody, he wasn't surprised to see his mother, father and brother in the living room. Michelle burst into tears when she saw them enter. Each had tried to comfort her but she was feeling left behind and left out of something extremely important.

Instantly, he and Darla realized their error in leaving her with the officers. They cuddled her between them and assured her that it was all over and that their family was safe now. Cody gave her a quick hug and told her to be brave.

"You are a Downing! We don't cry, Michelle."

"Cody you cried. I heard you on the phone."

"Well that was because I didn't know why they took me or if they were going to hurt me. I am home now and the bad people are in jail. So there is no reason to cry. Dad, did they put Patty in jail, too? She was nice to me and she gave me stuff to eat and helped take care of the babies. She wasn't very good at that, but she tried hard. Is she in jail Dad?"

"Yes Cody, she is in jail. She helped to take those babies from their home and they could have gotten injured or sick because of what she did."

"Just so you know, Dad, she didn't want to do it. That big man with the weird hair made her do it!"

"How do you know that?"

"I heard them talking and she said so. Dad, are the babies back home now?"

"Yes son, they are home and fine, thanks to your good care."

Cody was sitting at the table with his grandparents. His grandmother had dished up a big bowl of ice cream and he was talking to them and eating at the same time, relating the entire episode in detail.

CHAPTER THIRTEEN
MORE CHANGES

As the weeks passed, things seemed like they had gone back to normal, but many things were different. Jay was gone to New York much of the time. A security guard lived with them now and others patrolled the grounds with police dogs taking shifts.

The nursery was moved to the second floor with windows that appeared normal but opened only with an electronic code. The glass on all their house and car windows was changed to bullet proof.

When Susan was off duty, a new nanny named Janet was with them. The babies were never alone. Koza spent more time with them and never felt quite at ease out in her writing studio since they were back. Jay tried to tell her that she couldn't blame herself. Perhaps if she had been in the nursery at the time, she might have been injured or killed.

It was nearly a year before the new trial began. Cody and Michelle were taken to live out of state with their grandparents until it was over. By the time the last person involved with Harris was tried and convicted, the twins were nearly three years old.

One day, Jay arrived home with an undeniable grin on his face. He had leased land and a house. They were going to move.

"What are you talking about Jay? I thought you liked our little farm. Why do you want to move? "

"I like this place but I have found a place that I like better. I tried to buy it but they refused. They said it has been in the family since the original homesteaders settled on it, but they agreed to let me lease a large section of land and said that I could enlarge and remodel an existing house that is there."

"Jay, I don't understand. What about the animals and the people in town that are our friends?"

"Look Koza, here on the map is where the new place is. We are here. The construction on the house has already begun. You will love it. It is peaceful and safe and the boys will still have animals. They can have lots of animals. I was thinking that we can ask our neighbors to move in here as caretakers. They need this big house and he knows better than I do how to take care of the place and the animals. "

150

"Jay I can't believe you went ahead with all this without mentioning it to me. "

"I wanted it to be a surprise for our anniversary! I told your mother and she thinks it is a good idea. She is thinking of moving her shop to the town nearby. It is called Silverville. Isn't that quaint?"

"Who else did you tell?"

"Well Maddie and Michael know. There are several tiny cabins there and they could come on vacation and stay with us in our house or try roughing it in the log cabins."

"Jay, I like it here. The boys like it and we have friends here and the house is nice. I am in the middle of a new book and this just isn't a very good time to move."

"Koza, I feel this is something that we are supposed to do. Please come with me and see it. If you don't fall in love with the place I won't mention it again. You need a break. The boys can stay here with Susan and Janet."

"I don't know Jay, this is so disruptive. We have just gotten over all that New York court stuff, and now you want to uproot us."

"Koza, come with me. It will be like a small vacation. We have not had any time together alone since our honeymoon. Please Koza."

"Well, when you put it like that, alright, let's do it, but I am going to bring my computer. I really need to work on my book."

"Koza, I want you all to myself." His face was covered in a pleading frown. "Can't you give me one week?"

"When you say that I feel guilty, and it does sound like fun. When do you want to leave?

"Can you be ready by tomorrow afternoon?"

"Yes, I guess so. What kind of clothes should we take? "

"What you have on is fine."

"Jay! You are no help at all." They laughed and he held her close. "I have a million things to do if we are leaving tomorrow!" She ran up the stairs laughing and yelled back down, "Come on Jay. You can pack your bag while I pack mine. I need to write out instructions for Susan and Janet and shop for groceries and cancel my hair appointment. I have a lot of things to do."

"Koza, stop! This is exactly why you need a break. You don't need to do most of that. You are so frenzied all the time here. Ever since the day it happened, you have acted like you have to hold all the strings or your life is going to unravel!" Susan tapped on the open bedroom door and said that she had completed the list that Jay had given her.

"What list? Are you two carrying on a covert operation behind my back?" Koza was frowning but both of them were laughing.

"I wouldn't quite call it that. I asked Susan to get a list from Mrs. Calder two days ago and to be doubly sure that they had everything they needed for the boys and everyone else for the duration. Susan just called the store and the items on the list will be delivered.

"I took the liberty of having her also cancel your hair appointment. You can always call and reschedule it when you know you will be back."

"Jay Spencer, of Spencer's people, I love you. I know that you have hand-picked Susan and Janet and without that knowledge I couldn't leave our boys at all. I know that you are right. I need to relax and let them do the jobs they were trained to do. But I do want to take my computer. You will have to make that concession."

"Koza, if you promise to only use it when there is nothing else fun to do, like pay attention to your husband and hold his hand and ...."

He left the room with a foolish grin and Janet came in to help her with the packing.

"Koza, I have heard Mr. Spencer talking to the men on the phone and he seems quite taken by this place he has leased. He has already had plumbing done and electricity put in several buildings. I can't imagine why he would do that when they won't let him buy it." Koza stood with her case nearly packed, but was still unsure if she should take any fun dresses.

"We may want to go to town to eat or something." Janet giggled conspiratorially.

"If you promise not to tell him that I told you, I will share with you, all the projects I heard he was doing. He often uses me for secretarial duties and then his mind gets so involved that he forgets that I am there when he calls someone."

"Janet you must keep his confidence. He could fire you if he got upset over your spilling the beans."

"I know he could. That is one of the things they stressed in the classes we took, to never discuss the business of your employer with anyone else, but you are my employer, too."

"It is best if we let him have his way and surprise me with this place. He is like a child sometimes. "

"You are right of course. I have packed his case with the type of clothes that he said he wanted, but maybe I should just add a nice dress shirt and dress slacks and a pair of his good shoes. There that is everything. Do you think he will want his laptop?"

"Definitely not. He doesn't want me to take mine either, but I'd be lost without it. I think I have everything." Koza started to close the case and then as a last thought, she slipped in her prayer book and flat dress shoes. "I always seem to forget something important."

Janet smiled and one at a time she carried the cases to the top of the stairs and placed them near the wall, out of the way. Koza had gone down the hall to the nursery to play with the boys. She and Susan took them out to the large play area behind the house. The ground was covered with soft mulch to protect from bumps if the children fell. The guard dog came to them wagging and placed a gentle lick on fingers and faces and James hugged him tightly until the guard rescued him saying it was time for them to work. One small command and the large German shepherd stepped into the heel position and walked crisply away with the guard.

Just moments later the boy's giggles could be heard in the house as Jackie and her second litter of puppies were let in the gate to the play area and immediately the boys were down on the ground being covered with puppy kisses and having their fingers nibbled and sleeves tugged as the rambunctious pups climbed over the twins. Koza and Susan were laughing too hard to rescue the boys. Finally Jay's voice called a brief halt to the activities.

Where are Daddy's boys? I need some hugs. The twins struggled to stand up and free themselves from the pups but Koza and Susan let them fend for themselves. The boys wrapped around his legs and he lifted them up and kissed first one and then the other.

"We have time to swing before supper." The boys were fastened into their swings and Koza and Jay stood together pushing the swings.

"Higher Daddy, Higher Mommy" they both demanded.

"These guys are going to need a bath before they eat tonight. They are covered in dog slobber," said Susan laughing. "What do you think boys? Do you want to go play with your bubbles in the tub?"

As they returned to the house, Koza slipped her hand into Jay's.

"We do need to spend more time together, you and I, and as a family with the boys. That was fun."

"Yes it is always fun to be with you and the boys. Speaking of families, I want you to make an appointment for Jackie. I think two litters of pups are quite enough. She isn't that young and we can only keep so many dogs."

"Jay you are right, but all of these pups have been spoken for. I have found homes for all of them, and Brandy is the only one we kept from her first litter and she has had her appointment, so no problem there. When these pups are weaned, I'll have Jackie taken to the vet."

CHAPTER FOURTEEN
ON THE HICKORY

As they settled into their seats in the private jet the young man asked if they would like to have lunch served as soon as they reached the flight elevation.

"Yes Bradley that will be fine." Jay had planned everything with attention to detail, as always. Jay buckled his seat belt and closed his eyes as if he were planning to take a nap.

"Jay, open your eyes. Were you going to nap right now?"

"No Honey, I was just picturing you on the plane ready for take-off to Greece."

"You were a little frightened then of me and the trip, but now you are so self-assured. I am glad Koza."

"You are talking ancient history. I think I have figured out by now that you are my best friend and that I can trust you completely. I know that you have planned a wonderful surprise for me, but I have a surprise with me for you. Open your hand and close your eyes again."

Jay laughed out loud before he opened his eyes.

"I know what it is! You brought the little smiley ring. Didn't you?"

"Oh Koza, you are the perfect woman for me. I am so glad that I have you and the boys." He stretched the ring open a bit and slipped it on his smallest finger on his right hand. "Koza, I love you Honey, even more than when I gave you this ring. I didn't know that it was possible then, but it is." He kissed her then as passionately as he had the first time, with his whole heart.

They were sitting silently holding hands when Bradley brought their meal.

*****

"We will be landing in less than an hour Sir."

"Thank you Bradley." Koza was watching out the window when the private runway came into view.

"Is that where we are going?"

"Yes, we have a car waiting at the airport. Our place is out of town a few miles."

"I can see two different rivers."

Jay looked out the window beside her and pointed.

"That one is the Silver, and the other one is the Hickory. Our place is on the Hickory."

"Really? It will be fun to have it near. I wonder if there are fish in it. Jay, look at the big bluff! I am getting excited."

They landed shortly after that. Both of them and their luggage were easily transferred to the car that Jay had waiting. He didn't tell her that he had made that trip several times in the recent months, when he was on his way back from New York. Having his small private jet had made his life much easier.

Once we get there I will show her the before pictures, so she can really appreciate the changes. He mused as he drove over the newly constructed bridge on the outskirts of Silverville.

"I like this town. They have deliberately kept the historic buildings like the Blacksmith Shop."

"I wonder if they actually have a Ferrier there or if it is just for looks."

"Oh they have everything there that a horse owner would need. There are some beautiful horses in this area. In fact there are thoroughbreds on the "S and J Ranch" where we are headed. This entire area seems to hold a special feeling for the past and the standards that the pioneers represented. I don't think we will have to worry about anyone being dishonest or deceptive here."

"Jay how did you find this place?"

"They had an ad in a magazine that someone left behind at a restaurant I was in during one of my many trips. They were listing it as a rustic dude ranch and when I read the words, something inside me just clicked and I called and talked to the man that owns the place now. I convinced him that leasing it and allowing appropriate upgrades done in good taste would be to his advantage I have gotten to know the family quite well. He is a red haired great, great, great, great, grandson of one of the original settlers. His family has owned this place since the first homesteaders. It's amazing to me that somehow this place has stayed the way it has."

"This drive along the river has been lovely. I feel relaxed already."

"We drove through a portion of the ranch's original pasture land back a ways. There was a section here that they could not get their hands on when the original settlers were adding to the ranch. It was all added just a couple years ago when the current owners decided to sell. They had slowly purchased little pieces of property along here. All those cottages along the river used to belong to other people. Now the ranch rents them out to take care of some of the expenses on the ranch. We turn in just ahead." Jay stopped the car on the bridge and told Koza to get out so she could see something special. He held her hand and went to a large pile of rocks.

Above, just the trunk of an old oak tree stood. It was nearly as wide as it was tall. Close by, several huge oak trees moved their leaves in the breeze. Jay stood quietly, waiting for Koza to read the weather worn writing on the old trunk. "Josiah and Mary Slater, summer 1861." It's hard to make out all the letters, but I think that's what it says."

"Yes, this is where the original settlers were buried after an Indian raid. Their son, Benjamin, survived. He built this place with not much more than his bare hands, grit and prayer."

"That's quite impressive. I wonder how he managed all alone." They crossed the bridge and after a short distance he drove over another smaller bridge. He followed the gravel driveway along the river and then through an open gate.

"That big house at the end of the bluff is ours. They call it the Slater House. I added three bedrooms and four bathrooms. The porch was nice but too small to be comfortable if we have company so I had it extended out and down and made the steps wider and added fat posts." Jay handed her the pictures of the original house. "Do you like it?" He was eager to hear that she approved."

"Jay, I don't know what to say. You have kept the integrity of the original house while expanding it in every direction. This is a lovely place."

"It's not quite finished yet. They are still working on the kitchen but they promised me that it is useable, although they are doing some final touches." Koza stepped out almost hesitantly.

"Jay, do the owners approve of all the changes you have made?"

"Yes, they looked at the plans and were overjoyed. I threw in plumbing and electricity in the Jones house, too. They now have a new full bath and another half bath plus a modern kitchen."

"Is that good business Jay to be sinking so much of your money into someone else's property?"

"It's ours for fifty years plus we have the contract that says we can renew the lease and it is negotiable at that time for how many more years and at what price."

"Well, silly man, I just meant that our family might continue on for longer than that. Our boys are just babies, and we may have more children."

"They will have to plan accordingly. Honey our boys are only three years old. Come on, let's go in."

"This is all very grand. I never imagined a house like this, way out here in such a setting."

"Do you think you and the boys could enjoy the summer here?" She didn't answer, but instead smiled broadly and went up the stairs into the new foyer. She could hear people talking inside.

After exploring a bit farther, she discovered a large dining room and found herself being introduced to the cook. The carpenter backed up apologetically.

"This is Matt, and he can take credit for most of the work here in the kitchen."

"This is very nice Matt. I like the stainless steel and the tile is beautiful. I won't mind cooking in here at all."

"No, Mrs. Spencer, I cook. You eat. Mr. Jay said you need time to rest and play with your babies."

"Well then, thank you." Jay explained.

"This is Maria, the sister of our cook back on the farm. If you decide to come here for the summer, Mrs. Calder and our housekeeper get the summer off with pay. Maria is delighted to work here and Susan and Janet have already agreed to come to care for the boys whenever you feel like writing or... horseback riding." He swung open a large French door that opened onto a patio that made the corral and barns visible. "Koza let's go see the rest of the house and bring in our luggage."

"Yes Jay. Yes, I want to bring the boys and stay all summer!"

"But you haven't seen the rest of the place yet."

"I don't need to. It is lovely and peaceful here and you have gone to such lengths to make it possible. Jay I love you so much. I don't know how you envisioned this house for us, but I think it is perfect. I think we will feel safe here and the boys will love it, too. We will need to make a fenced in play yard like the one at home to keep them out of the river, but other than that I think it is perfect."

"Matt and the other men, finished the play yard last week. That's when I decided that my secret was far enough along to bring you here to see it. Come down the hall first and see the bedrooms and there's ours with a private bath. Next are the Nannies rooms. They have two bedrooms and one bath all connected to the nursery. The nursery has the same security features as our house on the farm. This door leads to the play yard. It has a gate on the side with a security code, so she can go through and take them for long walks or over to see the horses."

As they stood in the play yard admiring all the new play equipment and the beautiful view in every direction, the owner drove up the driveway and parked where they could see him. He walked to the fence and shook hands with Jay.

"Mrs. Spencer, welcome to the S. and J. Ranch. I am Eddie. I have heard so much about you that I was sure that it was you. How do you like the place?"

"It is lovely. You must be very proud of this ranch and your family heritage."

"Yes I am. We all are. Our family is spread far and wide, but they all manage to come back here when school or work permits. I have a son in the east in school and a daughter in nursing school. My Uncle and his family will be here for a few weeks' vacation in July, and my cousins will come soon for a week or more. Most of them think of this place as their free vacation spot, but they don't do much to help keep it going. I am glad you finally got here ma'am. I'll bring in your luggage and then I need to do some work in the barns. I'll see you later at the Jones house for your first night here. It's tradition." He grinned at Jay as he walked to the front of the house. "I will be gentle with your small case. I know that it holds a computer." He soon backed his small jeep up and pulled away slowly.

"He seems quite pleasant. Eddie has quite a sense of humor. You will soon see what I mean tonight at dinner."

"His wife is nice too. Her name is Ellen."

"Jay, do you want to unpack or would you like to go get the boys?"

"Are you serious?"

"Yes, this place is perfect. I know that they will love it here and so will their nannies. Jay I hope you won't mind but I want to bring Jackie and Brandy, too."

"That's fine with me, but we should unpack and go over to the Jones House tonight and fly back tomorrow first thing in the morning. I think Ellen has gone to a lot of trouble for us. We wouldn't want to disappoint them. They have gone along with all the changes that I wanted to make. The only thing they wouldn't let me do is run electricity to the original place they called the hut. You haven't seen that yet. There are so many things here that are fun to discover."

"I want to take a shower and change before we go over to their house. Are you going to?"

"No, my clothes are fine, and so are yours. They keep things simple here. I will just wash and shave before we go." Koza was quick with her shower and change. She came out with jeans and a plaid shirt. Her hair was pulled back into a pony tail. She had applied only a minimal amount of makeup. Jay had taken the opportunity to shave, and he was waiting for her. "I put all your folded clothes in the left dresser, and your dress and skirt are in the closet and so are your shoes. I slid your computer case in the back of the closet. I have us all unpacked. Let's walk over there and investigate as we go."

"Sure, I am ready, and thanks for doing the unpacking." Koza walked to the fence on the side of the house and looked at the horses clustered together under the trees against the bluff. "Aren't they beautiful Jay? I wonder how many of them are trained to be ridden. They have several fields but those are the only ones close enough to see them well. There is a beautiful paint horse over there that I like. We could go riding some morning. Jay have you ever ridden a horse?"

"No I haven't and I don't intend to either. With these short legs, just getting on would be a challenge." Koza giggled.

"Sorry, I didn't think about that."

"That's one of the reasons that I love you, Koza, you never think about me as little or different." They stopped on the small bridge that covered the water from the river, being channeled to the animals. Koza leaned on the railing.

"Look Jay, I wonder what they had in there. I can see pieces of clay tile all along the way. It wasn't a pipe because the pieces are flat not rounded. See over there is a piece on the side. It's curious isn't it?" He nodded but didn't comment.

"Would you like to peek in the hut? It is still light enough that if we pull the door wide open you will be able to see without lighting the lantern."

Koza glanced around and couldn't see a division of the property.

"Jay how much of this place did you lease?"

"Not much really. They have hundreds of acres. We have the Slater House and a small cabin on the other side of the long pen. Most of the place is full of guests or their family in the summer. Look in here Koza. They have turned it into a library. All those books were in one of the bedrooms in the Slater House until I suggested the shelves and a book migration. That gave us more room and made this place even more special. Ellen said she is going to catalog the books and put them in better order but she hasn't had time to do it yet. This hut already had a hiding place in the back. I think they wanted it in case of another Indian raid, so the carpenters built this set of shelves so they move and a person can still go into the stone room and go up the bluff and away without detection."

"I must remember that when our boys get big enough to hide from me. You said they call it a stone room?"

"Yes, a huge boulder fell from the bluff and crashed through the back part of the roof. The vibration from a buffalo stampede set it loose. The roof was repaired and the hut was actually built forward.

The Stone is too big to remove so they repaired and built around it incorporating a way to slip out unnoticed."

"That is a nice little place and I know that you had the shelves built. Didn't you?"

"Yes I got the idea to put the books somewhere else and this seemed a logical solution."

"This place is almost magical. Everything has so much history and it seems like it is safe and peaceful here. I really like it all Jay." They had chatted their way to the steps of the Jones house and Koza pointed out the flower beds on either side of the steps in front of the long porch. "They will have lots of pretty blooms soon."

Ellen opened the door with a big smile.

"Come in, I am so glad to finally meet you, Koza. Jay talks about you all the time. He brought me your first book. I will probably not get a chance to read it until fall, but I would like you to sign it for me. Please sit down wherever you feel comfortable. We will be eating in just a few minutes. Eddie is still in the barn with the new foals."

"How long have you lived here Ellen?"

"I have been here about twenty years, but Eddie was actually born here. His parents lived in the Slater House until a few years ago. They moved back east after our daughter left for college. They said it was too remote and too quiet. They are in a condo in Manhattan. That left us here alone most of the time. I am really glad that you have come. I understand that you have twin boys. This ranch needs children. It's big and there is lots of room for them to run and play."

"Thank you, I feel welcome here. I noticed the horses in the field by the bluff. Are they gentle?"

"Yes, there is a couple I wouldn't recommend for you right in the beginning, but most of them are very good. Eddie will help you pick one and saddle up, if you would like to ride tomorrow. There is a beautiful trail that goes through the woods and across a small patch of pasture and then you will come to a little water fall that sprays out of the bluff. There are cherry trees and willows. It is a lovely spot. Some of our visitors report seeing an old gentleman of the

Blue Stone People there. They are wonderful people and if you see one, they will welcome you."

"Oh, I wouldn't want to disturb a reservation."

"It's not a reservation. It is all part of the S. and J. but the original settlers of this land bought it and gave them the right to live there. The government tried twice to take them off there and they had soldiers block a convenient pass through the bluff that they used, but they just found another way. They completely subsist from the land and they help maintain the church near them on the Hickory. They are Christians. Those of us that go to that church take fruits and vegetables or animals to trade for the beautiful things that they make. The priest sells their wares for them."

"That all sounds so wonderful, but we are leaving in the morning. I want to go get my twins and bring them here now. We don't need to stay a week for me to know how special this place is."

While the women were talking, Jay had slipped out to the barn to see what Eddie was doing. Eddie had placed a bridle on a yearling and was just gently leading her around the corral. She was carrying a rather large roll of leather, stuffed with hay for bulk and a couple rocks and boards for weight.

"Hi Jay, meet Melody. She was born last spring. She is too young to ride yet but we are getting her ready. I use the same methods that the settlers did and the horses are never treated with violence. They are gentle and let us ride because they are our friends and want to please us. No whips and no spurs are allowed on this ranch."

"That's good. I don't agree with beating a horse or whipping it until its spirit is broken. When you think about it, that's an awful way to treat a beautiful animal, but so many ranchers still do it. It makes me sick!"

"I think it says something about a person that can do that and not feel something bad inside." Eddie released the bundle from Melody and removed the bridle. "Good girl Melody," he said as he slipped her a treat and patted her neck. She walked out to the field to join the other horses grazing nearby.

"You ready to go eat," he asked?"

"I am getting hungry. It has been a long time since our meal on the plane. I took Koza to the house so she and Ellen could talk and get acquainted."

They strolled along the path to the house in a comfortable silence. When they entered, the women were both laughing.

"What's so funny," asked Eddie. "Are you two conspiring against us already?"

"Well Eddie, you know you are the subject of my every thought, so ..." Ellen started laughing again and Koza joined in. Jay felt welcome to laugh too because he was sure they weren't laughing at him. He was wrong.

"Koza and I were discussing riding one of the horses, and I told her about Katie and her insistence that she could get on her pony by herself. She was only four at the time. She did and ended up facing the backside of the horse. Koza said that Jay doesn't ride. I said that if he tried he might end up like Katie! I am sorry Mr. Spencer. I meant no disrespect." They all laughed again.

"Jay, we do have an old pony out in the field if you want to start small!" They continued to laugh until they had tears in their eyes. "No disrespect intended," said Eddie, trying not to laugh again. But they all did.

Jay turned to Koza and hugged her.

"We haven't laughed like that for a very long time. Isn't this place a wonder? Even if I am the brunt of their jokes, I don't mind. It is good to laugh."

"Yes, it is. We need to laugh. It has been very difficult, but now we can put all that behind us. I promise, Koza, we will never have to live like that again."

"Everyone sit down at the table and I will tell you our unusual menu. We are having chili made from the original settlers handwritten cook book. We have crackers made by the fireplace, baked on hot stones and applesauce from our apple trees that they planted. For desert I baked a cherry pie from cherries we picked and canned from the orchard. Eddie, would you please say the blessing?"

"Sure honey; Heavenly Father, we thank you for all you have given us. We thank you for Jay and Koza our new friends. We thank you for our health and this beautiful day. Thank you for the bounty that this ranch provides and thank you for my lovely wife and the food she has prepared for us tonight. Amen"

"Amen."

As the meal progressed many of the stories of the ranch and its connection to the Blue Stone People were discussed.

"So what happened to Sarah, David and their daughter Pili? Do their ancestors still live near here?" Koza was so enthusiastically listening that she was unaware of the late hour.

"We better save that story until next time," said Jay. "If we are leaving in the morning I think we better go get some rest. Thanks Eddie and Ellen for the delicious meal and entertaining evening." He held her hand as they walked back to the Slater House. The porch lights were on and their path was lit all the way with the small lights that Jay had provided.

"Wow, Jay, when you think about the fact that we just got here this morning, it doesn't seem possible. I feel like we have become part of this place. I can see why you love it. There is something special about Eddie and Ellen, too. They don't act like they are owners of this huge ranch. It's more like they are honored to take care of it."

"I feel it too, Koza. I wish you could have seen him working with that young horse before supper. He was as nice to her as if she was his child. There's love here. It's everywhere. It's in the air and water."

"Now you are being a little dramatic, but I understand why you leased the house and did the remodeling." As they entered the house, Koza didn't head for the stairs, she walked through to the kitchen. "That meal was fun wasn't it? They had a story for everything, even why their house was built by the people of Silverville, and the pie that she baked came from the original wild cherries they picked and ate in the barn and kept the seeds. That was when the boulder went through the roof of the hut." Koza made a pot of decaffeinated coffee and they sat at the little kitchen table eating sugar cookies and sipping their coffee. It was as if they didn't want their day to end.

Koza wrote a note to the cook that she could take the day off, and that they would eat their breakfast in town. She placed the pen back near the pad of paper and phone.

"Jay, this kitchen is perfect. You thought of everything. He smiled accepting the compliment.

"Come on, Snow White, it is time to go upstairs." The bedroom windows were both open and the curtains moved in the breeze. Jay pulled the shades down and set his alarm to ring at seven. "That should give us plenty of time to be at the plane by nine."

"I don't think I will take any of my clothes. I guess I can leave my computer. We will be back in a day or two."

Their plane took off and a half hour into their flight, the pilot had to swing wide of the flight plan they had filed, to avoid flying directly over a very large and swiftly growing wildfire.

"Jay, I am going to take us up away from this fire." The pilot was frowning as he called the tower to tell them what they were experiencing and ask for permission to gain more altitude and to swing wide to the right.

Suddenly there was an extremely loud explosion and shudder, jarring them painfully against their seat belts, as they looked in the direction of the sound; they realized that their plane had collided with one of the emergency tanker planes carrying red slurry to the fire line. The two planes were meshed together and as the flames engulfed the engine and wing of their plane, they plummeted down to a forest floor already engulfed in flames. The last thing that Jay heard was Koza's scream. They died instantly on impact. The search team was unable to enter the area until the fire was quenched in that area.

CHAPTER FIFTEEN
THE CRASH

Robert Harris had been given Jay's trust when he had realized the shock and disgust on his face at the knowledge of what his son, Mark had done. Jay had used good judgement and his will was well written and filed properly by Robert. His boys would be well cared for and very well educated. He had also taken the time to have Robert prepare a college fund for Cody and Michelle Downing in gratitude for Cody's care of the twins during their ordeal. Joe didn't know about it until he was asked to attend the reading of the will.

In the months that followed the double funeral, Koza's mother, Terri moved her little shop to Merritt so she could live near their home on the farm. James and Rosie were there as much as possible. Madelyn and Michael and their daughter did all they could to fill the boys lives with love. Their baby girl, named Gloria, was two when they lost Koza and Jay. The family had all agreed that both Susan and Janet should remain in their positions as long as they wanted. They were needed. Janet's role changed as the boys grew older into one of household manager and advisor to them in the everyday decisions of life.

It soon became apparent that neither of the twins would be small people. By age fifteen they were very tall and athletic. Keith liked basketball and baseball, while James enjoyed the rough and tumble of both wrestling and football. They entered college with the offer of both sports and academic scholarships. Having been given a generous heart that paralleled their father's they passed up the scholarships allowing others to benefit. Robert spent long hours counseling the boys. He wasn't surprised when Keith chose business accounting and administration, and James, now known as Jim decided to go to Harvard to study law.

Life had moved on quickly and the family at the S. and J. Ranch, after a brief period of shock and sadness found that they were given back full rights to the property that Jay had leased. Two stipulations were included. That if the family ever decided to sell the ranch they were to inform the Spencer family before it was put on the market, and second that they be welcomed in the Slater House after giving appropriate notice for a reasonable amount of time to stay. Robert

Harris had decided at the last minute to include that, thinking that perhaps after the boys finished college, they might want to go see where they would have been living, had things gone differently. He was right but it was another ten years after college when the whole family decided that if it were possible they would all like to get together at the S. & J. Ranch for the Christmas holiday.

The years and circumstances had separated them and they thought that Christmas would be a great time to get together and reconnect.

Eddie and Ellen had grandchildren now and were happy to have them visiting often. It was easy for them to know how meaningful a family reunion would be for the Spencer's. The family would have the Slater House and two additional cabins, which had all the modern accommodations inside including two bedrooms and two bathrooms each. Plus they had maintained the cabin exterior appearance with care.

Several of the cabins on the other side of the Hickory River were rented year around but no other guests were booked for the holidays. Rosie had made it clear that if necessary she would pay extra, but wanted the place to her family. She had taken charge and food supplies would be delivered and she included extra to be delivered to the Jones House. Her preparations had covered all the usual Christmas food and she had remembered to order a tree for each place they would be using. She asked Ellen to oversee the decorations and to be sure that the food was put away properly after delivery. She wanted every detail right as Jay and Koza would have wanted it. She felt it was important.

She asked Eddie to string Christmas Lights around the roofs of every building even the barn. The hut, now the library, sported a beautiful wreath with red berries and a big red bow.

This was not a year of mailing small token gifts. Everyone would bring huge bundles of wrapped presents.

When she counted on her fingers the number of children that would be there she was surprised. Jim and his wife Trisha had three and Keith and Camille had four. Madelyn and Michael's daughter,

Gloria had recently remarried and her husband, Joe had sole custody of his three children. Gloria had one from her first marriage.

"I can't possibly keep track of all this in my head. I need to write it down. I don't want anyone to be forgotten."

"What did you say dear? I will be finished here in just a few minutes and then we can go shopping."

"James, I need to make a list of everyone that will be there, and how many and their ages. We could miss someone at gift time and that would be awful!"

"Rosie you have done a great job of planning everything. Relax. Would you like to use this little notebook? It is rather nice. My secretary gave it to me, but I never write anything down. I use the computer for everything."

"Yes, thank you dear. That is just what I need."

"That's it James! You solved my problem. I think we should give everyone an age appropriate computer, except Madelyn, she wouldn't use it in a million years. What could we give her?"

"Give her the latest phone. She is on that thing all day long every day. She says she has given her business over to her staff to run, but they don't dare blink without her approval. There you are dear, a technological Christmas and everyone can get a gift card to buy the programs they want. I think we could do our shopping online right here and be done before we go to dinner!"

"James, can it really be that simple?"

"Not really dear. There are many different kinds of computers for different purposes."

"Oh, did you have to say that, just when I thought this would be easy? Can't we just get them all laptops and let them get their own programs like you said? How different can they be?"

"Rosie, do you want to get them for the girls too?"

"Yes, I think so."

"Here call all the parents and write down the kids' favorite color. Then find out what grade they are in. Do you know all their ages? If you do then you won't need their grades." He handed her his phone and sat down at his office computer. While she was making calls, he pulled up three websites with computers. Some were powerful and fast, some filled with all the video capabilities that a gamer could ever want. He marked them and sat waiting for her to finish.

Keith and Cam's girls are 8 and 9 and she said that they both like pink and purple. Kelly is the eight year old. Let's give her pink and Taylor Kay will get purple, but what does all that mean? Do they even make computers for kids that young?"

"Yes, Rosie, look at my screen."

"Oh they are beautiful, but will they be able to use them?"

"I think so. Kids are using these things in school and at home for their homework now days. These are not heavy, so they can take them in their backpacks. Which ones do you think?" They are just good basic ones and they will engrave them so they aren't as apt to get stolen at school."

I like the pink one with the big butterfly on it, and the purple one with the big flower."

"Now let's do their boys."

"They are six and ten."

They continued on through their list until they had finished. Rosie was excited.

"If you will get the prepaid cards for them to ad programs and Maddie's new phone, we will be nearly finished. I may add a few things for the little ones, but nothing big. I was thinking we could do stockings and get mostly treats and one nice gift in each."

"Honey, please don't get carried away. Remember we will all have to transport a lot of it when we head home."

Trucks delivered many big boxes. Ellen directed them to the Slater House. Finally her curiosity got the best of her and she went in among the boxes reading the "from" labels. That's odd, she thought, many of them seem to be from companies that make technology products.

The cook and the housekeeper came out to talk to her.

"Rosie called us and gave us a list of names and a description of the items that she had selected for each one. She said if we would wrap and tag them she would give us a big bonus. She said one of the boxes is from "Joy Collections," and it is wrapping paper and bows and all the special touches we will need to make them beautiful. I just hope we get it right! I would feel bad if we mixed them up."

"You won't. Just open all the boxes first and put a name with the item. When you know what is here and have assigned all the names you can be comfortable gift wrapping them. I am going in the kitchen and make us a pot of tea and then I have some baking to do for her. That Rosie has not forgotten a thing."

"I think I will clear the dining room table and we can wrap the gifts on it. Some of these boxes are big!" Maria, the cook, had stayed on at the ranch and found the kitchen in the Slater House, very convenient. Ellen and Eddie couldn't pay her as much as Jay Spencer would have but she enjoyed the little cabin they allowed her to live in. She loved the ranch and said it gave her heart a good feeling. The current housekeeper, Kari did all the cleaning and washed the linens and towels. When guests were scheduled she was there to care for their needs. She lived with Maria and they got along well.

It took the two women most of the day to get all the boxes wrapped, decorated and tagged. Each was placed near the big tree in the dining room. Once the job was finished they were pleased with the result.

"It looks beautiful in here doesn't it?"

"Yes, let's put the Christmas cloth on the table and the center piece before we leave."

"Where should we put the leftover wrappings?"

"They may want a bit for this or that when they get here. I think I will store it on the floor of the linen closet. That's the only place I can think of that has room."

"That's a good place and we should put the tape and scissors in there too, for now."

The next morning they discovered the ground was coated with a dusting of snow.

Over the next two days the family arrived and was assisted in selecting their living quarters according to Rosie's suggestion. The youngest children were the most excited. Keith felt pressured and was sure that he was neglecting his work. Jim had snapped his briefcase shut at his office and said that anything inside could wait until he returned. Their personalities were extremely different yet from a short distance it was difficult to tell which one they were.

Eddie and Ellen enjoyed meeting each person as they arrived. Even with so many years having passed, they saw the resemblance of Jay in his father. Rosie was the only little person there but what she lacked in height she made up in energy. She was a constant source of ideas and suggestions for activities.

Christmas morning was a huge success and the technological age that had invaded the holiday was a source of joy to the recipients of Rosie and James's gifts. Wisely thinking of the problem of transporting gifts home Keith and Camille's gifts were gift cards to be used when people were back home. Jim and Trisha had not planned for efficient dispatching of gifts after the holiday. They bought sleds and cross country snow shoes for the young folks and various bottles of the very best imported wines for those old enough to enjoy them.

After the enormous and joyous Christmas dinner, everyone helped Maria to clear the table and then they each turned to their own type of activity. The men gathered in the living room, looking out at the gently falling snow and heavy gray sky.

The children put on their winter gear and tried out the sleds on the slope behind the barn. The snow shoes soon took the direction of the mysterious path in the woods. Ellen told them that it was there when she came and although nothing was done to maintain it, it stayed fresh and open. The young ones returned to the Slater House after their outdoor fun. They were red-faced, hungry again and tired. Maria knew just what to do.

With Kari's help the snow covered boots and coats were placed in the entry to dry while Maria served big bowls of turkey noodle soup, with fresh baked bread. Christmas sweets were piled on a huge platter in the middle of the table. She offered milk and cocoa to the youngsters and coffee to the adults.

As the sun lowered, it peeked through the clouds exposing patches of the evening sky. The snow had stopped falling earlier. The scene through the windows was one that revealed the busy day they had all had. A small snowman stood in the middle of the yard with a bright blue scarf and a cap sitting on top of his head at an angle. His eyes looked toward the house and he smiled. This man of snow had a story to tell if they had known the history of Sarah Slater but they didn't. Not yet.

"Jim, I will see you here for breakfast and then we can take that ride we mentioned." Keith and Camille walked their family down the path to the cabin they were using.

"Cam, I am so glad that you talked me into coming," said Keith.

"It is great to see Jim and my grandparents again. Aunt Madelyn doesn't seem to age at all, and Gloria looks just like her. Uncle Michael has aged. It has been four years since I saw them and I think they are not telling but he looks to me like he has been sick."

"I thought so too, but I wasn't going to mention it. He is a doctor and I'm sure that he would get the best care possible if there was something wrong."

"They haven't revealed it so I really think it is best to not say anything Keith. They want to keep it to themselves. That's their right."

"This has all been wonderful, like a great vacation but it is hard to imagine what a life here with Mom and Dad would have been like. Would you feel bad if I stay on for a few days? Could you fly back without me? I would like to spend some time here with Jim."

"Sure that would be fine. When I get back I will have to hit the ground running anyway. We wouldn't have much time together until New Years. I had a rough time getting a few days off."

"Thanks for understanding." Jim was having a similar conversation with Trisha. Her response was like Cam's, but she did say that since he was staying he should take charge of getting all the gifts packaged up and mailed back.

"Jim that's a good idea, when all of us are gone the place will return to normal, and you and Keith can get a better sense of the place. Most of us will be out of here by ten in the morning. Your grandparents are leaving before breakfast. Rosie certainly did a marvelous job of coordinating everything. The trees, the decorations, and the gifts were all perfect."

"Well, I would never have splurged on a PC that powerful for my office. They must have spent a fortune. Between that and the dinner and all the other food and goodies, it was as if this was home for a few days. I hope we can do this again sometime."

The children all insisted that the sleds and snowshoes should stay at the ranch and wait for them in the barn. They wanted to come back next Christmas and use them. That was a relief to the men who would have had to figure out a way to ship them.

Maria and Kari created a departure breakfast that everyone would remember for a long time. Rosie and James changed their plans so that they could sit down to one more meal with their family. Spontaneous applause broke out when the platters of green waffles and red pancakes were placed on the table beside the bacon, sausages and ham. Eggs were made to order and everyone was amazed at Maria's skill to quickly deliver everyone's preference. The butter and maple syrup were passed as they promised each other that they would be back.

The banter was light and a little difficult as they all felt the sadness of the necessary parting. Prearranged vehicles arrived taking them to the airport.

As the last person left and Kari assured them that nothing had accidentally been left behind, Jim and Keith looked at each other with sadness.

"It is strange, isn't it? This whole holiday felt like we were in someone's video. I mean it all didn't seem quite real to me."

"I know what you mean, but now we will be able to relax and see if we can feel what Dad and Mom were feeling when they chose this place. Ellen showed me pictures of what the ranch looked like when Dad first saw it. He was definitely a person with vision. She put the photos on the table in the hut library. I want you to see them."

"I would like that, but right now I want to get ready for that ride, lawyer boy. Do you think you can stay on a horse?"

"Ha, I think I will do better than a number cruncher!"

"That sounds like a challenge. We are not going out there for a race. I just would like to follow that trail in the woods and go to the orchard and stuff they told us about. The only thing I regret is that with Christmas falling on Sunday this year, we had the tree and gifts and we didn't make it down to the church for a service."

"Yes, Cam and I usually take the kids to church early and that way we have a late breakfast and the rest of the day left for family fun together. Actually it is the only day that we can enjoy together. Everyone in the family is involved with various activities. I wish it wasn't so."

"Our gang is the same way. We are all so busy that having a meal together never seems to happen. I don't know how Trisha keeps it all together."

"Well, women seem to have a way with organizing it all and getting everyone where they need to be, fed, dressed properly and on time."

"We really need a couple days here to just relax and catch up with each other's lives. Come on; let's walk over to the barn. I see Eddie has a couple of horses out and saddled for us."

"Good morning Eddie. Are those for us?"

"Yes they are ready and eager to go. They are both good mounts. This red one is named Ginger, after the first horse that was on the ranch. The other is Blue Moon. He is older, but don't be fooled into thinking he is too old to get frisky. He loves to run, if you boys are experienced riders he will give you a lot of fun."

Jim looked at his brother and they both laughed.

"Eddie we have not been on a horse since we were kids. We just want a slow ride so we can talk and relax."

"Wait here just a minute, I have an idea." Eddie went through the gate and slowly walked to the center of the field where a group of five horses were grazing. He patted first one and then another. Finally he selected one and slid up on her bare back and walked her to the gate where the men stood watching. "This girl is Gracie. She is sweet and mellow. She will let anybody ride her. I will take Blue to check the other fields and she can go with you for a little exercise." Eddie saddled Gracie and after a bit of instructions the two brothers were on their way.

The weather had turned mild. It was pleasant riding along the path in the trees heading up river on the back side of the bluff.

Although they saw nothing to cause it, they both felt a sensation of movement amongst the trees. They stopped at a small pond to let the horses drink. Keith was the first to mention it.

"Jim, did you feel like something was moving in the trees back there?"

"I hate to admit it. It sounds like we are a couple of alarmists but yes, I sensed motion all around us, but I couldn't see anything. There isn't even a breeze to stir the tree branches."

"Let's move on before we spook ourselves into not enjoying our ride. These horses have been good. They probably take this trail a lot with ranch visitors." Keith and Jim were not allowed to see the multitude of pure white horses that God was preparing for His army to ride in the last battle.

They continued on the path for a little farther and then the trees opened to a wide prairie vista. The bluff was far to their left and the forest wrapped around to the right.

"This is beautiful, but a little confusing. Eddie said when we get out of the trees we will be on the edge of the Indian camp. I don't see any camp."

As they moved forward they could see the sparkle of water coming out of the bluff and then the small lake and willows surrounding it came into view. In the distance they could see the water had formed a small shallow river that disappeared into the woods. They could hear the faint sound of a flute, or was it the breeze in the treetops?

"This is creepy! Where are the Indians?"

"Not here, that's for sure and these trees look ancient. I have never seen such huge trunks on willows."

"Look over there across the water. The trees in rows are probably the cherry trees that Ellen mentioned. I don't get it. I thought that the camp was active and that some Indians were still here." They ate their lunches that Maria had thoughtfully prepared for them and then headed back the way they came.

That evening they sat in the cabin that Jim had used with his family. They watched the news and then turned off the television.

"I don't want to watch a state of the union address. Do you? Seems like I already know things are falling apart. I don't need him to tell us how great things are and what a wonderful job he is doing. I didn't vote for him. Did you?"

"No. Let's walk down to the hut library and poke around. I am sore from that horse and tired, but not sleepy yet."

"Sleepy? Keith. You didn't eat turkey today! It is only seven o'clock!"

The path was well lit thanks to their father's planning. They pushed the door open to the hut and felt for a switch.

"Eddie told us that they asked Dad not to run electricity in here. Now what do we do?"

"We use the lantern. Over here on the table are matches in a bottle and an old oil lamp. I am glad that they left it the way it was."

"Well, Keith, you always did like all that nostalgia stuff. I like big screens, cellphones and computers. I love the computer that Grandma and Grandpa gave me. I can't wait to fire that baby up and load it to the hilt with all the neat programs I want."

"I like mine too, but I won't load it with as much as you probably will." As the lantern light reached the rows of books, they were both amazed. "Look at all these old leather bound books. It smells like a real library in here. They studied the photos on the table. The original house was not large, but it was nice."

"Hey Keith, for sure we know the settlers were Christians. I see two old Bibles and one of them liked to study science." Jim pointed at a physics book. "Keith. Look what I found. This had to be written by someone way back when this place was started." They sat together reading the journal until their eyes were burning. Jim scanned the shelves and found another journal. "Let's take these with us and go back where there is better light, and bring the older Bible too."

They strolled down the path to the cabin by the long pen. Keith made a pot of coffee and they sat reading for half the night. Once in a while they would comment, but mostly it was silent in the little cabin.

"This is the longest I have sat reading since I left college. I feel like I have been cramming for exams. We need to get some sleep."

"My eyes are tired too, but I can't put this journal down. I want to go back to the camp tomorrow. I think we are on the edge of a discovery that will change our lives!"

"Geez, don't be so dramatic! I will go back with you but only if Eddie lets us borrow his Jeep. I am sore from riding that horse. I don't want to ride that thing again tomorrow." Keith laughed at his brother's confession and then admitted that he could barely walk when he got off.

"There has to be an easier way to get back there. I would like to see the church and the first journal speaks about an image. Maybe if we time it right we will get to see it."

"What are you talking about, a ghost or something?"

"No, but it is supernatural."

"That sounds like something to stay clear of! The journal I have been reading is written about things that happened after the Indians arrived on the ranchland. It tells here that they brought with them people they had rescued from a tribe up north called the Abalinah. It sounds like they were really a bad brood. The Abalinah would raid other Indian camps and keep some of the young people as slaves. The person who wrote this journal didn't write as clearly. It says that God blinded the Abalinah warriors and all the adults in the tribe with a bright light so the chosen men from the Blue Stone People were able to rescue the slaves without killing anyone!" Jim turned to the front of the journal. "The writer of the second journal was Sylvia Thomas and she was one of the women rescued. She had been captured from a wagon train. She refers to a young leader they called Two Feathers. She mentions a relative of the original settlers of the ranch named Lauri Moody and her brother Mark. They arrived at the ranch about the same time as all that stuff was happening. She says she lived at the ranch for five years and then moved to Silverville and she and a woman named Rose Weatherly opened a bed and breakfast. I think it still exists. I saw a sign that read Rose's Place, on an old house right on main street as we came from the airport."

178

"She couldn't still be alive. Someone must have bought it and kept the name."

"I wish they had put dates on some of the stuff in here. It's hard to know how long ago any of it happened," said Jim.

"Ha! You mean if it happened at all! That stuff could all be fiction made up by people here at the ranch to increase their number of guests. Some of this stuff is unbelievable."

"Keith, do you really think it's all made up?"

"No, not all of it but I think they sprinkled in stuff from their imaginations as it goes along."

"This one starts out with Sylvia Thomas saying she is writing the journal for Mary Slater who is ill with a bad chill she got riding home from Sarah and David's cabin on Christmas Eve. Who wrote the first one?"

"Mary Slater did. She says she married Benjamin Slater after her husband was killed by an Indian raid on their homestead. She says she had two sons, Joshua and Adam by her first husband. She called him Slim Parker."

"We could go to town and check to see if they have records that go back that far. That had to be in the eighteen sixties. Hey I just had an idea. The church we wanted to look at probably has records. Maybe we could see how much of this they kept track of. I wonder how long the church has been there."

Keith opened the old dusty Bible. He hadn't read a Bible in years."

"Wow! Look at this, they recorded names of births, marriages, deaths and dates fill it up and then paper has been added to the back. The dates cover from eighteen sixty two to nineteen forty four. That's during WWII. I don't think they made this stuff up, maybe some of the stories in the journal but not this."

"We should put these back. We can always get them and read some more tomorrow." They pulled on their coats and headed out the door of the cabin. They found the air was cold and the sky was crisp and clear.

CHAPTER SIXTEEN
NEXT OF KIN

Keith had a strange feeling in his chest and then a sharp pain. The Bible he was carrying seemed to weigh an enormous amount. He clutched his chest and collapsed as they were walking over the bridge that crossed the water channel. Jim yelled and grabbed his phone to dial Eddie, but he came running. He had been sitting on his porch and heard the cry for help.

"What happened?"

"I don't know. We were heading back to return these books and he just went down!" Jim was shaking as he dialed for an ambulance. Keith opened his eyes and seemed to be in a great deal of pain. "Eddie, I think it is his heart. Get him an aspirin, quick!"

Ellen had come running when she saw Eddie bolt from the porch.

"What do you need? What can I do to help him?"

"Get him an aspirin and some water." She ran to her house and returned quickly; sitting down beside Keith she raised his head and helped him to swallow the pill. With his head in her lap she stroked his hair and talked softly to him.

"You will be fine. Help is on the way. Just rest now and they will be here soon to take care of you." In the dim light of the trail the books went unnoticed until Jim saw that they lay scattered there and in danger of being knocked off into the water. He calmly gathered them and handed them to Eddie.

"Please put these back inside. I don't think we will be reading them anytime soon." They could hear the siren on the ambulance, coming rapidly.

Just then the EMT vehicle arrived and professional help was all they thought they needed, until Ellen prayed.

"Heavenly Father, please help Keith to recover from whatever is causing his distress and pain. You are our creator and our healer. You are our Savior and Lord. Be with these young men as they work to help him."

They lifted Keith from her lap to a stretcher and placed him into the ambulance. Jim jumped in with him. He was feeling the pain in his own chest. He wasn't sure if it was real or imagined but he knew one thing for sure. He would never again leave his brother and live so far away that they couldn't be together as often as they wanted. Never ever, never ever; he had repeated the words in his mind to the rhythm of his own heartbeat, as he gripped his brother's hand so tightly that the EMT had to tell him to release it so that blood could flow normally. Jim apologized and laid his hand gently on his brother's leg. He couldn't completely let go of him. Not now, not ever again.

As they sped down the highway toward the hospital, Jim realized that he would have to call Camille as soon as he could. Then just as quickly, he decided he would not call until he had some positive information to give her.

Now for the first time he began to examine events of the past in a new light and thought about the way his grandparents had dealt with the loss of their son and his wife and without missing a step they had stepped up to take the responsibility of an international business and the job of raising small twin boys.

Not yet fully aware of the critical condition of his brother, Jim could examine what they must have gone through in the days and months that followed. He allowed his mind to look at his family in a new way. He slid into a dark frame of mind. He opened the door to the small room where loss lives. He had usually managed to keep that door closed. It was my father's fault, he thought as he allowed himself to enter that space of pain. He was so busy with his precious business and the fortune that he had created that it took up all his time. We were almost three years old when that plane went down, but I can't remember him ever holding me or telling me a story or doing any of the things that father's do. I can remember some things about my mother. How she always smelled like lilacs and oranges mixed together and how she would take us out to play on the swing. Suddenly he remembered a day when his father had been there and he had been talking to him and pushing the swing. He could remember a man with a big dog that walked around their yard and he always was near them when they were outside, but right now, he was focusing on remembering his father. He was there with us and we all were laughing, because the man had opened the gate and let the puppies in, but they left the next day and never came back. Tears had escaped Jim's eyes but he was unaware of them.

The ambulance had stopped and Keith was quickly transferred through an automatic door to the emergency wing of the hospital.

A woman handed Jim a clipboard and indicated a place for him to sit.

"Please fill this out and return it to the window. Are you his next of kin?"

"I am his twin brother. His wife flew out yesterday with their family. We were all here for the Christmas holiday."

"Well then I guess you can fill it out."

"I want to see him. I want to be in there. What are they doing for him?"

"I don't know. I am just the receptionist. They are probably doing tests. They always do tests. He is in good hands. Don't worry. They will take good care of him. It's hard for twins isn't it? I'll bet you two stick together like glue."

"Yes, like glue," Jim mumbled as he laid the clipboard on the counter and hurried to the door where they had wheeled Keith. He followed a nurse in but she stopped him.

"You can't come in here. I will let you know as soon as we find out anything."

The same nurse returned twenty minutes later to tell him that his brother had a blocked artery and they would be taking him to surgery to put in a stent.

"Is he going to be alright?"

"This is something we do quite routinely. I will keep you posted." After what seemed like an eternity to Jim the doctor came out and introduced himself.

"Your brother must be eating a lot of rich foods. We put in a stent for the vein that was ninety percent plugged and we opened two others that were operating at about half their capacity. He is going to have to change his eating habits. You look like you are in good shape. Keep active and eat right and you will both live a long life. It is amazing how much you look like him. Don't worry, in a few days he will be doing fine. We are running some tests to make sure nothing else is wrong. Meanwhile you should get some rest. He is going to be here a few days."

"Can I see him?"

"Not right now. He is in recovery. I will tell the nurse to let you peek in when he is taken to the Cardiac Care wing."

"Thank you, doctor." Jim gave a sigh of relief and sat down. He looked at his watch. It is four a.m. I better call Cam now and let her know. She said she has to be at work by six. She is probably up getting ready. First I better think how I want to tell her so she doesn't panic. The phone rang several times before Camille picked it up. She glanced at the clock. It read five fifteen.

"Hello," she said it hesitantly.

"Hello, Cam, did I wake you?"

"No, I was just heading for the shower. What's happening Jim? You may look like Keith but you don't sound like him. Is something wrong?"

"Well, yes and no. There was but now it is fixed. Keith had to be taken into the hospital. He had to have a stent put in a vein and two other arteries were half plugged and they were able to open those up."

"Jim is he going to be alright?" He could hear the tightness in her throat. She was working hard to keep her emotions in check.

"The doctor said that he would have to stay in the hospital for a few days to rest and he is doing more tests to make sure nothing else is wrong, but I think he will be good after he is out I will keep him here a few extra days and then I will fly back to your place with him. You don't need to come back. The operation is over. They took him in right away. He is in recovery right now. I will stay with him Camille. I promise you I will keep you informed if I get any further updates. The doctor did say that he will need to make some changes in his eating habits."

"I have been telling him that for years. He likes all the wrong foods."

"I doubt if Grandma and Grandpa are up yet, I will call them a little later. It's going to be fine. Don't worry. I will take good care of him." He hung up and knew that he couldn't really take care of him. He couldn't even take care of himself. He called Trisha.

"Hi Trish, I knew you would be up. We ran into a bit of a problem. Keith is in the hospital. Yes, What? No, he didn't tell me. You knew? Why didn't you tell me? I could have kept things a little less strenuous. He rode a horse all afternoon yesterday. What? He collapsed on the bridge as we were walking to the hut to return some books about nine, I guess. They operated right away. Yes, they put in a stent and opened up two other veins that were partially blocked. The doctor said he will keep him there a few days and then I plan to keep him here at the ranch a few more. I will fly with him back home. Then after that I will come home. Yes, I know it is a long time to be gone, but Trisha, he is my brother. He needs me too. Well I am sorry you are unhappy but that is what I am doing. Call the company and get a person to come in until I come home. Trisha, we own the damn company! Get help and stop acting like you are being put upon. I am sorry that you feel inconvenienced! I don't care about a New Year's Eve party. I love you Trish, but I love my brother too. This holiday together made me realize just how much I missed him. I always felt like a part of me was missing ever since I left for college. I have to go now. I will call you tonight."

Jim suddenly noticed that the few people there in the waiting room were staring at him. He had raised his voice to a level they could not ignore. He quickly apologized and left the room. He walked swiftly to the men's room where he threw up.

He does need me, he thought. We have always needed each other. He knew but I didn't recognize it until now. He asked me to come to Chicago when he got his job there, but I said no, I wanted to stay in New York, closer to home base. How could I be so stupid? He rested his forehead against the cool tile of the restroom wall, and then washed his face in the cold running water in the sink.

When he left there he appeared to be calm and collected. The storm that raged inside him would not subside so easily. The nurse had been looking for him. She approached with a smile.

"Mr. Spencer, you can see your brother now, but he is sedated. We want to keep him still so he will rest and heal. He is receiving an antibiotic intravenously and nutrients as well. When he wakes he should feel much better than he has in quite a long while. How long has he been experiencing the chest pains?"

"I don't know, he didn't tell me. I feel terrible that he kept such a thing from me. We live quite a distance from each other and our careers and families keep us busy." She nodded. It seemed more of an acknowledgement than an approval. His phone rang. He turned it down before answering it. It was Camille.

"Hi, I have good news Cam. He is in the intensive care unit now and out of recovery. No they have him sedated so he doesn't move around. They want him to rest. He is getting meds and nutrients intravenously. His color is good. Now that I am aware of what was going on, I can see a difference. He was gray before; now his face is pink and looks healthy. I am going back to the ranch to shower and change and then I will come back here. The nurse said he will sleep well into tomorrow. I will call the office, and let Grandma Rose and Grandpa James know if you want me to. What? No that is fine if you want to. Cam, I wish you had told me right away when you found out. I know but maybe together we could have got him some help sooner and maybe it wouldn't have come to this. I understand. I know he is. I am that way, too. I will and you take care of yourself. I will talk to you soon. No don't feel guilty for not coming back here. You can't do anything right now but the thought that you are home and safe and caring for the kids will be a comfort to him when he wakes up."

Jim's rental car seemed less than reliable. He wondered just how old it was. He had never been interested in cars. As long as they looked decent and got him from point A to point B on time he was satisfied. In New York he used a taxi. It was efficient and no hassle trying to park.

As he turned onto the bridge that crossed the Hickory River, he had a feeling of relief, as if he was coming home. That is silly. I am not attached to this place. If we hadn't gotten interested in their foolish stories Keith might not be in the hospital. Well I know that's not true. It is better that happened here than on a plane or driving in Chicago traffic.

When he was ready to leave, Maria met him at the car with a small cooler of food and healthy snacks. He thanked her and asked her to pass along the good news that Keith was doing well and that he would be bringing him back to the ranch for a few days to rest before heading home. He stopped at the library and collected the journals and the older Bible. He knew he would be doing a lot of sitting and waiting. These would be good entertainment while he waited.

After pumping all the change he had into a machine, he chose a Cola, thinking that he needed the caffeine. He had been up all night. Actually, he thought, I don't regret any of this. If he hadn't collapsed when he did, we might have just stayed another day or two and then gone our separate ways back to life as usual. This way he got the help he needs and we are really back together. I want to change jobs and move us to Chicago. I can imagine how Trish will take that idea. She doesn't take well to change. She is a teacher. She should be able to find a job there. She has a lot of friends and she won't like leaving that house. She has been working on it ever since we bought it. I can cross that bridge when I come to it.

He sat on the end of a large couch and placed the cooler at his feet. The Bible and journals he tucked safely against his thigh with his hand on top of them. Soon he tipped his head back against a pillow that was placed invitingly near. I'll just rest my eyes for a minute before I start reading, he thought. His phone persistently buzzed in his pocket and finally woke him.

"Trisha, oh hello, honey I guess I was asleep. I thought I would just rest but I dozed off." He looked at the time and realized that he had been asleep for over an hour.

"Jim, I think when you get back here we need to have a serious talk. I know this will sound crazy but I have been talking to Cam and I think we should consider moving to Chicago. She says there are several places in their area that are on the market. You know I have been working on this place and I think that with the new landscaping and extra bath that we put in, it will bring us a good price. We should actually make a profit."

"Trish, that sounds like a great idea! Oh honey, you have made me so happy. I will think about it and we can come up with a plan when I get back. Keith is still resting, and they said his tests came back with no indication of anything else wrong. I didn't sleep last night so I am in a waiting room just down the hall from him and I was napping. When he wakes, I will call everyone and let them know."

"No that was good, I am glad you called. Trisha, I love you very much. Thank you for suggesting that. It means the world to me that you are willing to move. This will be an adventure for all of us."

When Jim hung up and slid the phone back in his pocket he had a broad smile on his face. He was eager to tell Keith and wished he would wake up.

Instead, he called the Chicago office of Spencer's and was surprised when he got no answer. He looked at his watch and saw that it was just five there.

Guess I'll see what Maria has fixed for me in this little cooler. He was amazed to find green grapes, cheese, salami and crackers. In the corner she had tucked a bottle of water and a piece of chocolate fudge. She is a marvel. This is perfect.

After his meal, he made sure his hands were clean before he picked up the old Bible. He studied the names and dates. They corresponded with entries in the journal. It all seemed to come together and suddenly he believed all the stories. He asked the nurse if he could get a tablet or something to write on and she brought him a clip board with several sheets of computer paper and a pen. He started by making notes with dates, adding or subtracting years by using births or marriages. He felt strangely saddened when he read the account of Ben Slater's attack and head injury. He was connecting with these people on a personal level. A sense of loss came over him when he read the entry that related the death of the old cowboy that they had named Uncle. It was then that he noted that the cabin they were using was built for him.

He picked up the second journal and was very pleased when he found that Ellen had written in there about his father and mother and all the wonderful generous changes they had provided for the ranch. The last sentence was "They will be truly missed because we had grown to love them both." There were several empty pages left in the back of that journal. He wondered why she didn't keep writing. Then he noticed on the bottom of the last page a note in small print. "See journal #3." So there is more to read. I wonder where she keeps it.

The nurse stepped into the waiting room and told him quietly that Keith was awake. Her soft step and whispered message made him aware for the first time that he was not alone. A man sat across the room from him. His snow-white hair rested on the arm of a chair and he looked very uncomfortable. Jim motioned in his direction and the nurse said that he was waiting for his wife to come out of surgery.

It was with that thought that Jim quietly gathered his things and followed the nurse to Keith's bedside where he sat sipping water and being host to several tubes in his arms. She took his temperature and blood pressure and then smiled and left the room.

"Well, Keith how do you feel?"

"Good, I mean better than I did before all this happened. I need to call Cam and let her know that I am fine and that I will be coming home tomorrow."

"No, you won't! When the doctor says you can go home, he means you can go with me to the ranch. We will be there a few days and then I will fly back to Chicago with you."

"Cam will be worried sick if I stay here that long."

"Hey Cam is doing fine. She and Trisha have cooked up a plan to sell my house and we are going to move to Chicago. What do you think of that?" Keith's eyes filled with tears.

"Jim, I have missed you every day. I will help you find the best house possible. I am so happy that I feel like shouting!"

Jim leaned over and hugged his brother gently and then held his hand unashamedly as the doctor came in to talk to him.

"I am going to let you leave in the morning, but it hinges on a promise from you that you will follow my instructions completely. I have them printed out for you and a diet that you will need to stay on for the rest of your life. If you do, you will gradually lose some weight and you will look like your brother from behind as well as in the face. The most important thing to remember is no smoking!"

"I don't smoke Dr. Robert, and I will follow your instructions. I promise. I won't even stay in a room where people are smoking."

"That's good. I am glad to hear it. If you want to stick around and enjoy the company of this handsome brother of yours, that's the way to do it. I will be back in to see you in the morning to sign your release papers and to check you before you leave. I will leave these instructions here so you can read them several times before you go. I want you to know what is off limits before you head out." Jim took the papers from Keith's hands and started to read it.

"Keith, this isn't bad. This is the way I eat all the time. The only thing he has limited is dairy and red meat and fatty foods. You can do this without even thinking about it after you get used to it."

"You eat like a woman! I will have the salad and the baked chicken breast." He mocked his brother laughing.

"You can do it Keith and we will all help you."

"I know you will. I just hate having anyone fussing over me. I want to be around a while and it will be a lot better with you moving closer. Thank you, Jim. That's going to be hard to get Trisha and the kids to unplug from New York though. I have missed you so much that I can't even explain it. It was like part of me was gone and I couldn't find it."

"I know I have felt the same way. Cam and Trish came up with this on the phone last night. It blew my socks off! I was pondering the idea wondering how I could bring it up to Trish and she called me all excited about the same idea."

"I guess we will have to thank Cam on the QT. She knew how I was feeling for a long time. I know that she took this happening to me as a chance to leverage Trish."

"It is going to be so nice to be able to see each other whenever we want to."

"Why can't we get a huge house big enough for all of us and live together the way we used to when we were kids?"

"We aren't kids anymore, and Trisha and Camille both have different ideas on how they do things. I seriously doubt if they would go for such a drastic change."

"Keith as soon as we get to Chicago, I am going to call a realtor and tell them the size of our two families combined and ask if there is anything out there that we could make work."

"We could always add on as long as we had enough land."

"Good luck with that idea. Chicago is like New York on that. There isn't any land around the houses. Most of them are condos, stacked to the sky."

"That's ok; I am still going to try." Keith laughed and then winced at the discomfort he had caused.

"You never change. Once you get an idea you run with it."

"Well we can't make it happen if we don't try. I have some thinking to do and I will be back in the morning to get you. Rest while you can. It sounds like we are going to both be moving in the near future." Jim left the room with a big smile on his face.

Snow was hitting the windshield as he drove to the ranch. He called the airport to get an accurate reading on the weather.

CHAPTER SEVENTEEN
THE SPENCER FARM

Camille stood at the top of the stairs holding a laundry basket that was half full of toys and one sweatshirt.

"This is not good! I told you kids to count the number of new things you came home with and that I wanted you to put at least that many in the basket. You all have things that you haven't used or worn in months. Come on, be generous. There are kids out there that need the things you don't use. "

She shook her head and decided to go down to the kitchen to have a cup of tea.

"When I get back I want that basket overflowing." She yelled over her shoulder. She knew it wouldn't be until she forced the issue.

Trisha stood at the bottom of the stairs laughing.

"I had my kids doing the same thing while I am gone. The nanny from the company told me she had a secret weapon that works every time."

"I need to talk to her!" Cam laughed. The tea was hot and they stood at the big window in the living room each holding a cup, and watching the snow pile up on the single tree that reached up toward them.

"I don't know if I could move into a place that didn't have a yard," said Trisha. "I guess I will if I have to but if I have my wish, it will be some place big and old with a yard."

"Good luck with that," said Cam. "I called a realtor when we first talked about you possibly moving here. He could show us some places if we want. That would be fun."

"The company has a male nanny that I can call. He would probably do a better job at getting the kids to part with some stuff, too. I will call him. Brent said he could come if we needed him today."

"Great, let's do it. That would be fun and with the realtor driving we don't have to deal with the traffic or the snow."

*****

"Well that was a fun day, but a waste of time as far as finding a place to live."

"Trish, don't get discouraged. You will find something that works, but nothing can take the place of the Spencer farm. We all know that. If we had the courage we could all move there and live together. Our men could fly into New York when they have to be in person and the rest of the time they could work at home. I wish the guys would think of that so we wouldn't need to suggest it."

"Cam, it would be harder for Keith. His job is here. Jim likes to fly to the different offices. He gets bored in one place, but he could do that using the farm as home base."

"Keith has a clientele that it has taken years to build. I doubt if he would want to move away from them."

"We should relax and just wait to see what the guys say once they are here and rested."

"It will be a while before Keith and Jim can settle down and accept that they can't recapture what they had as kids. No matter how we do it, there isn't a way for them to be together every day. They chose different careers and that sent them to different colleges. They have been apart ever since. I wish there was a practical way to make it happen."

"Trish I think our kids will be the big stumbling block. They are into so many extracurricular activities that it will be nearly impossible to disengage them."

"Hey if we all decide we are moving, then we are moving and they will all have to accept it and adapt. I just thought of something. Why not take the kids back to the old Spencer farm and let them have a few days to explore and see what it is like. You and I can size up the place for possible additions and renovation. We don't have to mention that part to them.

"We need to call Jim and Keith and tell them to fly to the farm. I think you and I should take the initiative and get the ball rolling."

"Trish, this is exciting. I think you should call the folks at the farm and see what we need to do to make it possible for all of us to converge on the farm without causing them a lot of inconvenience. You know Grandpa Jay bought them a large house and it is on their land. I don't know how much they use it, but we could ask to see how much notice they need. Let's call them right now."

*****

Jim sat quietly reading and making notes until he realized that Keith was awake and looking at him.

"What are you looking at?"

"I was just thinking that someone in our family should have written a journal as things took place. We would certainly have a lot of good stories."

"Not all of them would be good. Actually most of them would be bad! I am glad they didn't. Sometimes it is better to not look back. What could we possibly write that wouldn't be painful? Dad's first wife was a nightmare. Then the attorney killed her, and to this day I think he killed Dad's brother. Then we were kidnapped. I am glad we don't remember that. We were just little babies. Then the worst thing of all was Dad putting so much love and money into this big ranch and when they left to fly back to get us, their plane crashed and they were both killed. We don't have a life full of adventures, like the people on this ranch."

"Maybe you are right but isn't it time we changed all that? We were happy until college. We chose to be apart at that time. Can't we reverse some of the decisions we made? Jim I want to take Cam and the kids and move back to Dad's old farm near Merritt and I want you and Trish and the kids to move there, too. We have the benefit of a steady income that is more than generous, from "Spencer's People", and we can do a lot of our work by internet. I could rebuild my practice. It would take time, but I am sure that Merritt can use a good lawyer. You could add a helipad and not have to commute by plane to New York when you were needed at the home office. That would probably take a lot less time and be far more convenient. Put a pad on the home office roof and all you would need is an elevator to take you to your office."

"Keith, don't get so excited. I know it could be done. What if we build two new houses on the farm? We could let our wives choose the designs and that way they would remain queen of their domain and have things their way."

"How long would all of that take?"

"I don't know. I would have to do some calling. Rest now and I will start by calling the girls and see what they think about the idea. The last thing they heard was that you were here at the ranch resting and that Trish and I were going to look for a place in your neighborhood.

Jim's mind was whirling with all the possibilities ahead. It included the battle with the kids. They won't want to leave their schools and friends. I wonder what the schools are like in the Merritt area. He walked out the door and headed to the hut library to return the two journals and the Bible. I think I will go see Eddie and Ellen for a little while. Maybe they can give me some insight into all the changes we are planning. On the way to the Jones House, Jim placed a call to Trish and ended up talking to Cam on the speaker. When he hung up, he was grinning. They love the idea and wish they could do it right now! He tapped on the door and Eddie opened it immediately.

"I saw you coming up the path. Is everything alright?"

"Yes, it is better than alright, it is great!"

"Hello Ellen. "

"I just thought I would ask your advice about some things that Keith and I are talking about. Were you going to bed soon? Am I interrupting anything?"

"No to both, and come on in. I have a lot of beef left from our supper. Would you like a sandwich and a cup of tea while we talk? I will make a pot of green tea"

"Thanks, I would like that. Maria made a light meal for us with vegetable soup and a salad. She is helping Keith to get used to his new way of eating. She is a gem. She had steamed salmon, too."

"Yes, she is, but although we shopped, we have to admit that Camille called and faxed us a copy of his diet and a suggested menu for the days he will be here. She is certainly efficient."

"Well that's good I guess. I am sorry that she caused you and Maria extra work though."

"That was not a big job. I had to go in and shop anyway. Frankly it is a good way to be reminded of the right things to eat. That beef sandwich isn't good for you." Ellen said as she refilled his tea.

194

"Thanks anyway, it was delicious." He paused and then continued. "You know that Keith and I are twins. We have been separated since we chose different colleges and getting together here for Christmas made us sorely aware of how much we missed each other. We have cooked up a plan to move both of our families back to the farm where our folks lived. We have been talking about building two new houses for our individual families. We figure that way our wives can pick the design and decorate them and still feel like they are in charge of their own home and family. At first we wanted to move back there and add some bedrooms, but we know that would not be convenient for all of us. That's why I am here. What problems do you think we will run into?"

"Wow Jim, I can understand why you would want to do that, but have you considered how that would impact your careers and what about your children?"

"That's why I thought I would ask for your input."

"Jim, have you talked to Trish and Cam about this? It will affect them the most."

"Yes they are willing to make the change, but they said that the kids will be hard to convince. It will impact them as much as us."

"Yes, it will. Probably more," said Ellen. "We are from a different generation so we can't imagine all the things that children from big cities are involved in but plucking them from that environment and putting them on a farm in the country could seem like isolation to them. Jim, do you have a pastor you can talk to about this? It will be more difficult than you think." Jim shook his head slowly. My mother was quite spiritual. Grandmother Terri took her to church just about every Sunday when she was growing up and my Dad was raised Catholic. We were given the option to go to either church, but I didn't go at all once I went to college. I don't know about Keith. He did say that he wanted to go to the church mentioned in your journals."

"You know I think that might be a good thing to do. Father Bernard is there. He is a wonderful man. He is wise and caring."

"Thanks Eddie, I will think about it, but right now I just want him to get strong and feel better. The rest can wait." Their conversation continued for a few minutes more and then Jim realized that it was getting late.

"We probably will go to that church even if it is just to see it and the area. Would you be able to lend us your jeep so we could drive there? I don't think we want to ride the horses anymore this trip."

"Sure, but give him another day to recuperate before you go down there."

"Yes, I intended to wait. He read about an image on the rocks that looks like a lion. The second journal is quite mysterious in parts. I guess we both would like to be there at Sundown so we can see it. Have either of you been there and seen the lion?"

"We both have, I recommend that you be sure his heart is strong before you go there at the right time."

"Eddie, so you think it is real and not a story."

"Oh, it is real! Just be there as the sun starts down over the trees and sit on the bench by the cave. Look above it and be prepared to be amazed."

"What about the rest of it? Do you think all those stories actually happened?"

"They did. I have checked them out. The church in town has records of most of it and the names and dates match up. There is one mystery that no one seems to have an answer to and that's where the Indians went and what happened to Sarah, David and Pili their daughter. No one wrote down anything about what happened to them. Their cabin is still in the trees just up river from the church. It is still in good condition. The Indian's cabins are deteriorated. The priest at the church has maintained the cabins near him but the Indian camp was on the other side of the bluff. Eventually it will all be totally gone and no one will be able to see that they were ever there. It is sad in a way. I would like to know what happened to them."

It was two days later before Keith and Jim took the jeep and headed up the road to see the church. They read the records that the priest brought out in a heavy, leather bound volume.

He proudly showed them the drawings created by the two Indian women. The virgin and child paintings each were protected in a case covered with glass.

In another case on the wall, was a small white rabbit's fur blanket. A corner of it had been pinned back, revealing the white snowflakes on the back side of the leather.

"This one has always caused me to want to follow their route and see what I would find there now. This is the map that they used to find the Abalinah. Their scouts drew it before the chosen warriors went to rescue the slaves. They were successful in their mission and the Lord punished the camp by blinding all the adults with the exception of a guard and a herdsman. That story is here in the record book if you have time to read it."

"Father Bernard, I understand that we are supposed to go outside if we want to see the image of a lion. We were told about it by Eddie and Ellen at the ranch."

"Yes, 'The Lion of Judah", appears above the cave just before sundown. He only appears on clear days. You are fortunate to have a nice sky today. Let us go there now. We can sit and talk and wait for the lion."

Keith smiled at Jim with a slight twinge of disbelief. He didn't quite believe all the stories as Jim did. He hadn't spent hours poring over the journals and comparing names and dates with all the local records.

"It is later than I thought! We must hurry or we will miss it!" The priest stopped in front of the cave looking up. He dropped to his knees just as Jim and Keith stepped around a huge pine tree. There above them was the image of the Lion, looking directly down at them. Slowly the men lowered themselves to the smooth stone that covered the area. Neither spoke. As the image faded they looked at the priest and then at each other.

"It's true. All of it is true. Dad must have known that. That's why he wanted to live on the ranch and be part of it." The priest shook their hands and walked them to the jeep.

"It is awesome isn't it? I wish we had taken pictures so we could show the girls."

"No", said Father Bernard, "I think this is something they should experience in person. I have discouraged people from taking photos."

"Keith lets come back here next Christmas and bring everyone to the church. This is something we should share."

CHAPTER EIGHTEEN
ALL ARE MOVING

Keith and Jim flew back to the old farm as their wives had instructed them. They had called it a mini vacation. It was difficult separating the kids from their teams, friends and activities even for a few days. The new semester had started at school and they didn't want to miss a thing. The sleeping arrangements were like a camp out and the children were especially enjoying that part of the visit until the morning of the third day, when their parents gathered them all at the table to inform them that a decision had been made and they would all be moving there permanently after several more rooms were added. The rest of the day was spent with sullen faces, bad attitudes and the older ones were glued to their cell phones most of the day.

The following morning the two families flew out to return to the usual routines in New York and Chicago, while the remodeling was hurried along by long distance calls and quick on-site trips, mostly by Jim. The two brothers were separated for a while during the renovation of the farmhouse.

Trisha and Camille continued to pare down their belongings to a more manageable amount. They moved in a little at a time, sending some things to nearby storage until school was out.

That summer, the wives took charge of the transition and with a little help from company employees, they actually made it happen. As seasonal sports ended the children were disconnected and familiarized with the local schools and teams available to join. Successful tryouts and making new friends that summer helped to change the dark moods of the youngsters.

By fall the benefits of living in the community around Merritt began to be appreciated even more by all of them. The children had fallen in love with the horses available and soon several new additions were made to the farm. A brown and white paint stole the heart of the girls. She was gentle and actually came to the fence when they were outside. She wanted their attention.

Keith had the most difficult time transitioning until Jim brought a Tech to the office they had included in the renovation. He was able to download several programs that made it possible for Keith to retain all his clients and serve them well over the internet. Finally by Christmas they were all happy to be home on the Spencer Farm. School activities and work responsibilities kept them all away from the S. and J. Ranch until many years later.

Keith and Jim took Cam and Trisha to the Ranch for a summer vacation.

The mystique of the place seemed gone. The people living on the ranch were still Eddie and Ellen but they seemed very different. They had aged and were slower and tired.

It was summer, hot and dry. This is the worst draught in 50 years they heard over and over when they spoke with people in the town of Silver Ville. The name's spelling had been changed to reflect the growing sophistication of the area. Many of the buildings had been replaced with new ones. The town had grown up in their absence. Keith and Jim were not happy about it.

"It is just not right. They didn't know what they had. Now it's gone and it will never come back." They had just settled into a booth in the dining room of a new restaurant that had taken the place of one of the old stores. Keith had been grumping ever since they landed.

"Keith, quit complaining. If this place was anywhere else you would be delighted to try everything on their menu. Try not to order the steak, please. You are gaining weight again and it isn't from the food at home. I worry about you."

"Hey, I am on vacation."

"You don't act like it. People on vacation are supposed to have a good time and a happy face. You don't seem to have either."

"I am sorry Cam. It's just that nothing is the same. We wanted you and Trisha to have a good time and to see and feel what we did. I wanted to use their horses and go for a ride and then go to the old church and have you girls read the stories that we did."

"Keith, you are talking about those old journals again. I've read all that stuff. Are you forgetting that Jim made copies of every page while you were in the hospital?

"I wish you hadn't because then it would all be new and exciting like it was for us. This blasted weather isn't helping either. It is so hot that I can't get my breath." The waitress approached the table and took their order. Cam and Trisha each ordered a large chef's salad and an iced tea. Jim said he wanted to have the perch dinner and a cold beer. Keith looked at Cam and defiantly ordered the biggest steak on the menu.

Jim was sad to see the friction between his brother and Cam. He decided to play mediator.

"Keith, the last time we were here you had heart trouble. Cam is just trying to take good care of you. Why do you fight it? When you don't take care of yourself, you hurt all of us. We love you, you know." Keith sat silently staring into space for a moment and then waved at the waitress. She hurried over.

"Is it too late to change my order?"

"No, not if we hurry."

"Tell the chef that I want what he is having."

"Good choice. It is delicious."

She hurried away.

"I feel better already! He said laughing. Cam patted his hand and nodded.

"What would you all say if I said I want to change our plans? I was looking at this brochure from the lobby and if we leave early tomorrow, we can drive north on the road that goes beside the Silver River, take a right on the Wagon Trail Highway and visit a lake and an Indian village that has been rebuilt. The scenery sounds beautiful the way it is described. They say that we pass huge boulders called the Big Rock Country and drive through a virgin forest with a high bluff near the road that leads to the village."

"It sounds like a tourist trap to me," said Jim, "but if you really want to go. I don't mind. Just remember to take plenty of cash. They will probably have lots of stuff for sale."

"What do you think Keith? Do you want to go see an old Indian village? Maybe someone there will know what happened to the real Indians that were on the ranch land. They couldn't just disappear."

"Sure I'll go. I didn't want to ride a horse again. As long as we can rent a nice car with cold air, I will go. I wonder what the temperature is today. I am roasting."

The trip was farther than they thought and by the time they arrived they were tired and hungry. The lake was not impressive. The hot dry weather had diminished it to a small brown pool. It was obvious that the five tents were not made by Indians. The exteriors were painted with garish circles and triangles in blue and green enamel. Two gift shops stood front and center with a food cart nearby that offered Indian fry bread and lemonade. There was nothing authentic in sight.

Jim was particularly disappointed until he saw an old man with long, white, braided hair sitting under the trees. His skin was furrowed and dark from the sun and his trousers and bare feet were covered with the red dust from the land. His head leaned against the trunk of the tree where he rested. His chest held the evidence of a wealthy history. I didn't see anything like that in those gift shops, thought Jim. The old man's eyes opened and locked with Jim's. He didn't look away. Jim spoke respectfully as he entered the shade of the ancient trees.

"Good afternoon, how are you?"

"I am fine. I am home. It is you that is hot, tired and hungry. Sit here. We will talk. I sense many questions in your mind. Ask them."

Jim smiled and lowered himself to the grass near the man.

"This is a little cooler. Thanks."

"Begin."

"Well I am not sure just what I should ask you. I am not from this area, but I did stay at the Slater and Jones Ranch when I was a bit younger and I have read the journals there with the accounts of an Indian people that became Christian and went with a priest to rescue young people that were held as slaves. Do you know the story?"

"Yes, I know the story. It is true."

"Is this their village?"

"No, not this." He waved his hand at the tents and gift shops. "It is made for people like you who come and go and never come again but the land is their land. It lasts forever."

"Where did the people go after they left? Were they the same people that moved to Ben Slater's land?" He nodded and smiled.

"They went far to the north. They live there now and with their help and love the people who once held the slaves have learned a better way to live and prosper."

"I am glad for all of them."

"Yes, as am I. I stay to watch and guard the spirits of the ancient ones and their treasure."

"Really? What treasure?" The old man got up slowly and groaned a bit from the effort. He smiled a sly smile at Jim and walked into the trees. Cam and Trisha were enjoying their costly snack and each carried a sack from the gift stores. "What did you girls buy?"

"Jewelry," they answered together. He chuckled and suggested they join Keith in the car before they ran out of fuel.

"I saw you talking to that old man. What were you talking about?"

"Nothing much, but he said that he is here to guard the spirits of the ancient ones and their treasure."

"I wonder what his name is."

Cam picked up the leaflet from the seat of the car.

"This says that Chief Rising Eagle is occasionally seen walking the land that he once fought to keep. It says that he died of a rattle snake bite on his neck while he slept in his tent.

Although he was not seen by his people; after they left, he has occasionally been seen by others visiting the area."

"I am glad that we didn't see any snake! The scratchy grass was bad enough. My toes feel like I have pickers in them. I shouldn't have worn these sandals I guess."

Keith backed the car up and turned around as soon as everyone was settled.

"He was no ghost. But I saw the jewelry on his chest. That was real. That piece of amber in his necklace is worth a good sum. That was real turquoise too."

"Keith you should have come over there and talked to him. He was friendly."

"No thanks, I am eager to get back to town. You girls will be lucky if you don't both get sick from eating that stuff."

"It was fine. She pulled it out of boiling grease."

They talked and joked about the ghost that talked to Jim and he shook his head as if he believed them. Later they returned to the ranch to enjoy a lovely meal and the comforts of the cool evening. A tap on the door just after they had gone inside brought them an exciting gift.

"I should have brought this down from the attic when your family was here for Christmas those many years ago. I thought of it but then we got busy and I forgot again.

"This was in your parent's bedroom when they left to fly home and get you boys. May they rest in peace. What an awful thing that was when the news came of their plane crash, we couldn't believe it? We had grown to love your folks. I sent everything else back but missed this. We had guests after that so it ended up being put in first one closet and then another, and finally someone stuck it in the attic. I know it should have been packed up and mailed to you. I don't know why I didn't. Something just kept me from doing it. I hope it isn't anything important." She stood holding the computer, looking apologetic.

"Don't worry about it, Ellen. We just thought that it had burned up in the crash. My mom was always carrying around her computer. She wrote stories. We have a few at home that she wrote. Thank you for bringing it down to us tonight. We will see you in the morning before we leave. Goodnight."

Keith cradled the computer against his chest as if it were a baby.

"This is a wonderful thing. If we are careful, we might get this old thing to open up and give up the stories that mom had on it."

"We need to talk to one of the techs back home. They will replace the battery and do their magic. This is a rare gift!"

It was the following Saturday when Jim walked into the farmhouse carrying that old computer with a cord in his hand and a smile on his face.

"Kids, all of you, come here!"

"The kids are not all here dear. We have one at practice and one at the mall."

"Well I guess I can wait. Eric has copied everything on here so we can't lose it. There is one story that is complete and just needs a little editing I think and a second that is a partial. Eric is making copies of the second one for us in book form with blank pages at the end. I am going to give all the kids a copy and ask them to write an ending. Maybe one of them will come up with a really good conclusion and show they have their Grandmother's talent."

"Keith I like that idea. I hope they think it will be fun and don't look at it like it is more homework."

"They won't when they know who wrote the first part."

"Did Grandma Koza give that new story a name?"

"I think it is just marked "work in progress," but the name is on the completed one.

"I want to read that one!"

EPILOGUE:
The mysteries of the S. and J. Ranch are many. If you would like to know more about the supernatural happenings mentioned in this book, you will find "The New Life Series," interesting reading.

The Christian fiction in that series is written to offer the reader a wholesome entertainment, starting back in a simpler but not easier time. Their example of spiritual strength and "never quit" attitude is refreshing and inspiring. The adventurers follow the trail to a new land and challenges they never imagined.

In book one "**More Than Survival**", follow Benjamin Slater as he copes with the wild isolation of the new frontier and the lessons of self-preservation. He experiences the pain of loss and joys of accomplishment. He travels, "**Life's Many Journeys**," in book two and learns to appreciate "**The Land's Heritage**," in book three.

In Book four, you will find out "**The Story of Sarah**"

As you read the books, Ben develops into a man of physical and spiritual strength. His problem solving mind is challenged many times.

When Sarah, his sister returns to him, they are finally "**Together**," in book five. You will find out how her life affected the Indians that took her and how they became "**The Blue Stone People**," a chosen nation in book six.

A change of scene takes you to the camp of the Sentu and three survivors enter the story, in book seven "**Teewahpanyee the Boy, Two Feathers the Man**," Willow and Water Bug bring new strength and young blood to an old people. With Willow at his side in book eight he becomes leader of "**The People of The Lion**". They are chosen by the Lion of Judah to be rescuers, and are rewarded in book nine by being allowed to discover "**The Lion's Den.**"

In book ten, the land that Ben Slater's father chose had miraculously remained with the family as time has gone by and generations were born. In a day beyond today, the series skips to the final times after the rapture. A new heroine stands up bravely to the soldiers of the anti-Christ. She finds Ben's Bible, Mary Slater's journals and the gift of faith. Emily spreads the word and struggles to survive the time of tribulation as she finally realizes that this is "**Just the Beginning**" for those who believe.

More Than Survival
Life's Many Journeys
The Lands Heritage
The Story of Sarah
Together
The Blue Stone People
Teewahpanyee The Boy, Two Feathers The Man
The People of The Lion
The Lion's Den
Just The Beginning

AN INVITATION

If you do not know Jesus, as your savior but you would like Him to be, please pray the following prayer. Invite Him into your heart. Commit your "New Life" to Him. He will be your constant companion, counselor, comforter, and protector. The Holy Bible tells us that He will never leave you or forsake you.

"Dear Jesus, please forgive my sins. Give me grace and strength Lord, so that I will not commit them again. Come into my heart so that I can start a "New Life" with you as my companion. I want to live according to your will and commandments. Bless me Lord and lead me in a life that is pleasing to you. In Jesus' Holy name I pray. Amen"

If you prayed that prayer, you are saved. You are born again. Your soul is whiter than the snow that caps the highest mountains. The angels in Heaven are singing with joy as they write your name in The Lamb's Book of Life.

Get a Christian Bible and begin to read it. Find a good Bible believing church and start attending, so that you can learn more about Your Heavenly Father. What a wonderful God we have.

If you wish, you can sign and date your Bible as an outward sign of your salvation and tell someone that you have committed your life to Christ.

I will pray for you. God bless you. Louise Bouck

About the author

Louise Bouck is a follower of Jesus Christ. She has been married to her husband, Dale Bouck for more than fifty years. Together they have raised six children.

Until an early retirement from her fulltime job in 2000, little time was available to allocate to writing or art. One of the many interests that Louise enjoys is painting on location. The lush greenery of Michigan, her home state and the abundant flowers in her grandmother's greenhouses and flower shop all encouraged her eye to appreciate the colors and beauty of nature.

Later after moving to Arizona, the rugged landscape of the mountains and desert stole her heart and took her artistic soul in a new direction.

Paintings in many media cover the walls of her studio as she has deliberately turned her creative side more to the written word. Hesitantly she withdrew from the art gallery where her work was sold and left the position of resident artist at the local Historical Museum. Louise has written ten books in a series of Christian; Bible based stories that she has now released on Amazon as eBooks and paperbacks for the first time as she works on still another story and another painting.

Some of her artwork may be included as cover art on her eBooks. She hopes that you will enjoy them all and be blessed. ⍰